OUT OF HORMONE'S WAY

Also by Jane Isenberg
in Large Print:

The "M" Word
Death in a Hot Flash
Midlife Can Be Murder
Mood Swings to Murder

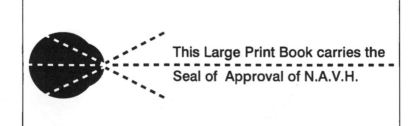

This Large Print Book carries the
Seal of Approval of N.A.V.H.

OUT OF HORMONE'S WAY

A BEL BARRETT MYSTERY

Jane Isenberg

WHEELER
PUBLISHING

Published in 2003 by arrangement with Avon Books, an imprint of HarperCollins Publishers.

Wheeler Large Print Softcover Series.

The text of this Large Print edition is unabridged. Other aspects of the book may vary from the original edition.

Set in 16 pt. Plantin by Minnie B. Raven.

Printed in the United States on permanent paper.

ISBN 1-58724-396-2 (lg. print : sc : alk. paper)

OUT OF HORMONE'S WAY

Acknowledgments

To spin a popular adage, "You can take the writer out of New Jersey but you can't take New Jersey out of her books," at least not out of this one, which takes place in the Meadowlands as well as in Hoboken and Jersey City. Thanks to Bonnie Shepherd, Director of Communications at the Hackensack Meadowlands Development Corporation, my husband and I got to cruise down the Hackensack River with author-naturalist-artist John R. Quinn. John pointed out and explained the many wonders of that historic stream and the surrounding area. Less cheerful, perhaps, but no less crucial to the story is the information on chemotherapy for breast cancer patients that oncologist Deborah Smith graciously provided. I'm also indebted to cancer survivor Miriam Isenberg, who shared her recollections of treatment with me.

Once again I turned to Johanna Hagelthorn and Elaine Foster for insights into parenting and child development and to Jimmy Shamburg, former Deputy Police Director of Jersey City, for details of police procedure. Phyllis Lehrer provided a useful photo essay and

Denise Swanson e-mailed advice and encouragement. Ruth and Dave Tait, Joan and Joe Rafter, and Elaine Foster have generously housed my husband and me during visits to New Jersey to do research.

My editor Jennifer Sawyer Fisher demonstrated her usual skill in smoothing out the rough spots in the manuscript, and great patience and good humor while helping me come up with an appropriate title for this book. My agent Laura Blake Peterson knows how to keep me grounded in reality rather than overwhelmed by it. It is a privilege to work with both of these women.

Over the last decade writing group members Susan Babinski, Pat Juell, and Rebecca Mlynarczyk have all become the readers I see in my head when I write. I am especially indebted to Susan for her understanding of dyslexia. Pat and her husband Tom continue to welcome me into their home when I visit New York for writing group meetings.

My daughter Rachel Stoner and her husband Brian provide advice, moral support, and invaluable glimpses of another generation, as do my son Daniel Isenberg and our friend Shilyh Warren. My husband Phil Tompkins remains the genie behind my website (www.JaneIsenberg.com). He is also the gentle but honest first reader every writer longs for and the patient proofreader every writer needs.

Author's Note

I began writing this book many months before September 11, 2001, and finished it shortly afterwards. I believe it is important to recall and celebrate the many roles the Twin Towers played in the lives and psyches of folks in Hoboken and Jersey City before September 11. Therefore, at the risk of prompting painful memories, I decided not to remove references to the World Trade Center. To people just across the Hudson it was more than a part of the beloved Manhattan skyline. It was a place to work, play, shop, eat, work out, get a haircut, and take houseguests. Tragically, for two hundred of these people it was a place to die.

Chapter 1

To: Bbarrett@circle.com
From: Woconnor@circle.com
Re: Big Favor
Date: 04/04/01 07:16:44

Bel,

Little family emergency here, so I need a big onetime favor. My mother fell and went to the ER via ambulance last night, so I'm booked to fly to Fort Lauderdale in two hours. Don't worry. Harold, our kinder and gentler department chair, is actually arranging for an adjunct to cover my classes. He was pretty civil about it. Actually, what he said was, "For Christ's sake Wendy, River Edge Community College will not fall apart if you miss a few days of class." I know he's right, BUT the Urban Kayaking Club meets this Saturday at nine at Laurel Hill Park in Secaucus. I really hate to miss that. It's the orientation meeting.

I left the UKC membership list and brochure on your desk under a one-pound bag of M&M's. Remember I told you that seven students have already signed up and we met once on campus and elected officers? You know how hard I worked to get the club approved by the Student Activities Committee and to write the grant proposal. Well, the grant stipulates that a faculty member be present at all club meetings. I've arranged for a park ranger to be there Saturday and brief us on the area and talk about basic kayaking safety. We don't actually hit the water until the kayaks are delivered on Tuesday, so all you have to do is show up, welcome the students, introduce the speaker, and tell everybody I'll be there next Saturday. My brother's meeting me in Fort Lauderdale and I expect to be back within the week. Just this once? Please, Bel? I owe you big time. That pound of M&M's is just the first payment. Mucho thanks.

Wendy

"Wendy's really got her hands full with her mother. The poor woman fell and Wendy had to drop everything and fly to Florida," I reported to my friends Betty and Illuminada as Illuminada maneuvered her Volvo around the Tonnele Avenue traffic circle and out of Jersey City on the way to our appointment in Englewood.

"Gina told me. She also told me about you

standing in for Wendy at the Urban Kayaking Club's orientation meeting. Gina said you were at Laurel Hill Park first thing Saturday morning in raggedy jeans giving a lecture on the history and geography of the Meadowlands." Betty, an unabashed control freak whose not-so-secret goal is total world domination, was chortling and shaking her head. I wasn't sure whether she was laughing at the idea of me out of context and out of bed early on a weekend morning or at Gina's legendary ear for gossip. As executive assistant to the president of River Edge Community College, Betty has a clerk-typist all to herself. This long-suffering woman is notorious for having her multiringed finger on the pulse of the college. If it happened at RECC, chances are Gina knows about it.

"*Caramba*, Bel. You really took that speech you gave at your adult bat mitzvah seriously, didn't you?" asked Illuminada. I couldn't see the twinkle in her eye from where I sat in the backseat of her car, but I could tell by her tone that it was there. She never tired of teasing me about my belated decision to study Judaism in an effort to connect with my spiritual and cultural roots. "You talked about doing good deeds or mitzvahs in the spirit of the foremothers or something highfalutin like that and the next thing I know, you're playing Smokey the Bear on Sabbath mornings. Sol must have loved having you go

13

to work on the weekend." As CEO of a busy private investigative agency and adjunct instructor of criminal justice, Illuminada tends to view everyday life as a desperate race against time.

"Actually he did," I replied. "He came with me." Now it was my turn to laugh as I added, "Betty, tell Gina she better get a fact checker. It was Sol who gave the talk on the Meadowlands, not me. A park official showed up, but he only stayed long enough to explain that he had a scheduling conflict and had to leave. So Sol just started to talk. He was great! The students were really attentive. A couple even took notes. And Jason Carillo, the UKC president, taped the whole thing. Who knew Sol was such a Meadowlands maven?"

"Well, girlfriend, you should have figured he'd know about anything that's got to do with the environment. Since his retirement from Rutgers that dude's been on a one-man crusade to keep the developers and politicians from bordering your precious Hoboken waterfront with high-rise, high-rent view busters," said Betty turning to glance at me in the backseat as she spoke. "And, for better or worse, the Meadowlands *is* our environment too," she decreed.

"*Dios mio,* with all due respect to your life partner, what the hell is there to tell about the Meadowlands?" asked Illuminada. "Look

14

at it." She took one brightly manicured hand from the wheel and swept it in a dismissive arc, swiping Betty's dreads and making them ripple. Illuminada had just merged with traffic onto the New Jersey Turnpike heading north. We were only a few miles from the view that Tony Soprano, New Jersey's most famous commuter, had turned into a national icon just by driving home from work once a week. Suddenly we were surrounded by those vast vistas of reedy vegetation that most Americans see only from the window of a plane approaching Newark Airport.

"Believe it or not, the Meadowlands has an interesting history." I spoke a little louder than usual, eager to defend my native state. "Sol said the whole area where we are right now was once a tidal estuary carved out of the earth by a glacier during the Ice Age." Betty stared out the car window as if trying to reconcile this geological sculpting session with the utility poles edging the tracts of reeds undulating alongside the turnpike.

"Well, *chiquita,* it's a long way from the Ice Age to the Outlets," Illuminada said. "And that's what I know best about the Meadowlands." Again, while I couldn't see her smile, I could hear the amusement in her voice. Illuminada's idea of a relaxing weekend afternoon was elbowing her way through a crowd of other shoppers at a sale. The Secaucus Outlets were her stomping grounds.

"Me too," Betty echoed. "I've been to Secaucus a million times to shop, but I never even heard of Laurel Hill Park till you mentioned it," she said with a chuckle. It was good to hear. Since her son Randy got laid off in February, Betty hadn't laughed much lately. She didn't like to talk about it, but Randy's so far unsuccessful job search had gotten to her.

"It's the first new park in Hudson County in seventy-five years," I added, repeating what Sol had told me last week when I had confessed the same ignorance. "It's right at the foot of Snake Hill."

"Snake Hill?" Betty's dreads swayed as she executed a mock shudder. "Sounds really appealing. Seriously, the only places in the Meadowlands I ever go are the Continental Stadium when they have Springsteen's comeback concerts and the Secaucus Outlets."

"*Dios mio,* Bel, remember when Betty and I spent all day at the Outlets helping you find those funky shoes for Rebecca's wedding?" Illuminada asked. I pictured the round-heeled black satin flats with ankle straps that I'd first spotted selling for a small fortune at Nordstroms in Paramus. It was a good thing Betty, Illuminada, and I had already honed our sleuthing skills together because it had not been easy finding those same shoes at a more affordable price and in my size.

"You're right, girl, that was a loooong day,"

Betty responded with another chuckle.

"We finally zeroed in on them at His 'n' Hers Shoes, remember? I was feeling like one of Cinderella's stepsisters by the time we found them in an eight narrow. That place has great buys. We should go and look for sandals when it gets a little warmer."

"They do have buys," Betty agreed. "But I'm not sure we want to go there for a while. Gina was at His 'n' Hers with her daughter last night looking for an end-of-season bargain on boots and, would you believe, somebody found a body in the parking lot?"

"Good grief, what happened?" I asked, trying to imagine having a shopping excursion interrupted by the discovery of a corpse.

"For once Gina didn't stick around to find out. She pulled out just as the police arrived. But don't worry, sooner or later she'll have all the details."

"Some poor woman probably shopped till she dropped," Illuminada said before sheepishly adding, "Sorry. I couldn't resist that one."

By way of registering her disapproval of Illuminada's tired joke, Betty turned to look at me and said, "Moving right along, Bel, it sounds as if your morning with the UKC worked out okay then?" Having posed her question, she faced forward in her seat.

"I hope so. The weather was awful, but the kids seemed enthusiastic and Sol was dynamite! I'm going to suggest that Wendy invite him back to speak," I said. "Unfortunately, they didn't get the briefing on kayaking safety from the real Smokey Bear type, but Wendy can tell them all about that next week. That woman can kayak upstream blindfolded in a hurricane."

"*Dios mio,* I just don't understand why some people's idea of a good time is to slather themselves with insect repellent and paddle up and down a river. Raoul really likes Wendy, but he calls her a green queen. I'm amazed that any city kids at all signed up for the UKC," said Illuminada.

"Well, they did. I know one of them, Belinda Judd. She's in my Basic English II class this semester. She's very sweet. Unfortunately, she's dyslexic. In fact, she told me she thought she was signing up for the Urban Kickboxing Club, but after she realized her error at the meeting they held to elect officers, she decided to stay." Recalling how a red-faced and stammering Belinda confided her misconception to me, I frowned. Life is difficult for those who don't read well. Belinda's problems matching sounds and symbols occasionally caused her to mispronounce or avoid certain words, making her seem far younger than her eighteen years. She looked young too. Last Saturday, wearing only a denim jacket, the short, baby-faced woman had stood shivering in the raw morning air and gusting wind. She reminded me of a child who had refused to bring hat or gloves to the playground and was now sorry. In spite of the recent administrative memo advising faculty that any physical contact between faculty and students might invite a charge of sexual harassment, I had enveloped Belinda in my red wool ruana. The two of us huddled in our cozy bright cocoon waiting for the others to arrive.

"I give up," said Illuminada impatiently, reminding me of my obligations as a raconteur. "Why did she stay, Bel?"

"She told me that she has a boyfriend, but she's getting tired of him and she thought Jason, the UKC president, was quote, really hot, unquote, so she decided to hang in and try to get his attention." Even though Illuminada and Betty couldn't see me, I was smiling and shaking my head at the hormonally driven antics of the young. "He *is* kind of appealing — tall, dark, and very businesslike with his tape recorder and binoculars. He's part techie, part nature buff. The nature buff part wants to get out of Union City to someplace green."

"Well, Belinda's dyslexia shouldn't be a problem in a kayak," said Betty, practical even in the face of young love.

"I'm not so sure of that," I responded. "Dyslexics can have trouble with directions. And guess who was elected UKC secretary?"

"Oh no," said Illuminada, shaking her head. "But I suppose the others don't know she's dyslexic. How would they?"

"They don't. Besides, I bet none of them wanted to be secretary. The other guy who was willing to be an officer, Jason's buddy Basil, is too macho to be secretary, so he's vice president. And his girl, Deatra, at least I think she's his girl, she's way too cool." As I spoke, I recalled Deatra's serious and aloof demeanor and the measuring look she had given me when I introduced myself. A tall, lithe young woman with a complexion of dark chocolate, she wore her sleek black hair so short it gleamed close to her head like a second skin.

"Bel, is Deatra tall and striking with hair that looks like a skullcap and big hazel eyes? Do you remember her last name?" Illuminada asked.

"Yes. Deatra Cain," I answered, relieved that for once I could remember somebody's name. "Why? Did you ever help her out?" Northern New Jersey sometimes seemed to be populated entirely by grateful women who had hired Illuminada to help them obtain child support, child custody, or evidence of infidelity or workplace harassment. She had almost as many former clients as I had former students.

"Only in the most general sense. I had her in class a couple of semesters ago. She's a criminal justice major, and she was an excellent student. But she's a real city girl. Wants to be a cop," Illuminada said. "I never would have figured her to be even remotely interested in kayaks or the outdoors."

"That's just the kind of person Wendy wants to reach. She's determined to share her bliss with kids who haven't had much exposure to nature. That's the whole point. She thinks they should experience the Meadowlands before, as she puts it, it's all 'malls and multiplexes.' Then if they don't like it, well, they've had a taste," I said, now feeling slightly defensive about my longtime office mate's passionate advocacy of the UKC.

"I hate to interrupt you mid-rant, but we're here," said Illuminada. "Do we have time for lunch first or should we wait until afterward?" she asked as we exited the turnpike in Englewood. She headed for the town's main thoroughfare, a street lined with upscale boutiques, cafés, and restaurants that could easily distract us from our mission. And we definitely had a mission. I smiled to myself, well aware that the ever clock-conscious Illuminada knew exactly what time it was and when our consecutive appointments at Englewood Imaging began.

My smile became a grin when Betty voiced my thoughts in her most take-charge manner. "Oh come on, girl. You know damn well our appointments start at one and it's ten of. Let's get it over with and then have lunch." Illuminada raised her elbow in what, from the backseat, I took to be a mock salute and steered us in the direction of Englewood Imaging.

Chapter 2

DO NOT USE POWDER OR ANY TYPE
OF DEODORANT ON OR ABOUT THE
UNDERARMS AND BREASTS.

Once we had entered the deliberately cheery waiting room, we hung up our coats, filled out forms, and settled ourselves in the rose and white chintz-covered chairs. We were primed for what had become a rite of spring for us, having our annual mammograms. Doing this together had been my suggestion. A coward about many things, I had no trouble letting radiologists make metal sandwiches out of my boobs once a year. No doubt the fact that my mother had survived two bouts of breast cancer and two mastectomies had something to do with my willingness to let the technician flip my very own floppies between the metal plates of the machine on a yearly basis. It was definitely the lesser of the two evils, and I'd been doing it since I was forty.

That's why a few years ago I had been rendered slack-jawed with shock when Illuminada and Betty both confessed that neither of them had ever had a mammogram. Long ago, colleagues and subordinates at RECC had nicknamed Betty "Ramrod" Ramsey in recognition of her steely demeanor and refusal to recognize any authority other than her own. And the petite and elegant Illuminada was notorious for her take-no-prisoners attitude toward deadbeat dads, wayward spouses, and pilfering employees. Students preparing for careers in law enforcement thought twice before telling "hard-nosed" Professor Gutierrez that their pet pit bull or ferret had eaten their research paper or that the essay in question had gone up in smoke when their apartment burned to the ground. As a notoriously empathetic English prof, I heard these excuses frequently.

"I do breast checks myself every so often," Illuminada had said. "And Dr. Hererra's always bugging me about having a mammography, but he does breast exams too. And there's always Raoul." She had grinned at the mention of her handsome husband. *"Caramba!* How many people do I need checking out my boobs, anyway? Besides, I heard they squeeze them flatter than pancakes between pieces of metal and it hurts like hell." This from a woman who carried a gun and could use it.

"Yeah, that's what I heard," Betty had chimed in. "That's why I keep putting it off. But you know, I don't do breast checks either. What if I found something?" She laughed nervously. "Girl, I'd be so scared if I found a lump, I don't know what I'd do." This from a woman who made a living by knowing exactly what she and everybody else should do and making sure they did it.

I had bribed Betty and Illuminada into having their first mammography by suggesting that we go together and promising to treat them to lunch at Baumgarten's, a renovated luncheonette in Englewood that features Asian stir fries, fifties comfort food, and sinful desserts. That first outing was such a success that we'd made it a yearly event, a sisterly celebration of survival instead of a solitary confrontation with mortality. Having transformed this medical procedure into just another excuse for a lunch date, all three of us were almost comfortable with the whole experience now.

So when the medical assistant called out Betty's name, she stood and smiled cavalierly as she left the waiting room. I was called next and while I waited, naked to the waist under the pink and white flowered cover-up I'd been instructed to don, I saw Betty pass by the partially open door to the room I was in. Even if she hadn't given me a thumbs-up, I'd have known from her grin that she and her breasts had been declared "normal," as in cancer-free, for another year.

While the technician arranged each of my arms, armpits, and breasts in the awkwardly precise positions required for this particular photo op, I willed myself into a doll-like state, limp-limbed and pliant. I was a veritable Chatty Cathy, making what I hoped was appropriate small talk with the technician about weather and traffic. But my facade of breezy sociability was not easy to maintain for one simple reason. Once I had stepped across the threshold of that second small pink and white room, I knew I had cancer. With my German Jewish genes, how could I not? With my mother's history, how could I not? I'd escaped the premenopausal breast lump, but now I was over fifty and postmenopausal. And I'd been taking estrogen for years along with the devilish progesterone. Necessary to prevent uterine cancer in women taking estrogen, progesterone had recently been associated with an increased risk of breast cancer. This finding posed a mind-and-body-boggling dilemma. In response to this catch-22, I'd halved my dosage of both medications, but it was probably too late.

As if all that weren't damning enough, I've been known to feast on fatty foods. And I didn't eat nearly enough broccoli or do enough yoga. On top of that, I lived in an urban/industrial area where I breathed polluted air. Even New York's mayor was not immune to our airborne toxins and was battling prostate cancer. Hell, closer to home —

my home, that is — Hoboken's mayor had recently undergone surgery for both brain and lung cancer. What's more, I didn't always drink filtered water. I had cancer, and it was my own fault.

As soon as the technician finished the mammography, I put on the pink and white cover-up she'd left me and sat waiting for the radiologist to read the films. By this time I was completely convinced that I had inoperable cancer of both breasts which had metastasized throughout my entire body. I had mere months to live. Tears welled in my eyes as I mentally informed Sol, my mother, Rebecca, and Mark of my imminent demise. When the smiling radiologist entered the room to tell me that there had been no change in my mammography from the year before and that, in other words, I was fine, I experienced a flash of incredulity and then felt waves of relief pulse through my body. Brushing away tears of gratitude, I struggled for composure as I dressed and reentered the waiting room.

Betty was there, but Illuminada was still inside. Betty and I grinned at each other. Then, looking across the room where two other women sat, their grim faces framed by pink and white flowered wallpaper, Betty said softly, "Do you suppose somebody's done a study of what color scheme is most soothing to women waiting to hear if they have

27

cancer? I mean really, girl, whoever decorated this place should rethink the Laura Ashley look. All this pink and white makes me nervous."

At that moment Illuminada emerged from the inner office, white-faced and shaking. Betty and I were so taken aback by her transformation that for a moment we sat in silence watching her make her way toward us, a little unsteady on her feet, like someone walking under water. "Oh my God. What happened?" I blurted, winning the prize for dumbest question of the year.

"Let me get your coat, and we'll talk in the car," said Betty, ever the pragmatist, leaping into constructive action and taking us with her. For once I was glad she was in control since I had been instantly transported back into my cancer fantasy of a few minutes ago. Except this time it starred Illuminada. My friend was living through my ultimate nightmare. She had a lump. She had cancer. She —

"Do you want me to drive?" asked Betty, still in control of herself and the situation.

"*Como mierda,* Betty, of course not. I'm not dead yet. It's just a little shadow of a speck that the radiologist thinks they ought to check into. She did one of those extra tests, that's what took so long, you know, a . . ." Illuminada hesitated, searching for the elusive medical term.

"A sonogram," I said, inserting the word as soon as Illuminada paused. I had dredged it up from the deep recesses of memory, where it had remained buried since my most recently diagnosed friend, Marilyn, had used it under similar circumstances. Like my mom, Marilyn was fine now. Thinking about my mom and Marilyn made me feel a little better. Breast cancer needn't be fatal. Illuminada might very well be one of the lucky ones.

As I was repeating this to myself, I heard Illuminada say in an uncharacteristically shrill voice, "What about lunch? I'm hungry. I am having lunch. Care to join me, *senoras?*" Hearing our friend speak in the choppy sentences of a Dick and Jane reader, Betty and I looked at each other.

"Don't you want to call Dr. Hererra now? And talk to Raoul? And figure out how to deal with your mother and Lourdes about this? Are you going to tell your mother?" As usual Betty was zoning in on what she perceived as the problem with one of her to-do lists from hell. It wasn't going to work. Illuminada's "shadow of a speck" was just one more example of how little control we have over our bodies, our lives, anything. At that moment Betty's list offered puny protection from the deadly cells that were probably multiplying by the minute in Illuminada's body.

"No, Betty, I'm not, not now. It's nearly two and I'm hungry. Don't you have time for a quick lunch?" Illuminada looked even more upset than she had the day she told us that her daughter Lourdes had dropped out of pharmacy school. Her tone was sharp, but her question came out as a plea. Both Betty and I heard it.

Although for once in my life I wasn't hungry, I gave Betty a quick look. "Of course. I don't have class until six, and I'm actually completely prepared," I lied, thinking of the stack of essays I had hoped to read and respond to that afternoon.

Betty fell into place, saying, "I told Woodman I'd be back late today. I knew we were having lunch. We always do. I'll just give Gina a call and see that she's got work lined up." Betty took out her cell phone and punched in the number of Gina's extension as we entered the restaurant.

Sobered by Illuminada's news, we had no appetite for the excesses of the menu but instead opted to share a relatively spartan chicken and veggie stir fry with brown rice. While we waited for our lunch, Illuminada pulled out her handheld organizer, looked up a number, and tapped it into her cell phone. We heard her leaving word for Dr. Hererra to call her about setting up a needle biopsy. When she finished that call, she said to Betty, "Happy now, *chiquita?* I've called my doctor."

"How do you feel?" I asked, hearing how stupid this question sounded even as I asked it.

To my surprise, Illuminada answered without pointing out how moronic the question was. "I've only known about this for a few minutes, but already I'm tired. It's taking all my energy to make myself believe that this is happening. I never felt anything. Raoul never felt anything. There's no family history. *Como mierda!* How could I have a lump? I want to pretend it's a mistake and not true and just forget it."

"Can't say I blame you," I said.

"Me either," added Betty.

"My mother will hear the word *cancer* or even *lump* and start with the saints and *orishas* and all that Santeria stuff. Innocent chickens will die before this is over if I tell her." Milagros Santos's penchant for the more arcane rituals of Santeria drove her daughter crazy. "*Dios mio,* give me strength." Illuminada squared her shoulders. "No, I'm not going to tell her anything until I have the needle biopsy and we know for sure what we're dealing with. I can't handle it if she goes off on me," she said, her tone again full of pleading. Now, though, she was pleading with herself for permission to spare her mother the bad news and so to put off Milagros's predictable reaction, never mind her own.

31

When our food came, we dutifully picked at it. In between tiny mouthfuls, Illuminada kept repeating, "*Dios mio,* I can't believe it." When her cell phone buzzed, we all jumped, but it was only her secretary calling to apprise her of a new development in a case.

Suddenly she was in a hurry. "I've got to be in a lawyer's office in Jersey City in half an hour. I'll drop you off. Here, this one's on me," she said, throwing a bill on the table and putting on her jacket. "I'll tell Raoul tonight and we'll tell Lourdes after the needle biopsy if there's, you know, anything to tell." Illuminada shrugged off this possibility. "Right now I'm going back to work." Now that she had called her doctor and shared her plan to inform Raoul and to put off telling her mother and her daughter, Illuminada's eagerness to get back to business seemed like a good idea. It sure beat going home and dwelling on the small speck that cast such a large shadow.

Chapter 3

To: Bbarrett@circle.com
From: Woconnor@circle.com
Re: Row, row, row my boat . . .
Date: 04/10/01 23:09:16

Bel,

I just e-mailed Harold asking him to hold on to the substitute. My mother was X-rayed again yesterday and the new films show she's broken her right hip as well as her wrist. I was afraid of this. She's being operated on again as I type. My brother never made it down here, surprise, surprise. He has a "prior commitment" to try a case. Like I don't have a "prior commitment" to my students or to the UKC? Tell me, what commitment is prior to your mother? But that's a story for another time. I'm trying to find somebody to help Mom when she gets out of rehab, but I haven't yet. I want to hang around and see how she comes through today's surgery and how the rehab goes. She was kind of confused yesterday and in a lot of pain . . . but what am I telling you this for? You've been down this road.

I'll cut to the chase. BEL, WILL YOU PUHLEASE TAKE THE UKC KIDS KAYAKING THIS SATURDAY? The kayaks should have been delivered to the Student Activities Office. Someone from there will load them into the van and drive them to Laurel Hill Park by nine on Saturday morning and pick them up again at noon. Odilia (you know, the new secretary to the dean for student activities) will arrange for it if you remind her right away. The driver is to be paid out of the grant.

Now, Bel, I know what you're thinking, but get over it. Remember when we took our kids kayaking in Pennsylvania? You were terrific! You can do this and take a load off my overactive mind and give seven inner-city students a once-in-a-lifetime outdoor experience or you can refuse and ruin the lives of eight people. Thanks.

Wendy

Wendy's e-mail came at a bad time. I had just gotten home from my evening class and logged on to my computer while waiting for Sol to return from a meeting of the board of the Citizens Committee to Preserve the Waterfront. I had hoped to answer the inevitable e-mails from students inquiring about assignments, requesting extensions, and explaining absences. I figured keeping busy would prevent me from dwelling on Illuminada's speck or shadow or lump or, God forbid, tumor at least until Sol returned when I could tell him about it and, I hoped, take comfort in his reassurances that she would be okay. It didn't sound like Wendy was okay though. Only the last line of her e-mail message had even a trace of her defining wry humor.

When I heard Sol's key in the lock, I put two containers of leftovers from our Passover Seder into the microwave and pushed the timer and power buttons. It had not been easy to prepare even a small Seder after kayaking last week, but we had managed. And even after sending Ma and her housemate home with care packages, we still had plenty of brisket and potato kugel left. "So how did the mammography session go?" Sol asked, giving me a hug. He moved toward the sink where he washed his hands before foraging in the fridge for salad greens. "No more chicken soup, right?" Sol's voice was wistful.

"No. I sent the rest home with Ma," I said, answering his second question first. "I'm fine, but . . ." I saw his smile glow and then darken. "Illuminada has a 'shadowy speck' that may be something. She has to have a needle biopsy." I poured us each a glass of wine and continued, "She's pretty upset."

"I don't blame her, but it's a good thing she found out now rather than when the speck has become a tumor," Sol said as I had known he would. His deep voice lent resonance and credibility to his words. "If it's malignant, they can remove it before it spreads, and she'll be fine. If it's not, she'll be reassured and relieved. It's better to know. They say early detection saves lives, and it sounds like this is one of those cases. Here's to her." When he stopped repeating what I already knew but needed to hear over and over, he raised his glass in a solemn toast to Illuminada's health.

I raised mine too, but that night, wine held no allure, and after a perfunctory sip, I put my glass down and said, "Wendy just e-mailed me. They finally figured out that her poor mom broke her wrist *and* her hip," I said. "The doctor operated on her hip today. Would you believe Wendy's brother, the hot-shot lawyer, is too busy to make it to Florida? So Wendy's down in Fort Lauderdale coping with all this on her own. She's not going to be back until maybe next week." I responded to the buzz of the microwave and removed the containers of food.

"Poor Wendy. She's had a tough time. How long ago was it that her mom had gall-bladder surgery?" Sol posed the question as he served salad. I dished out the brisket and kugel. Although the food smelled delicious, I approached the table with a sense of obligation rather than my customary enthusiasm.

"Last July. At least that happened during the summer when Wendy didn't have to worry about work. But I have to admit Harold is being pretty decent. She just asked him to keep the adjunct he hired to take her classes for another week. He'll do it. After all, he has a mother too." I sighed, thinking of how unprepared my friends and I were for the inevitable reversing of roles as our parents aged. It is so hard to realize that the person who taught you to make a U-turn and helped you with your college applications now needs your help to complete a simple insurance form or drive to the supermarket. If this predictable progression of the generations caught us off-guard, the specter of losing a peer hit like the detonation of a forgotten land mine. To remember that buried threat was to acknowledge the mortality of our agemates, ourselves.

"And let me guess. You're going kayaking in the Meadowlands on Saturday morning, right?" Sol asked, his deep voice now jovial and his words accompanied by a grin. He was trying to cheer me up. "Wendy certainly helped you out when your dad died and Rebecca was in that accident. You owe her."

"Oh God, I guess I do," I replied with another sigh, remembering my own marathon of personal loss and anxiety. It had been complicated by the brutal murder of a RECC colleague whose suspected killer had stalked me for months. Wendy had covered my classes while I flew around the country in a state of shock ministering to my mom and my daughter. But that wasn't why I would help her out on Saturday. "I do owe her, but aside from that, Wendy and I have shared an office for almost twenty years. Hello? Wendy's my friend. Besides," I added in a more philosophical and cheerful tone, "kayaking is great exercise."

"I've never seen you kayak, even in Maine, but Wendy thinks you can do it," Sol said, refilling his plate.

"Wendy thinks I can kayak because years ago when our kids were young and portable, she and I took them camping beside a lake in Pennsylvania. I only went because we had no air conditioner, there was a heat wave, and Hoboken was a miserable hellhole." I sighed again at the recollection of the steaming city sidewalks and the hot, humid air that had driven me to accept Wendy's invitation to take our cranky kids camping. "We only drove as far as the first campgrounds on the other side of the Delaware, but the kids all loved it." I paused in my narrative to take a bite of brisket. I still wasn't very hungry.

"So did you two rent kayaks?" Sol asked.

"Not right away. We sat in the shallow

water gossiping about RECC the way we always do while the kids waded and splashed. Then I saw the water snake. It was black and about twenty feet long and swam with its head out of the water, kind of like an anorexic Loch Ness Monster. I was terrified. I catapulted out of the lake." Encouraged by Sol's rapt attention, my inner drama queen was beginning to surface. "The serpent was gliding, sinuous and silent, like a stealth submarine, in the direction of our defenseless, nearly naked babes. And you know what Wendy said?" I paused, playing to my audience.

"Yup," said Sol with another grin. "She told you water snakes were harmless and avoided people, right?"

"Right," I answered, managing a smile for the first time since Illuminada's mammogram. "Anyway, I got my kids out of the water and rented a kayak. For the next hour I paddled Rebecca, Mark, and me around and around that lake. Then it rained, the heat broke, and we headed back to Hoboken." My story finished, I added, "So that's why Wendy thinks I can kayak."

"How long ago was that?" asked Sol.

"Well, I bet it was damn near twenty years ago," I said, pouring a little oil and vinegar onto my salad. "But you know, I'm not in bad shape. Remember when Betty and Illuminada and I were investigating the killing

of that dot com whiz kid and we went undercover cleaning offices? I held my own
then and that was only a year or so ago."

"True. And you know you'll share a kayak
with a student, so you probably won't even
have to pull your own weight," Sol said.
"And you'll have life preservers too. But
you'll have to be careful about the tide. Remember, the Hackensack River and the salt
marshes are tidal."

"Right," I replied. I had been hoping Sol
would offer to go with me again, but then I
remembered his promise to spend most of
the coming weekend baby-sitting for his
granddaughter in upstate New York. Besides,
I thought, taking in his paunch, I was probably in better shape than he was. "I'll e-mail
Wendy and get her to tell me what direction
to take after we launch the boats. And I'll
ask the ranger too. We definitely need a route
that takes the tides into consideration." Sol
nodded, recognizing the sense of my plan. I
continued, thinking out loud. "And while I'm
at it, I'll try to get the ranger to come back
and lecture on kayaking safety and maybe to
give us a few tips on what sort of flora and
fauna we might see. I like to look at pretty
birds, but I don't know one from another.
And as for kayaking safety, my motto is 'Do
whatever you have to do to stay afloat so the
water snakes don't get you.' "

Sol smiled. "Sounds foolproof," he said.

"Besides, I don't think you want to go swimming in the Hackensack River either. They've gone a long way toward cleaning it up, but there's still a ways to go." I shuddered, remembering the color of the water.

Sol and I rinsed the few dinner dishes and loaded them into the dishwasher before collapsing onto the sofa, where we immediately reached for our nightly fix of news. We were newspaper junkies, two throwbacks craving pages of printed headlines and stories rather than succinct sound bites accompanying flashes of sensational video footage on the small screen. Sol exuded contentment as he tackled an unread section of last Sunday's *New York Times*. As usual this behemoth bulletin was still demanding his attention well into the week. As Sol grunted and groaned in almost ritual response to the circus that has become our nation's political life, I settled down with the equally entertaining local news, a predictable but always engaging potpourri of politicians getting indicted, convicted, imprisoned, released, and then petitioning to run for office again.

Politicians weren't the only headliners though. There was an equally predictable population of psychopaths who routinely and fatally shot, strangled, stabbed, poisoned, and suffocated their hapless victims. That's why I hadn't really been surprised earlier by Gina's account of a murder at the Outlets. Nor was

41

I surprised now to see that it had made the front page. The victim, a young Colombian-American woman, Maria Mejia, had been found stabbed to death in the parking lot of her place of employment, His 'n' Hers Shoes, presumably on the way to her car after work. Because her purse was missing, the local police officer summoned to the scene assumed that she had died resisting a thief. There were no suspects or witnesses yet. I wouldn't have paid too much attention to poor Maria Mejia's untimely demise had it not been for Gina's heads-up. But now, reading about it in the paper, I felt a chill.

I poked Sol, who was holding the *Times* with one hand and his head with the other, distressed by events in Washington, the Middle East, Africa, and Asia. "Sol, look, some poor young woman was just murdered at His 'n' Hers Shoes. That's the outlet where I bought the black flats I wore to Rebecca's wedding," I added, hoping that if I put this killing in a personal context, he would pay attention. "Right in the parking lot. In Secaucus. At the Outlets. Betty said Gina was there when it happened," I added, trying harder to interest him in this odd confluence of conversation, shopping, and death. "Look," I insisted, finally placing my copy of the *Jersey City Herald* over his *New York Times* so he couldn't help but eyeball a headshot of the late Ms. Mejia.

"What the hell did she do? Shop till she dropped?" I winced as the familiar bad joke rang out for the second time that day. "Jesus, Bel, she's not the first and she won't be the last. The Meadowlands has been a body drop since forever. Before Jimmy Hoffa." Even as he spoke, Sol gently but firmly pushed my paper out of his way and immersed himself once again in The Big Picture.

I didn't bother explaining that Maria had not been a shopper but an employee. Nor did I say how discomfiting it was to read about this murder on the same day I'd been reminiscing about shopping at His 'n' Hers Shoes in Secaucus. Sure, it was just a coincidence, but an eerie one. I was chilled by the killing itself and by the fact that the killer was still out there somewhere. *Not at Laurel Hill Park, I hope,* I muttered to myself as I moved closer to Sol.

Chapter 4

BOYFRIEND SUSPECTED IN SECAUCUS SLAYING

Failing to come up with any other leads, the County Homicide Squad has called in Hector Ramirez, boyfriend of the victim, for what they described as routine questioning. "We're covering all the bases," Detective Ralph Falco told reporters yesterday as he and two other officers led Ramirez to the waiting squad car. Ramirez is a security officer with GuardNJ at the Meadowlands Outlet Center where the deceased, Maria Mejia, was employed as a cashier at His 'n' Hers Shoes. She was found stabbed to death in the store's parking lot last week . . .

I was holding the paper in my hand when the phone rang. "Bel, Hi. I'm so glad I caught you home. I didn't want to e-mail you about this."

Wendy didn't have to identify herself. After sharing an office with her for so long, I had no trouble recognizing her voice even though

I hadn't expected to hear it on this particular Sunday night. I immediately jumped to the wrong conclusion. "About what? Oh my God, Wendy, your mother . . . I'm so sorry. When —"

"No, Bel. Yikes, I keep forgetting how you tend to imagine the worst. My mother's pretty uncomfortable right now, but she's still with us, thank goodness. That's the good news and the problem," Wendy said, sighing into the phone.

"What problem? What could be a problem if she came through the surgery okay?" I asked, but in my gut I knew. The problem was that Wendy couldn't and wouldn't simply deposit her mom in a rehab facility in Fort Lauderdale and return to New Jersey to resume her own life. And Wendy's brother, true to form, was not going to materialize in Florida. So I listened without surprise as Wendy explained that she would have to take an unpaid leave for the duration of the semester, abandoning her classes, her committee work, her husband, Jim, their extended family, and, alas, the RECC Urban Kayaking Club.

"Jim flew down over the weekend and we talked," she said. "And I just got off the phone with Harold." I heard her sharp intake of breath before she went on. "I've arranged to take an unpaid leave for the rest of the semester." Wendy used the same this-is-the-only-sensible-solution tone she used when asking a student to revise an unacceptable paper. I knew she was trying to convince herself. "I've got to stay here until my mother is on her feet again and then we'll have to make some decisions . . ." Wendy's voice trailed off.

I heard my own words streaming into the silence left in the wake of her unfinished thought. "That's a really good idea. Don't worry about the UKC. It went fine yesterday." I tossed aside the newspaper and sat down. No need to trouble Wendy with tales of an unsolved murder in the Meadowlands. "The kids are really into it. And I had a good time too. It was lovely out on the water." Wendy couldn't see me cross my fingers as I told this whopper, but Sol could, and he was shaking his head at my duplicity. "I'd really like to finish out the semester with them. Would that be okay with you?" Sol looked at me from across the room, a smirk turning up one corner of his mouth. He waggled his index finger at me. I wasn't sure if he was chastising me for my legendary inability to just say no or for exaggerating my enthusiasm for spending chilly Saturday mornings in a kayak on the polluted Hackensack River with a group of nautically challenged city kids.

"Bel, I'm really, really grateful. If anybody can keep those kids coming back so the club

46

doesn't fall apart while I'm gone, you can. And just think how good it will feel to have me in your debt when I get home." I was relieved to hear a bit of Wendy's customary humor filtering through the fatigue and anxiety that had raised the pitch of her voice and caused her words to rush out in breathy spurts. "So tell me, how did it go? Did the kayaks get there okay? How was the weather? Did everybody show up? What happened?"

"It was a perfect day. There were a few clouds but no rain." Wendy did not need to know that a windy, raw, and cloudy forty-three degrees is not my idea of pleasant weather for kayaking. "Odilia took care of getting the kayaks delivered." Wendy has enough on her mind without learning that the work-study student whom Odilia had hired to deliver the kayaks to the park had neglected to bring the paddles and life preservers. We had to wait for forty-five chilly minutes while he went back to Jersey City for them.

I'd used that time to take stock of the group. In addition to Jason, Basil, Belinda, and Deatra were Shisele Norman and Sandeep and Vekash Sharma. Shisele was light-skinned and fine-boned with penetrating hazel eyes and dark curly hair. I'd heard Wendy mention her many times. Shisele had taken Wendy's Intro to Children's Lit and Intro to Film classes, and Wendy spoke of her in the glowing terms profs reserve for the student who actually allows us to play Henry Higgins to her or his Eliza. Sandeep and Vekash Sharma, first cousins, were both slender, quiet young men with luxuriant black hair and glasses. I was waiting for the right moment to ask why they had joined the UKC.

"Are they okay? They cost enough," said Wendy, forcing me to refocus on the kayaks rather than the kayakers.

"The equipment is impressive, four shiny brand new two-person kayaks complete with nice light paddles and cushion life preservers. Basil took photos. In fact, he's photographing everything to show you when you get back. I haven't had my picture taken so much since Rebecca's wedding," I said, recalling how Basil had posed us carrying our life preservers in one hand and clutching our paddles with the other at each stage of our decidedly awkward and prolonged launch. Wendy did not need to know that, yoga enthusiast that I am, I had done six rounds of sun salutations early Saturday morning to ensure that I would be flexible enough to get myself in and out of a kayak unassisted and with a certain amount of dignity. "And we're keeping a log for you, but pretend it's a surprise," I said. "It's a group project, but Belinda's really the one who spearheaded it."

"How's Belinda doing? Is she having fun?" Wendy inquired.

"I hope so. She's the only one I worry about. You know, she kind of reminds me of that girl in *West Side Story*. Remember the tomboy who wanted to be accepted by the gang? I think her name was Anybody's." I heard Wendy grunt so I knew she recognized the character I was describing, and I went on. "Belinda's like that. All the others paired off, and she was left without a partner, so she and I kayaked together. She was kind of disappointed that Jason went with Shisele, but she gave it her all anyway." I could have told Wendy how Belinda and I had at first paddled in opposite directions because Belinda, like many dyslexics, had trouble distinguishing right from left, let alone port from starboard, but I decided that anecdote would keep. And besides, I had solved the problem by calling "wristwatch" when I wanted us to head left and "no wristwatch" when I wanted us to veer to the right. It had taken us only about half an hour to coordinate our paddling so that we didn't go around in circles.

"God, Bel, you make it sound like an episode of *The Love Boat*," said Wendy with what sounded like a smile in her voice. I hoped I was hearing right. "Did you see any interesting birds?"

"Jason was in the lead kayak with his binoculars, and he saw a hawk," I said. Why fill Wendy's already worried head with disturbing images of Jason struggling to paddle while using the binoculars? She didn't need to envision him and Shisele borne rapidly under the turnpike and downriver toward Bayonne and Kearney by the considerable current. And Wendy certainly didn't need a replay of me screaming over the amplified din of the turnpike traffic above us, "Jason, forget the freakin' birds and paddle!"

Wendy and the park ranger had both advised us to cross the river right at the launch site, where it was fairly narrow under the turnpike, and kayak through the less turbulent Saw Mill Creek, a large intact salt marsh, directly opposite Laurel Hill Park. I decided not to share with Wendy the story of how Belinda and I had nearly capsized when we suddenly found our vessel heading for two tires lashed together with rusting wire cable jutting out from what looked like the partially submerged remains of an old wooden bridge. Belinda had proved remarkably strong and, with me too terrified to scream directions, she had paddled us around the deadly detritus.

"We did better once we got across the river and into the Saw Mill Creek. But I felt as if we were out there all alone because those islets of tall reeds totally dwarfed us and we couldn't always see the other kayaks," I explained.

"You better believe it. Those are phrag-mites," Wendy interjected. "They can grow as high as fourteen feet! They're nonnative plants that grow where ditching, diking, or draining has disturbed the wetlands and created uplands. They don't —"

"Whatever," I said, unconsciously borrowing from the lexicon and speaking in the manner of my students when they were tuning me out. I wasn't in the mood for a botany lesson just then, so I didn't want to encourage Wendy, who, like Sol, could discourse for hours on a single leaf. "Jason bragged later that he caught sight of two cormorants, and Shisele saw a whole bird family in the reeds. Basil also said he got a picture of what Vekash thought was another hawk, but Sandeep thought it was a small plane coming in for a landing at Newark Airport." I chuckled at the memory of Sandeep's sly put-down of his cousin. "Man, I didn't know hawks had lights on their tails."

"Well, that's pretty good for your first time out. Too bad Belinda didn't spot something," Wendy said.

"Well, frankly, ever since she spotted Jason, she hasn't looked at much else. She just gazes at him, and I doubt that he knows she's alive. Although toward the end of the morning when we were back at the park, I noticed him talking to her, so maybe she did get his attention. I tried to eavesdrop, but

51

there were some dirt bikers nearby as we were leaving and they made a lot of noise."

"Bel, you're incorrigible. I think Jason's got a girlfriend, but for Belinda's sake I hope you're right."

"Of course, I am. Now you just take care of your mother and yourself and don't worry about RECC. The adjunct Harold got to sub is working well with your classes and Captain Bel is in charge of the UKC," I said brightly. I ignored Sol, who had walked over to our kitchen wall calendar. Picking up the marker attached to it by a string and heaving a deliberately exaggerated sigh of resignation, he slowly and deliberately scrawled a big black *X* on all the Saturdays on the page.

Chapter 5

Bear Prosefor B,

I am going to miss klass tonite to go to a job intvu! I've been looking rof a job for a mile so I can't wiss this chance to get one. Im sorry sit at the same time as your klass. I no I need help with my rdg and spelling. Mish we luck. Thanks fr going mith we in the kiack. Here are my KCU Log nots, I don't spell so good, even on the compututer, so I hope you wont mind pruf reading them for me before I turn them in too Jason plese don't say anything ok? don't worry I wont tell anybody wat you sed wen the tires alwost got us!

Your student,
Belinda Judd

Until I checked my mailbox and saw Belinda's nearly illegible handwritten note, I had been upset because she hadn't shown up for her six o'clock developmental reading class. Well aware that she needed all the help she could get, Belinda had not missed any classes so far this semester. That's why her unannounced absence had taken me by surprise. I was already worried about Belinda. In fact, since RECC had no special needs counselor or tutor currently available, I'd e-mailed the director of counseling in an effort to alert him to the severity of Belinda's problem and to ask for help on her behalf. For although Belinda struggled valiantly to keep up with her small group's discussion of the novel *The House on Mango Street* and the short readings in our textbook, there was no way she was going to be able to pass the course without a lot of specific academic support.

Some parents provided this support for their dyslexic kids who were then able to compensate and function well in school. But Belinda lived with an aunt and a cousin, and the aunt, who worked in the cafeteria of a local hospital, had no extra money to pay for tutoring. Some of the better elementary and secondary schools also offered this type of assistance for special needs students. But Belinda had not had this advantage, either, in the special education classes in the decidedly unbetter Jersey City public schools she had attended. Like the few other white and native English-speaking students who found their way to RECC, Belinda would not have been accepted elsewhere except, perhaps, at one of the few colleges that offered special programs for learning disabled students. RECC was her first, last, and best hope for higher education. All this flashed through my mind when I found Belinda's note attached to a sheaf of printouts in my mailbox. Shaking my head, I wondered what sort of job she was seeking and hoped she could find something that would reward the grit and effort it must take her to read ads, fill out applications, and go on interviews.

I didn't see her until the following Saturday when she arrived as I was getting out of my car at Laurel Hill Park. Except for the dirt bikers who were roaring around the foot of Snake Hill, we were the only people there. Belinda was carrying her book bag and wearing a smile that lit up the gray morning. "I got the job! Look!" Still beaming, she took off her book bag, opened it, and, in a charming imitation of a magician producing a succession of rabbits, pulled out a navy blue blazer and matching slacks, black oxfords, a light blue shirt, a black belt, and a clip-on pager. "See! My uniform," she exclaimed, carefully folding the clothes and then stuffing them along with the shoes and accessories into her book bag. "I'm a security guard," she proclaimed with obvious pride as I looked at the generic costume she showed me.

I couldn't help noticing that her hair, which I recalled as lank and blond, had been permed into a fluff of soft golden waves framing her heart-shaped face. Her lips, now tinted a faint rose, echoed this shape. Belinda seemed transformed into a human Valentine. I wondered if it was the new job or her desire to impress Jason that had wrought this metamorphosis. Maybe it was both. Community college years are often the catalyst for major changes, cosmetic and cosmic, even in students who don't stay long enough to graduate. Before I got too lost in my reflections on the value of the two-year college experience as a growth promoter, I responded to Belinda's announcement. "Sounds great, Belinda. You must have made a wonderful impression." I saw her stand a little taller as my words found their target. "Where are you working?"

"The Outlets. You know, right over there," she declared, pointing in the wrong direction. "What's the matter, Professor B? Did I get it wrong? It's over there maybe," she said, misinterpreting the frown I'd been unable to repress at the thought of her working at the Outlets and pointing again in another direction, still not the right one. Faced with what Belinda thought was my disapproval, she stopped smiling.

"Oh, I just had a bit of a twinge in here, that's all. I must have slept funny," I said, rubbing my neck to embellish the lie even as it left my lips. Practically speaking, there was absolutely nothing wrong with Belinda working at the Outlets. Just because a cashier had ended up dead in the parking lot of His 'n' Hers Shoes did not mean the whole place was inherently dangerous. Lots of RECC students worked at the Secaucus Outlets.

At the thought of Secaucus, my nose wrinkled involuntarily, and for a moment I was back in my girlhood in nearby Passaic. Then it had seemed as if all that stood between me and the magic of Manhattan was the Meadowlands, and then the Meadowlands was synonymous with Secaucus. In those days Secaucus reeked of garbage hauled in from New York restaurants to feed the voracious pigs that were the little burg's economic mainstay. Even grown-ups held their noses driving through. That this pigpen of a place had morphed into a modern mecca for busloads of modish and budget-conscious shoppers amazed me. The Secaucus Outlets, a conglomeration of discount designer stores, had emerged in the eighties like a bargain center Brigadoon on a onetime tidal estuary between the Hackensack and Hudson rivers that, according to Sol, had hosted everything from plantations to pig farms . . .

Belinda's next words snapped me back to

the present. "They need extra security guards now 'cause somebody found a body in a parking lot at one of the stores out there last week." Belinda was apparently unfazed by this grisly discovery. She spoke matter-of-factly as if turning up corpses were an ordinary worksite occurrence like shoplifting. "They're going to train me. And it's so cool. All the other guards are really friendly. They asked me out for a beer after my first training session. We go out every night after the stores close, just to talk, you know," Belinda said, clearly pleased to be included in the social activities of her new colleagues. "But don't worry. Like I told my aunt, I do my assignments before I go to work. And I can get the hours I want off for school and the Kayaking Club too." I was relieved that, unlike many RECC students, Belinda would not find herself forced to miss classes in order to keep a job. Wendy would also be relieved that Belinda had so far managed to protect her UKC time. Keeping track of appointments is a problem for some dyslexics, but Belinda seemed determined to manage her increasingly complex schedule.

"I'm glad they'll accommodate your other commitments. And just think, maybe you'll get employee discounts at some of the stores," I said, giving her shoulder a quick squeeze before moving on to greet the others, who were arriving and drifting over to the launch site where the kayaks were being unloaded.

As I turned away, Belinda grabbed my sleeve and said quietly, "And Professor B, thanks for correcting the log. Jason wants it to be perfect when the other professor comes back, the one whose mother is sick." I smiled at her and nodded as we walked over to the waiting kayaks.

Basil was handing out leaflets and Jason was explaining them. At first I thought the flyers offered more safety tips, but I was wrong. "Me and my man Basil, we got these at the Environment Center," Jason said, tossing his head back and then combing his fingers through his luxuriant black hair, gestures he repeated frequently. "This first paper gives a history of the area. It tells about how backinthedays a lot of this area gradually dried up and turned into a cedar forest. There are still some stumps you can see. So keep a heads-up for these stumps." He raised a leaflet level with his face and pointed at a line drawing. "It also tells how backinthedays the Lenape Indians lived here." Jason pointed to the ground at our feet. "They fished and trapped until the Europeans came and, you know, duh," he intoned, shrugging his shoulders as if the fate of the Lenapes after the arrival of the Europeans was almost too obvious to mention. Caught up in the drama of history and his pleasure in an audience, he continued. "It says the Hackensack River was a trade route in colonial times. The dudes who owned plantations and small farms, they used to ship goods all up and down this river." It was when he paused to point in the direction of the water that Jason noticed Deatra checking her watch and making little effort to mask a yawn.

Realizing that his audience's attention was waning, he summarized the contents of the other two leaflets. "This paper here shows the birds and animals. There's a sketch of each one and a paragraph about it. The last paper has plants. That way we'll know what we see. They got a lot of good stuff over there at the center," he added. I felt a pang of guilt. Wendy would have obtained, copied, and distributed this material to the membership. Then I relaxed. It was actually better for them to find it themselves. The process was called research, I reminded myself. Clearly Jason had relished discovering the leaflets and sharing them. Perhaps he would be a teacher someday.

"Thanks," I said, as I scanned the lists for familiar birds and plants. "Are you going to test us on this material?" I inquired playfully.

"Maybe," Jason answered seriously, not about to have his contribution to our morning's adventure trivialized by my attempt at humor. "Listen up," he called with that enviable assurance of a born leader. We gathered around him again. "When we get over to the marsh, start looking for what's on this list. If you got a camera, photograph it, man," he said, directing this mandate to Basil, the only one of us with a camera. Basil nodded. "When we get back, we can report on what we seen, okay?"

Then breaking away from the group but not from his role as alpha male, Jason grabbed Belinda's denim sleeve and propelled her toward the boat he had selected. "C'mon. You goin' with me," he said gruffly. The smile she flashed him in response to this rather primitive invitation was a whole different facial expression from her earlier ones. Her newly rosy lips opened slightly and curved upward, her brown eyes gleamed, and her chin tilted toward him. I heard a click. Using Basil's camera, Deatra had photographed Belinda's open upturned face. I was not the only one who had seen and appreciated the young woman's radiant smile. Deatra winked at me, her first communicative overture venturing beyond mere politeness into complicity. Her wink sealed a bond between us, two women of the world, recognizing puppy love. Later I noticed Deatra shaking her head as Jason and Belinda pushed off in their kayak, and I was reminded of Wendy's speculation that Jason had a girlfriend. For that matter, Belinda had mentioned a boyfriend. I found myself shaking my own head as well.

Meanwhile Shisele was pulling my arm playfully, "C'mon, Professor B. It's you and me this morning. Let's go watch us some birds. Professor O'Connor gonna want to know what birds we seen."

Our river crossing was decidedly less harrowing this week because everybody was more adept at paddling, there was hardly any wind, and, best of all, just as we launched the kayaks, the sun came out and shone down on us all morning. The warm bright rays may not have affected the mechanics of our trip as much as our improved paddling and the decreased wind, but they utterly transformed the view. Sunlight polished the occasional oil slick sullying the surface of the river into a kaleidoscopic patch of purple and aqua. At the same time it illuminated the gradual greening of the vegetation along the shore. As the sun burned off the wisps of fog and cloud that had curtained the Manhattan skyline last week, the trademark towers of the Big Apple three miles away were transformed into a glittering Emerald City.

The sunshine also elevated the mood of our intrepid little band. Like many young people, especially those with roots in the tropics, the UKC membership definitely subscribed to the warm weather fashion statement that less is more. To them the early spring sunshine was an overdue invitation to peel off layers of fleece, denim, and down, as much to cool off as to showcase their toned, youthful bodies. By the time we had paddled across the river, the entire crew professed to be sweating from their exertions and the heat and began to undress. I smiled as Deatra and Basil simultaneously stripped off their Polartec jackets, baring their sculpted arms to the sun as they paddled into the phragmite jungle. Jason smiled as Belinda shrugged off her denim jacket and then rolled up the sleeves and knotted the hem of her orange RECC T-shirt, condensing it into little more than a tight, bright bolero. Even Sandeep and Vekash took off their windbreakers and turned up the cuffs of their khakis.

As a concession to the warm weather, I unzipped my vest halfway, recalling that as a young woman, I too had worshipped the sun at a makeshift altar in the backyard. There, half naked and coated with Johnson's baby oil, I had knelt before a handcrafted aluminum foil reflector and prayed for a tan. I had gotten the tan all right, but that early and innocent exposure to the sun had caused precancerous growths to blossom amid the new lines on my face. Removing them was practically a full-time job for my dermatologist, whose idea of humor was to inform me that I was responsible for putting his kid through private school and then to direct a blast of nitrous oxide at my face. These recollections prompted me to realize that I had not brought along sunblock. Repressing inevitable thoughts of Illuminada, I resolved to bring some sunscreen next week.

Rounding a bend, I saw Basil and Deatra passing the camera back and forth, he snapping pictures of an occasional flurry of birds flushed out of their hiding place by our noisy approach, she taking candid shots of members of our fleet or of the dazzling postcard-perfect horizon. In fact, the only nature that held any appeal to Deatra seemed to be human nature. Jason was using his binoculars to view passing birds and shoreline plants while Belinda paddled. Nearby Sandeep and Vekash paused every now and then to dip a net into the water, pull it up, and examine its contents, a briny bouillabaisse of beer cans, decomposing vegetation, and fragments of fiddler crab shells. Then, after harvesting the beer cans to recycle, they lowered the net again. Shisele and I slowed to a stop and she consulted the leaflet Jason had distributed. "This here is Spartina," she said, waving her arm in a circle wide enough to encompass the green marsh grasses just beginning to tuft the islets all around us. " 'It can grow in the salty water,' " she read somberly, " 'because a membrane at the root cells blocks large quantities of salt from entering the plant while special glands on the leaves excrete the salt that does enter.' Too bad we don't got no camera," she said, looking up from the paper.

"I'll bring a camera next time," I promised. "I meant to bring it today, but I completely forgot. I'll have to write myself a note on a Post-it and stick it on the dashboard of my car," I continued, wondering how I was going to remember to do this. "I should bring some sunblock too," I added.

"Yeah, you the one they call Professor Post-it," said Shisele with a grin. "I heard about how you got Post-its for everything." By this time we were both paddling hard back across the river and had once again glided into the stretch of water blackened by the shadow of an old railroad bridge directly overhead. The deafening whoosh of a passing train muffled the sound that should have served as a heads-up, so the sudden rush of soft-bodied flying creatures swooping past our faces, necks, and shoulders came as a discomfiting surprise.

"Bats!" I shrieked, flailing one arm around my head and clutching the paddle with the other before I remembered that the din of the train would swallow my words and that I was supposed to model calm in crisis. The disgusting winged and undoubtedly rabid rodents were gone before I caught my breath.

Shisele turned around to smile benignly at me, saying, "Look like pigeons to me. Don't need me no paper to recognize a pigeon. They out here for a break from the city just like us. We scared 'em is all." I felt only slightly foolish, especially when I imagined the ribbing I would get from Wendy and Sol about not knowing a bat from a bird.

When we got back, Vekash approached Jason, saying, "Man, when you were at the Environment Center, did you notice any brochures on the creatures living under the water? My cousin and I, we are very interested in these. It would be okay if we went to the center ourselves to make inquiry?"

"Sure, dude. We didn't see nothin' like that, but maybe they ran out. If they got any, bring enough for everybody, okay?" And the three young men slapped one another's upturned palms amiably in what has become a globally hip substitute for the handshake. Jason clearly relished the deference accorded to him by his constituents.

As people gathered up their shucked clothes and loaded the kayaks into the waiting van, I overheard Belinda confiding to Deatra, "I have to really hurry. I don't want to be late for work. I got a new job!" A sense of purpose and importance lent an unusual authority to her voice.

"Go, girlfriend. I remember how you said you been lookin' for one. Where you workin'?" asked Deatra in the longest string of words I had yet heard her utter. I was not surprised to detect an island lilt that shaded and shaped her speech.

I noticed that Belinda did not point this

time, but instead said, "Sescauscus. The Outlets. I'm a security guard."

Deatra hesitated only a moment before replying, "Oh, Secaucus. Yeah, girl. I hear dat's what dey be needin' out dere." Then after another barely perceptible pause she said, "Well, good luck."

Chapter 6

SUSPECT IN MEADOWLANDS MURDER RELEASED AFTER ALIBI CHECKS OUT

Hector Ramirez, fiancé of the woman found April 9 fatally stabbed in the parking lot of His 'n' Hers Shoes in Secaucus where she worked, was released today after his alibi checked out. "I would never hurt Maria. We were going to get married. That girl was my life," declared a grief-stricken Ramirez leaving the police station. He had been detained there while Detective Ralph Falco questioned security guards and the bartender at the Rat Trap, a local watering hole frequented by security personnel at the Outlets where Ramirez worked . . .

The *Jersey City Herald* with the article explaining that Hector Ramirez had been released lay for days on one end of the island counter in our kitchen with other unread newspapers, unopened bills, and unwelcome junk mail before I had a chance to read it.

When I wasn't teaching or preparing to teach, I was totally preoccupied by my concern for Illuminada. Like many New Jerseyites, the Gutierrezes used local doctors for diagnosis but hightailed it across the Hudson at the first indication of a medical problem more complex than a hangnail. So Raoul had accompanied Illuminada to an early morning appointment in Manhattan at Eleanor Roosevelt University Hospital's Breast Center for a needle biopsy. The news from New York was qualifiedly bad. Illuminada's "speck or shadow or spot" was, in fact, a small lump, a malignant tumor.

"Yes. It's malignant," Illuminada said when Betty and I met her at the RIP Diner where RECC faculty and students often snack and schmooze. Only a slight quiver in Illuminada's lower jaw betrayed how she felt about this dreaded diagnosis. "According to the oncologist, I have several treatment options." The constriction in my chest when she said the word *oncologist* lasted only a second but caused me to stop and put my teacup down mid-sip. "I could have a mastectomy, you know, just get rid of the whole boob and not have to worry so much about a recurrence. Or I could have a lumpectomy." She practically spit out the sharp syllables of the ugly words signifying removal of all or part of her breast. "Either way, they have to take some lymph nodes to see if the tumor has metastasized."

Betty reached out and stroked our friend's arm. I was about to squeeze the hand that Illuminada was using to tap out a muted drumroll on the table when she jerked her arm away, recoiling from Betty's touch. "*Como mierda!* It's not the end of the world. You two look like you're at my funeral already. Give me a break." I refrained from the hand squeeze. Illuminada signaled the waitress and ordered a refill of her coffee. "Want anything? Now or never," my friend quipped, a snide reference to the fact that the service in the RIP was so slow that one could expire from starvation while waiting for someone to take an order.

Betty was still recovering from Illuminada's rebuff. I was shocked to hear Illuminada insulting the waitress even as the poor woman was serving us. We usually waited until our server was out of earshot before criticizing her. While Betty and I were saddened and worried, Illuminada was angry. I saw that as a good thing. Perhaps her anger would propel her through whatever "treatment option" she selected. I hoped so.

Illuminada was not a micromanaging control queen like Betty, but she usually got what she wanted when she wanted it, and when she didn't, she made no secret of her displeasure. I remembered how furious Illuminada had been when her daughter dropped out of pharmacy school. Rather than acknowledging that Lourdes's secret decision to leave school had hurt her and threatened her dreams for the young woman's future, Illuminada had lashed out. She read the kid the riot act at the top of her lungs in two languages and refused to speak to her for months. And she was pretty hostile to Betty and me too, projecting onto us her rage, concern, and disappointment. I surmised that Betty was also recalling this as she and I exchanged a covert glance.

"Is there any way that we can be helpful?" Betty asked, just as if Illuminada had not rudely rejected her earlier effort to provide comfort.

"*Dios mio,* of course there is. Stop treating me like I'm a goner," said Illuminada. "And don't tell my mother. If the lymph nodes are clear, I bet I won't have to have chemo or radiation, and then I won't have to tell her." I grimaced, wondering how old some of us had to be before our mothers stopped being part of the problem and became part of the solution. That led me to realize that a chat with my mother, who had twice survived breast cancer, might be just what Illuminada needed. On second thought, since there had been few "treatment options" at the time, my mother had had two radical mastectomies, and Illuminada might find that prospect daunting. I know I did. Breast cancer was a legacy from hell. I wondered if Illuminada

71

had told her daughter yet, but decided to hold off on asking.

"So what did you decide on, the mastectomy or the lumpectomy?" Betty asked almost casually, as if she were inquiring what dress Illuminada had decided to wear to a party, the black silk or the gray knit.

"The lumpectomy. Raoul wanted me to go for the mastectomy to lessen the chance of recurrence, but I told him it was my boob and I was holding on to as much of it as possible for as long as possible," Illuminada said, keeping her tone light. "I'm not worried about the procedure either. It's not very invasive, they say." Sipping her coffee, she put the cup down and smoothed her sleek black hair away from her face with one hand, like an old-time movie star.

"When are you scheduled to have it?" I asked.

"I'm not. Not yet," Illuminada answered, consulting her watch and rummaging in her purse for her wallet. I could see that she was preparing to leave.

"What do you mean, not yet? You can't put this off. The longer you wait . . ." Betty was sputtering. Barely concealed anxiety about rapidly multiplying cancer cells taking over Illuminada's body suddenly overpowered Betty's effort to stifle her inner dictator and made her voice harsh.

"I can do whatever I want, Betty," said

72

Illuminada icily as she stood and threw a single on the table. Then, relenting a little when she saw Betty's eyes fill, she added, "Sorry, I can't schedule this myself. The Breast Center has to coordinate it with the hospital and they just haven't done it yet. Maybe that's why I'm a little touchy. *Dios mio,* you two know how patient I am." Illuminada, who thought everything should have been done yesterday and who Raoul joked was always in such a rush that she brushed her teeth during sex so she didn't waste any time, rolled her eyes, aware of her understatement. "They'll let me know by the end of the week." With that, she turned and left, calling over her shoulder, "If the cancer doesn't kill me, all this waiting will."

"You okay?" I said to Betty as soon as Illuminada was out of earshot.

"Yeah, more or less. I just wish there were something we could do to make this easier for her," replied Betty, signaling to our waitress that we wanted menus. "Meanwhile, I'm going to have lunch. I won't get out again today and I'm not ready to go back to the office right now. Do you have time to eat?"

"Yes, of course," I responded automatically. We ordered tuna sandwiches and while we waited for them to arrive, Betty said, "She must be so scared. Girl, her life may never be the same again. Getting cancer must be like losing your innocence, you know, like

73

when you learn that your father has a mistress or your mother had an affair and your daddy is not your daddy. You can never feel really young again after something like that."

"I don't know about that," I said. "My mother is pretty young at heart, wouldn't you say?" Now my eyes were filling up as I pictured my mother. Sadie Bickoff was a two-time cancer survivor who had lost two breasts and one beloved husband. But, as she put it, she beat the odds and had rallied to make a new life for herself in Hoboken with a housemate she had met in the ladies' room at the Senior Center.

"Yeah, girl, your mother is a piece of work," Betty replied. "That woman knows how to have a good time. And she makes money doing it," Betty added, reaching across the table to poke my arm. It was a well-documented fact that my mother's winnings at the casinos in Atlantic City financed most air travel in our far-flung family. I had to chuckle.

"And look at Marilyn," I said, eager to add to the roster of fun-loving cancer survivors. Betty stared, not registering who Marilyn was.

"You remember. My friend Marilyn." In response to the blank look this not very helpful factoid elicited, I continued. "When we were investigating the murder of Dr. Garcia, Marilyn was an accountant in the RECC business office. You remember. She had a thing with one of the trustees."

Just as I was about to give up, Betty made a pretense of smacking the side of her head with the heel of her hand and said, "Oh yeah. She's the one who Dr. G found had a college car without any legitimate reason. I didn't know she had cancer." Betty's eyes misted over for the second time that day as they did every time she thought about her beloved Dr. G, RECC's first woman president, the person whose murder had brought Betty, Illuminada, and me together. "I remember her now. She's not here anymore, is she?"

"No. That's the point. After her bout with breast cancer, she completely turned her life around. She gave up on loser guys, quit her job at RECC, and moved to a little town in New Hampshire with some friends who design a line of clothes that are sewn by local women. She does their books, their marketing, and some selling. I think she has a few other clients too. And you know what? She loves group living and being in the country." I paused for breath. I was trying to reassure myself as well as Betty that Illuminada would not only recover from breast cancer, but that she would retain her zest for life.

"Too bad we don't have a murder to solve right now," Betty said. "That would take her mind off her real troubles." Betty sighed.

"Illuminada's got plenty on her plate at work all the time. You know that," I said. "She doesn't need a murder to distract her." *But maybe you do,* I thought, recalling Betty's concern about Randy since he had been pink-slipped by the on-line brokerage firm he worked for. She had hovered over him, offering unsolicited advice, expertise, and contacts, as he followed job leads, interviewed, and revised his résumé. One day after a particularly painful rejection, he had exploded at her and told her to back off. She had, but it had not been easy for her, consummate control freak and devoted mother that she was, to be both rebuffed and helpless while her only offspring took his chances solo in an unpromising job market. Something told me not to ask how his job search was going.

When I got home that night and finally tackled my pile of unread newspapers, I saw the article about Hector Ramirez being cleared of suspicion of the murder of Maria Mejia. Recalling Betty's words, now I almost wished that she, Illuminada, and I were out there trying to figure out who did do it. Maybe Illuminada didn't need to be distracted while she waited to have the cancer excised from her body, but I sure needed something to worry about besides my friend.

Chapter 7

Belinda Judd
Basic english 1
Professor barret
April 23 2001
Jurnal

The job I got is is so cool. I like it a
lot. I tell peoeple were things are
and look out for shop lifters. I
spotted one the other day and I told
the boss and he got her. I get to talk
to a lot of peoeple, the time goes reel
fast. I reely like the boss and I have
a lot of frends there. Every nite a
big groop of us goes out, its so cool.
I don't always get everthing they say
like the blu mall of license or
fucking (sorry, professor B) more
so I just lisen. Sooner or later I'll

figur it out. Evrybody takes turns paying for beer even the boss. last nite I paid. And I'll still finish reading the House on Wango St befor the test . . .

But I was worried. I put Belinda's journal down with a long sigh. I had just read and graded her essay exam on *The House on Mango Street*, and she had failed. Belinda would not be able to move into college-level classes until she learned some strategies to help her to better compensate for her dyslexia. Her dismal performance on the test had prompted me to schedule a conference with her to see if I could help. This semester I was teaching only four days and one evening a week and using Fridays to conference with students and catch up on papers.

Belinda arrived in uniform and on time that Friday afternoon. Her militaristic attire was at odds with the low-level radiance emanating from her halo of hay-colored hair and sparkling eyes. She did not walk but rather glided into my office. One of the upsides of teaching at RECC was witnessing young love blossom, particularly and predictably, in spring. So I was not at all surprised when Belinda floated down into Wendy's chair and said, "Jason really liked my log notes. Thanks for helping me proofread them. Here's the ones for last week." She fished a disk out of her book bag and handed it to me.

I took it, saying only, "You're welcome." Then by way of a preamble, I asked, "The new job still going well?"

"It's awesome." Of late I have heard young people use the word *awesome* to describe everything from the Taj Mahal at sunrise to the offer of a stick of gum, but I have seldom heard it spoken with as much, well, awe, as Belinda had invested in pronouncing it. She actually intoned the syllables.

"That good, huh?" I said with a smile.

I hated to be the bearer of news that would burst her bubble, but maybe being in love and having a positive work experience would make Belinda's academic problems seem less overwhelming to her. "I'm glad. They're lucky to have a smart and hard-working young person like you," I said, trying to make a positive segue into the purpose of the conference. "That's what I want to talk to you about." I took a deep breath. "You know, Belinda, the special needs counselor at RECC left to take a position at another college and we haven't hired a replacement yet. And the special needs tutor just had a baby and is on leave. So right now we don't have anybody on staff who's really equipped to teach you strategies to improve your writing." I was trying not to let my anger at this state of affairs show. But at times like this which are all too frequent when one is teaching students who have failed the New Jersey Basic Skills Test, it seemed to me as if RECC's open admissions policy did little more than guarantee challenged students the right to fail.

Smiling inanely, I continued. "But I think you're mature enough to get some help for yourself."

"I didn't do good on the test, did I?" Dyslexia may have interfered with Belinda's ability to read and spell, but it hadn't prevented her from getting my all-too-familiar message. Years of post-test conferences like this one had taught her to translate teacher-speak. I watched in dismay as the young woman's glow faded. Her shoulders hunched, her eyes lowered, her lips curved downward. She was literally deflating in front of me.

In deference to her obvious intelligence, I decided to skip the ineffective sugarcoating and get right to the pill. "No, not very. Not as well as you might have done. Because of your dyslexia you have trouble sequencing your ideas and, as you know, you didn't finish the exam. And of course spelling is a problem." I handed Belinda the test paper and paused to give her a chance to glance at its margins filled with my green-inked scrawl and to take in this familiar yet unwelcome information. "But, Belinda, here's some good news. I learned on a website that students with dyslexia can use voice-activated computers very effectively. The computers spell correctly."

Belinda's face brightened. "Do we have one of those in the lab at RECC?" she asked.

"No, not yet," I said, bracing myself to bear her disappointment. Before her face could fall too far, I added, "But I'm going to inquire about our getting one. Meanwhile, remember when we were kayaking together and you were having trouble with left and right?" Belinda nodded. "Well, remember how we solved that problem by labeling the hand wearing a watch as left and the hand with no watch as right?"

Belinda nodded again. Keeping her eyes on the floor, she spoke softly now, "I remember about that at work too when I gotta tell people where to find things. People are always askin' us security guards for directions. It does help me."

"Well, that's a coping strategy I found on a website devoted to learning difficulties." Wendy has accused me of being a cyber self-help junkie, but there were websites on the Net addressing everything from managing menopause to mothering the bride, and I had used them to get me through some trying times. Maybe Belinda could too. "The site lists a lot of materials and coping strategies," I said. "Here's the address." I handed her a piece of paper I had ready. "I think you're smart enough to make good use of it. Meanwhile I'm going to assign you to a regular tutor who will discuss your reading with you and maybe even help you access that website. And you and I are going to meet every week to go over the UKC log and make sure everything is in the right sequence before I proofread it. Maybe we can figure out a way you can organize ideas better."

Belinda raised her misting eyes to meet mine before saying simply, "Thank you. I'll try. I really want to graduate and get an even better job. I always wanted to be a firefighter. Or maybe I could help people like me someday." I was relieved to see that neither Belinda's euphoria over her current job nor her disappointment over her low test score had dimmed her ambition. I hoped that with help she could achieve her career goals. I scribbled a Post-it note reminding me to inquire about RECC getting a voice-activated computer.

Eager to restore some semblance of the aura of bliss that the young woman had brought with her into this conference, I asked a little too cheerily, "Wasn't it lovely out in the Meadowlands last week? Did you and Jason have a good time?"

"Oh yes. We had a real good time." Belinda's rush of words told me that she was as eager as I was to change the subject. She probably had a lot of experience dealing with

82

low grades and well-meant suggestions. She was only too pleased to elaborate on her morning with Jason. "And you know what the coolest thing is? He asked me to go bird-watching with him on Sunday morning at Liberty State Park," Belinda exclaimed.

"What fun!" I responded. Wendy would be ecstatic to learn that UKC members were exploring more of nature on their own. "What birds did you see?"

"Oh, Jason forgot his binoculars, so we had to go to his house to get them," Belinda said. "Nobody was home, so we started, you know, messing around, and then well, you know, we realized it was too late to go to the park. I had to be at work by one."

It was a struggle not to reveal how surprised I was by Belinda's candid account of her date with Jason. But this wasn't the first time I had marveled at the urge students had to confide in their English profs. For decades, in essays, journals, and free writing, students had been revealing to me what I considered intimate details of their personal lives. But they were usually more discreet in conferences. Belinda's inappropriate update was, like Belinda herself, almost childlike. I felt both privileged and burdened by her unsolicited report.

Oblivious to my ambivalent reaction to her narrative, Belinda smiled. Simply alluding to her tryst had reignited the spark in her eyes and brought a faint blush to her cheeks. "But that's cool. We're going to go again next Sunday." Belinda was grinning when she left my office. She called, "See you to-morrow!" over her shoulder as she made her way down the hall.

Chapter 8

To: Bbarrett@circle.com
From: ShiseleN@juno.com
Re: Practice speech on Snake Hill
Date: 04/26/01 10:44:03

Dear Professor Barrett,

I got a favor to ask. You know I'm taking speech with Professor Donato and doing my informative speech on Snake Hill (my grandma told me that's the real name for Laurel Hill at the park where we launch, so I researched it in the library and it really interesting). So anyway, Professor Donato say we got to practice before a live audience and I'd like to practice my speech to you and the other UKC members this Saturday while we waiting for the kayaks and everybody to get there. It's only about a five-minute speech, but I think people in the UKC gonna like it, especially we being right there and everything. And then you could give me some feedback maybe. Cause I know you teach speech.

BTW I checked this out with Jason and he cool with it.

Yours truly,
Shisele Norman

Wendy would certainly be pleased about the ripple effect of the UKC. Students were discovering the joys of nature and history, and their findings were enriching their academic experience across the disciplines. Shisele was not the only one inspired by our forays into the Meadowlands. Sandeep had been reading about the effects of pollution on the Hackensack River for a research paper in College Comp I, and Vekash was doing his on the Lenape Indians. Even though RECC didn't have a photography club or a darkroom, Basil and Deatra were honing their shutterbug skills outdoors and could probably be persuaded to mount an exhibition in the student lounge. Seeing them get so much out of their experience almost compensated for the Saturday mornings I had signed over to the UKC.

Shisele's speech turned out to be a winner. She had pulled into the parking lot right after I did, so she began her talk with me as her only listener, standing alone in the chilly April air. I hoped the damn dirt bikers would not roar by until she had finished. She stood a little apart from me, cleared her throat, and began. "Professor Donato, classmates, welcome. I have a question for you. How many of you have ever driven north from Jersey City on the New Jersey Turnpike? How many of you ever heard the Prudential Insurance Company's ad for 'a piece of the rock'?" Then pausing dramatically, leaning forward, and speaking in an exaggerated whisper, she asked, "How many of you here afraid of snakes?" By the time Shisele posed the last question of her brief introduction, Vekash and Sandeep had arrived and joined me in the audience, and so all three of us raised our hands.

Moving an index card to the back of the collection she held in her hand and offering a smile of greeting to the intrigued newcomers, who soon included Basil and Deatra, Shisele continued. "Laurel Hill Park in Secaucus where the RECC Urban Kayaking Club launches its kayaks from every Saturday morning while you still in bed is where you find Snake Hill." We all turned and looked at the hump of graffiti-scarred rock rising behind Shisele that had been, until she spoke its menacing name, an innocuous gray backdrop for our weekly rendezvous. Now we seemed to see it for the first time. "You all can go right by it on the New Jersey Turnpike. It be only a few miles from the Empire State Building."

Perhaps intimidated by the larger audience, Shisele was speaking with her eyes on her notecards, but after a few sentences she looked at her listeners, referring to her notes only occasionally. "Snake Hill was formed by the lava from a volcano deep inside the earth around the time of the dinosaurs, so it got a long history. The books I read say it got its name backinthedays when they was Dutch people living here. They called it" — and here she read carefully from her notes — "*slangenberk,* which could mean either snake hill or rattlesnake hill 'cause they was a lot of snakes there, some poisonous, some not. They had a lot of water snakes in the area too." I was not thrilled to hear this and allowed myself the environmentally incorrect hope that the pollution that had sullied the waterways had also decimated the aquatic reptile population. "The area around the hill was very good for growing crops and had many plantations worked by slaves. The book say that for punishment the masters sent slaves who acted up to spend the night on Snake Hill." Shisele rolled her eyes and shuddered.

According to Shisele's sources, Snake Hill had been much higher until it was quarried for traprock used to build roads and skyscrapers. She recalled that in the past the hill had been the site of a poorhouse, three different churches, a lunatic asylum, a prison, and once even a hospital for children afflicted with eye problems. She related how an adman working on the Prudential account commuted past Snake Hill every day and was inspired by it to coin the phrase "piece of the rock." Shisele even explained how the hill got the nickname Fraternity Rock when college boys scaled its summit and tagged it with Greek graffiti. She ended her talk by relating how, in an effort to improve the area's image, Hudson County officials had renamed Snake Hill Laurel Hill in 1915, but the new name hadn't stuck. Now that they had created the county's first new park in seventy-five years around the ancient volcanic outcrop, maybe it would.

We all clapped, including Miguel, who had arrived with the kayaks he delivered every week and, captivated by Shisele's words, stood riveted in place on his way back to the RECC van. I heard a click as Deatra snapped a picture of Shisele with Snake Hill behind her. "Bravo! Bravo!" yelled Basil. "Who you got for speech?" And before I even got to congratulate Shisele on her choice of topic, her thorough research, and her generally poised and engaging delivery, we were launching the boats. It was when I saw Jason look around, shrug, and then get into a boat with Shisele that I noticed Belinda had not yet arrived.

"Where's Belinda? Would somebody see if she's using the restroom, please?" I called out.

"I didn't see her. Here, Basil, gimme dat camera before you get it wet. You go by yourself. I'll go wid de professor today." With an almost casual flick of one foot Deatra pushed off Basil's kayak. Basil indicated that he accepted her decision with a good-natured grin and a wave of his paddle. "Later, babe," he called as he turned the boat around and began the river crossing.

"I didn't see dat Belinda girl today. Maybe she sick," said Deatra. "Or maybe she at work. You know she got dat new job she was goin' on about las' week. Can't jus' start a new job and take off on de firs' weekend," she said sensibly as we pushed off.

"I hope you're right." I was a little worried that my tough talk about her exam had hit her hard, and I hoped she hadn't quit school. "Except that I know she expected to be here as recently as yesterday," I added, recalling Belinda's cheery "See you tomorrow!" as she left my office.

Deatra was paddling vigorously across the river with not much help from me, so I was almost glad when, once we reached the relative tranquillity of the Saw Mill Creek, she turned around and said, "You want to paddle? I gonna take me some real pictures of dose folks for the RECC yearbook. Me and Basil, we the photography editors. Don't say nothin'. Dey be surprised when dey pictures come out in de book." I nodded,

90

pleased to be in on Deatra and Basil's conspiracy. I paddled obligingly for several hours, closing in on the other kayaks as Deatra took close-up and candid shots of all the other club members except, of course, Belinda. Basil mugged outrageously for the camera, and the Sharma cousins struck oddly formal poses. Deatra managed to catch me unawares several times in spite of the fact that she sat with her back to me in the front of the kayak.

I was beat by the time we recrossed the river and beached the boats. A distant roar and a spiral of dust barely visible below the spot where the turnpike span nudges Snake Hill indicated that the dirt bikers had arrived, but there was still no sign of Belinda, who I had hoped might be waiting for us in the park. Maybe there would be a message from her on my answering machine or one of her inimitable notes in my mailbox at work.

My concern stayed with me as I drove home, reviewing possible reasons that Belinda might miss an opportunity to spend time with Jason. Was she ill? Maybe Deatra was right. Belinda probably had to work. After all, Saturday mornings were pretty busy at the Outlets. Maybe they had just told her she could have this time off and then, once she was hired, reneged on that promise. GuardNJ, Inc. would not be the first employer to complicate a student's life that way.

On the other hand, maybe the kid had a family problem. RECC students had no shortage of family difficulties to contend with while they pursued their education. Or maybe she was with her boyfriend. As I drove out of the world of waving reeds back toward Hoboken and the beginning of what was left of my weekend, I resolved to set my mind at ease by calling Belinda.

Chapter 9

To: Bbarrett@circle.com
From: Rbarrett@uwash.edu
Re: Kayaking Granny
Date: 04/28/01 23:08:44

Dear Mom,

I guess it's pretty cool that you're kayaking every Saturday this spring even if Sol sounded a little steamed when I called the other night. Mark and I still talk about that camping trip from hell you and Wendy made us take to some reptile-infested mud hole in Pennsylvania. Wasn't that the time you strained your shoulder and had your arm in a sling for weeks? And Mom, are you really doing this in the Meadowlands? In the Hackensack River? Why not just kayak in an open sewer?

Seriously, I'm glad you can help Wendy out. It sounds like she's having a tough time with her poor mom. I know you'll never get old and sick and interrupt my life. You're always going to be like you are right now, a cool kayaking granny. BTW, your granddaughter, the one and only Abbie J, is really enjoying the books her Great-Grandma Sadie sent her, the ones all about potty training. She looks at the pictures while I change her diapers.

Any word from my baby brother recently? Last I heard Dad was still trying to talk him into going to law school but Mark was still set on backpacking through South America when he gets tired of Buenos Aires and/or saves up some money. I gotta feed Abbie J before I go to work. Keep paddling. Keith says hi.

Love,
Rebecca

When I got home, Sol was waiting with homemade pea soup and plans for the two of us to spend a relaxing afternoon strolling through galleries in Chelsea. That's why he was less than empathetic when I told him that I was worried about Belinda. "My God, Bel. Let it go. You just spent your whole Saturday morning with your precious RECC students. Is it too much to ask that you give me an afternoon? Isn't it my turn now?"

"That's the problem," I replied curtly, not in any mood just then to deal with Sol's unresolved entitlement issues. "Belinda didn't show up today, so I didn't spend any time with her. But when I saw her yesterday afternoon, she said, 'See you tomorrow!' and then

94

she didn't show or call or leave a note or anything. That's not like her. I'm very worried about her. She's so eager for acceptance and easily hurt. And on top of that she's kind of naive."

I guess my voice must have been getting shrill because when Sol next spoke, his own tone was gentle. "Easy, Bel," he said, placing a bowl of soup in front of me on the counter. But it was only after he had brought over a bowl for himself, a warm loaf of brick-oven-baked whole wheat bread, and a stick of butter that Sol addressed what was really bothering me. And when he did, his advice was familiar and simple. It was the same advice I'd given myself on the way home from Laurel Hill Park. "So call her. See what's up." I sensed that he made this suggestion in an effort to salvage at least part of the weekend by setting my mind at ease. His next words confirmed my suspicion. "Then we can go into Manhattan and walk around for a while and even catch a movie. And just maybe, if you play your cards right, I'll give you another sushi lesson. How about it?" Sol was determined to make a sushi eater out of me.

"Good idea, but I don't have her number here. I should have gotten it on my way home, but I didn't think of it. And I don't even know how she'd be listed in the phone book. There are quite a few Judds. Damn.

I'll have to go to my office," I said, cursing myself for not having thought to take the UKC members' phone numbers home with me. I asked students in my classes to fill out information forms at the start of each semester so if I ever needed to get in touch with them, I could. But I kept these filed away in my office and usually made phone calls to students from there. Unfortunately, Belinda was not very comfortable using e-mail and didn't have a computer at home, so we didn't keep in touch that way.

"Didn't you say she worked at the Outlets? Why not call her there? That's probably where she'd be today," Sol suggested sensibly. I knew that he wanted to avoid having me slice yet another chunk off the dwindling spring afternoon by going to RECC, but I had to admit his suggestion was a good one. After walking my fingers through the phone book, I made the call to GuardNJ, Inc.

Belinda had not reported to work. "She didn't show up at work today. I'll have to go to my office to get her phone number. Come with me. If I reach her, we can go into Manhattan right from RECC," I offered. I could tell he thought I was overreacting.

"Jesus, Bel. She could be with her boyfriend or her girlfriends or anyplace for that matter. I just don't see what the big deal is."

But Sol could tell that his plan had backfired from the set of my jaw and the beseeching tone of my voice when I said, "It'll only take a minute for me to get her number and make the call. And then I'll feel better."

Rosetta, the weekend security guard at RECC, clucked sympathetically as Sol and I passed her on our way up to my office. "You better be buying yourself some more of those Post-its," she called after us. Ever since I had begun to measure my life in senior moments, I had become a familiar figure to her because I often dashed in to retrieve a book or set of essays that I had inadvertently left behind. I stopped by the empty English Department office and probed my mailbox, disappointed to find only the predictable notices and memos but no note from Belinda. I entered the tiny space that is my office, leaving Sol to pace up and down the hall. The sight of him walking back and forth increased the sense of urgency I already felt, so I yanked open a file drawer and found the folder for Belinda's class. Since her last name began with *J*, her form was near the middle. I pulled the paper out and quickly scanned its lines of childlike scrawl in search of her number. As soon as I found it, I grabbed the phone and poked in the digits.

It rang twice before a chirpy-sounding woman answered. I spoke slowly, modulating my voice into some semblance of professorial plausibility. "Hello. This is Professor Bel Barrett, one of Belinda's instructors at River

Edge Community College. May I please speak with Belinda?"

"I'm sorry, Professor. Belinda's at work. Want to leave her a message? Lemme get something to write with. Hold on a sec please." I was glad of the moment or two that the other woman, presumably Belinda's aunt, spent trying to find a pencil. Should I tell her Belinda was not at work? No. Maybe she checked in at work after I had called there. Maybe the person who answered the phone at GuardNJ, Inc. hadn't known who Belinda was and was too busy or lazy to find out. Was it really any of my business where Belinda was? Should I alarm this total stranger with my half-baked worries? "Please ask Belinda to call me at home when she gets in. She has my number," I said, still trying to figure out what else to add. Finally I went with a version of the truth. "Belinda didn't show up for her Kayaking Club session this morning, so I wanted to see if she was all right," I continued lamely. "Thank you." Was it my imagination or had the other woman hesitated just a second before thanking me and saying goodbye? Had some of the chirp gone out of her voice?

"Well, it's her problem now. You did what you had to do. She knows Belinda didn't show at the UKC, and if she wants to see if the kid made it to work, she can call there herself," said Sol as we entered the PATH

98

train for New York. "You've gone above and beyond what Wendy or anybody would have expected you to do if that's what you were worried about," he added.

But, of course, that wasn't what I was worried about. I was worried about Belinda.

Chapter 10

To: Bbarrett@circle.com
From: Rbarrett@uwash.edu
Re: Now's your chance
Date: 04/29/01 20:06:12

Mom,

You're going to be so psyched! You and Sol are going to have your precious grand-daughter all to yourself for five whole days in June! I've been selected by two profs to go to a PT conference on new therapies for rehabilitating stroke patients in the other Washington next month, all expenses paid. Isn't that awesome? It'll be a pretty intense week, but what a sweet résumé builder! And everything's cool. I'll fly into Newark and you can meet my flight and bring Abbie J back to Hoboken while I take the shuttle to D.C. Then we can reverse that scenario when the conference is over. I figure you should be done with classes and kayaking by then. And Sol can help. Abbie J really bonded with him when he sang "Monday, Monday" to her while she was in the tub the night of your bat mitzvah. Keith wanted to keep her here, but Louise can't sit for her every day and half the night while he's at work, so that won't fly. Besides, I know how much you miss her and want to spend time with her, so what do you say?

Love,
Rebecca

P.S. Don't bother borrowing Wendy's Portacrib. Abbie J can sleep with you and Sol. And I'll pump and freeze ahead of time and pump and dump while I'm in D.C., so no problem there. All you have to do is a little childproofing 'cause Abbie J's into everything.

Instead of replying instantly to Rebecca's welcome message and her bewildering P.S., I dashed off an SOS to an on-line support group for grandmas. Then I scanned the remainder of my e-mail, responded only to those students requiring immediate attention, and rushed off to Jersey City on Monday morning. I'd spent an uneasy weekend. I was still worried about Belinda. The good news was that while my concern for Belinda's welfare had in no way displaced my concern for Illuminada, obsessing about the former had distracted me from obsessing about the latter. I'd arranged to meet Betty and Illuminada for an early breakfast at the RIP Diner before class. I hoped to hear that Illuminada had scheduled her lumpectomy.

The sleepy waitress had barely taken our orders and turned to walk away when Betty, her voice brusque and businesslike, asked, "Well, Illuminada, I want to know when you're scheduled for."

Illuminada, who looked drawn, replied with remarkable restraint, "And so you shall, *chiquita,* I promise. But I haven't even called yet. I'll contact both of you after I make the appointment." She glanced my way, graciously including me in her promise. "Now let's talk about something else," she said in a tone of voice that brooked no protest. "Bel, why did you suggest we get together this morning? You know how I love to start my day in this gastronomic paradise." Her sharp black eyes darted around, taking in our decidedly humble surroundings. Her sarcasm was not lost on me.

"I confess. I couldn't wait another moment to see what was going on with you." I lowered my head as if embarrassed by this admission of perfectly normal concern. Before Illuminada could interject, I went on, "But now that you've answered my question and since we're here, I do have a problem that I'd like to unload. I'm really worried about one of the UKC kids."

"Let me guess! A kayak capsized and a student fell into the Hackensack River and disintegrated. Now his or her parents are suing," Betty quipped before she tore into the scrambled egg sandwich that had just arrived.

Now it was Illuminada's turn to yank my chain. "No, I bet one of them was kidnapped by the ghost of Jimmy Hoffa. Isn't he supposed to be swimming with the fishes out there in the Meadowlands somewhere?"

"Unfortunately, you're half right," I said with a nod to Illuminada, who was nibbling daintily on an English muffin. "Belinda Judd, the student I mentioned to you who's in my Basic English I class, the dyslexic one, well, she's disappeared just like Jimmy Hoffa, except she's not dead. At least I hope not." *No, Belinda isn't dead. She's probably "messing around" with Jason like the lovestruck eighteen-year-old she is,* I thought with a shiver that rippled through my back and shoulders, taking me by surprise.

"You mean she just vanished while you were kayaking? Did she paddle off into the smog never to be seen again?" Betty asked, still not taking me seriously. She could be a royal pain sometimes.

"No. She never showed for UKC Saturday morning," I explained. "So I —"

"Bel, do you really expect every kid to show up every week? On Saturday mornings? To kayak? You know better than that,"

Illuminada interrupted to chastise me.

"Actually I didn't at first, but they have all shown up every Saturday so far. Remember, they signed up for this. And it's not a course. It's an extracurricular activity. And they like kayaking on the river and in the creek. It's fun." I was a little put out by Illuminada's city-centric cynicism.

"Anyway I had a conference with Belinda on Friday afternoon and when she left, she said, 'See you tomorrow' loud and clear. The last time she missed a class, she left a note in my mailbox," I explained. "So I was concerned, and Sol said I should call her to set my mind at ease. But I didn't have her home number, so then Sol suggested I call her at work, and I did. They said she hadn't shown up." I paused a moment to ingest a forkful of cheese omelet.

"Sol must have been annoyed that you were so worried about this kid," said Betty. "I know how he feels about all the time you put into RECC, especially on the weekends." Betty was right. Sol's resentment of the time and energy I invested in my work was no secret in our small circle.

"Well, he was, but he's used to it." I smiled thinking of Sol's many virtues, not the least of which was his willingness to put up with my workaholism as long as he could complain about it. "He went back to the office with me, and I found Belinda's home number and called her there." I paused. "She wasn't home. I spoke to her aunt. Belinda lives with an aunt," I explained when I saw Betty's eyebrows arc in an unspoken question.

"She could be with a guy —" Illuminada interjected.

"She could, indeed," I replied, cutting Illuminada off. "But her aunt said Belinda was at work," I informed them, hoping that now they would see why I was worried. "It would be good to be sure she was with a guy and that she's okay," I added.

Peering at me over the rim of her coffee cup, Betty immediately asked, "Did you check your message machine at work? Maybe she got home and got your message from her aunt and called you there to tell you why she didn't show."

"Of course," I replied. "I checked it several times including this morning. There are no messages and she didn't call me at home either. She might have left a note in my mailbox, but I doubt it. I checked that on Saturday when I went to RECC to get her phone number."

"No problem," Illuminada said crisply, annoying me by reducing my concerns to this catchphrase. But then she went on, "I'll have somebody call the JCPD and see if her aunt has reported her missing." She reached for her cell phone. "Hell, I'll call myself," she added. "It couldn't be easier. That number is programmed into my phone." She punched one number into her cell, and when somebody answered, she began to speak. "Illuminada Gutierrez here. *Si, amigo*. No, I do not want to marry you. No, I don't want to do that either. I just want information. Because if you don't, I'll tell your wife about — that's better." Illuminada winked at Betty and me. It was clear from her side of the conversation that our extremely attractive friend had one of her many conquests on the line and that he was hitting on her.

"Now listen up," Illuminada pressed. "Has anybody reported a Belinda Judd missing? Eighteen, white, a RECC student. No, I'll wait." Cupping the phone, she looked across the table at Betty and me and said, "He's checking." She tapped a rhythm sequence on her placemat with the cerise fingernails of the hand that was not holding the phone and glanced at her watch. I pushed away the plate of half-eaten omelet and sipped my tea. Then Illuminada's fingers froze just above the table and she repeated, " 'Belinda Judd was reported missing by a relative on Saturday. She has not shown up at home since Friday or at work since Thursday.' That's it? Okay, thanks. *Si, si*, I'm real sure about that." She clicked the phone off and replaced it in her briefcase.

"Damn. That's what I was afraid of. But I

bet she's with Jason. I'm going to call him," I announced, now pushing away my empty teacup. "She may have connected with him sometime Saturday afternoon. Her aunt may not know anything about Jason because Belinda has another boyfriend. I bet anything she broke up with him and called Jason." When Betty and Illuminada both raised their eyebrows this time, I continued. "Remember I told you she fell hard for Jason, another one of the kayakers, and that's why she stayed in the UKC when she found out it wasn't a kickboxing club?" As I spoke, I envisioned Belinda's upturned face smiling at Jason. "I hope that's where she is even though she's going to get her heart broken." In my eagerness to reassure myself, I spoke faster. "Jason doesn't really care about her. I'm sure she's just a casual thing to him. I'm pretty sure he's got a girlfriend. Poor Belinda."

"Well, girl, you have to be the original bleeding heart. So call now and put yourself out of your misery," said Betty, shaking her head at my well-known tendency to feel the world's pain.

"I don't have his number on me. The only one I grabbed at the office on Saturday was Belinda's."

"I keep telling you, you need one of these," said Illuminada, brandishing her Palm Pilot. "You could keep all your students' numbers in here and your calendar. *Dios mio,* I would be lost without this thing," she exclaimed, holding the little black object to her mouth for a mock kiss.

"Me too. I also record all my expenses," said Betty, adding her endorsement. "You really need one. And they're getting cheaper every day."

I suspected that they were right and had been hoping for some time that Sol and the kids would come through on my birthday, but it hadn't happened yet. To stave off further commercial announcements, I said, "I'll call as soon as I get into the office. There's still a few minutes before class." I had no Palm, but at least I had a plan. "And you call your doctor," I said to Illuminada as we stood up to leave.

"Yes, you do that, girl," echoed Betty as we walked out. " 'Cause I can't take much more of this waiting."

Chapter 11

HELP JCPD FIND:
BELINDA DAWN JUDD

MISSING SINCE FRIDAY, APRIL 27, 2001. LAST SEEN WEARING NAVY BLUE SLACKS AND DENIM JACKET ON HER WAY FROM RIVER EDGE COMMUNITY COLLEGE VIA # 5-6 NJ TRANSIT BUS. JUDD IS AN 18-YEAR-OLD WHITE FEMALE, 5'4" TALL, WEIGHING 135 POUNDS WITH BROWN EYES AND BLOND HAIR. SHE WEARS A GOLD NAVEL RING AND HAS "ANDY FOR-EVER" TATTOOED ON HER LEFT SHOULDER.

Anyone with information on
the whereabouts
of Belinda Dawn Judd should call
Investigator Frank O'Leary
at JCPD Missing Persons,
201-555-9324.

As Betty and I entered the RECC building that housed our offices, I was jolted to confront a large and grainy photograph of Belinda taped to the door with the above plea from the JCPD. "That's her!" I exclaimed to Betty, who obligingly stopped in her tracks to examine the photo and read the words beneath it. I followed her example, perching the reading glasses I wore on a chain around my neck onto the bridge of my nose to decipher the fine print. "My God!" I exclaimed again. "Frank O'Leary's handling this case. He was a student of mine, a criminal justice major," I added. "He was a really sharp kid, and he worked in the pharmacy when Dr. G was murdered, remember? He wanted to be a cop so badly. He married his sweetheart and they had a baby. I still have the paper he wrote about *Macbeth*. To this day I use it as a model of what a literary paper should be —"

"Bel, save it for your autobiography," Betty snapped, rolling her eyes. For reasons I failed to grasp, my friends were not as interested in the details of my students' lives and accomplishments as I would have liked. Betty's tone was less impatient when she added, "I just hope he's good and can find Belinda Judd. Even if he is a rookie, at least the JCPD is on the case." Then with a sigh, she added, "But I can tell you, girl, I'm going to have one hell of a day because of this mess." She sighed again as we approached the stairwell. In the name of fitness both of us opted to climb the stairs to the fourth floor where my office was. After that Betty would trust her fate to the one rather creaky elevator that was working and ride the next ten floors to her office in the presidential suite, dubbed the Penthouse by faculty and students alike.

"Huh?" I responded, already too winded to phrase more eloquently my curiosity about how Belinda's disappearance was going to affect Betty's workday.

"That sign mentions RECC. The cops will be here asking questions. There's probably going to be a newspaper article," explained Betty, gasping for breath herself. I didn't answer until we got to the fourth-floor landing, when she continued. "And President Woodman's going to get calls from the board. The trustees themselves are all over the front pages every time one of them is charged with graft, so, girl, you know how they hate the press. And they'll get on Woodman and he'll get on me. Mark my words. See you later. Go off and spread knowledge," she called as she disappeared into the already crowded elevator.

At least fifteen minutes remained before my first opportunity to "spread knowledge," as Betty had so facetiously put it. Once I had settled into my office and assembled the books and papers I needed for my nine o'clock class, I looked up Jason Carillo's phone number and called him. A machine answered and Jason's voice began to recite a long hip-hop riff about saving the earth. Impatient, I put down the phone. Before I could decide whether I wanted to call back and wait out Jason's message so I could leave one of my own, the phone rang.

"Professor Bel Barrett speaking," I said, prepared to listen to a student with an excuse for not attending class or a question about an assignment.

"Professor Barrett, this is Frank O'Leary, Investigator Frank O'Leary of the JCPD. Remember me?" Frank's voice was hearty, but I thought I heard an undertone of apology in it.

"Of course I remember you!" I replied. "How are you? How's your family?" Frank had always reminded me of my son, Mark, and I couldn't prevent the warmth I felt from flooding my voice. In fact, I didn't even try.

"Cool. Everything's real cool. We're all fine. And how are you doing? Still a slave driver?" His friendly allusion to the high expectations I had of my students reminded me of how at the semester's start, Frank had sat slouched in the back row of his Introduction to Lit class daring me to engage his interest.

"Of course. I'm meaner and nastier than ever," I answered with a smile that belied my words. "But I want to hear about you."

"Like I said, Professor B, I'm with the JCPD now," he began, and again I picked up a tinge of regret.

"Congratulations, Frank! Have you finished

your classes at State yet?" I was hoping he'd graduated, knowing that getting a four-year degree had long been a goal of his.

"I finish next month. But . . . well . . . I'll fill you in on all that. Right now, I need to ask you a few questions about a student of yours, Belinda Judd. When can I stop by to talk with you?" No wonder Frank was hemming and hawing and sounding apologetic. He wasn't asking *if* he could talk with me but rather *when*. I didn't care. I was relieved to learn that he was investigating Belinda's disappearance and eager to help in any way I could.

"Well, I've got a three-hour class that starts in just a few minutes," I answered. "Then I'll be in my office for a few hours before my next class. How about around one o'clock?"

"Cool. That works. Where do I find you? Still in the same old closet?" Frank inquired.

"Yes. Same old, same old," I replied, glancing around the tiny cluttered space. "But my office mate is on leave this semester, so we'll have it to ourselves. See you later." I put down the phone, wondering what Investigative Officer Frank O'Leary wanted to ask me about Belinda. Probably something about the UKC. Before I could speculate further, it was time to gather my books and leave for my Cultures and Values class. There, in the course of deconstructing Barbie as a cultural icon, I forgot all about friends with tumors and missing students for three whole hours.

After class I wolfed down a tuna sandwich I'd brought from home and was busily creating a final exam when there was a knock on my office door. I swiveled away from the computer to greet Frank O'Leary. He filled the doorway. The lanky teenager I remembered had been replaced by a tall, broad-shouldered, square-jawed man. But his grin was the same, and the twinkle in his eye was still there too. I was glad that the responsibilities of marriage, fatherhood, part-time study, and full-time work had not extinguished that twinkle. I stood and hugged him, only taking in his uniform, badge, and gun when I actually felt them against my body and my encircling arms. In his turn, he surveyed me, no doubt noting that I too had filled out a bit since our last encounter.

I gestured to Wendy's chair, and he seated himself there. "Well, Professor B, you look the same as ever," he lied. "I know you're going to ask about these, so take a look." He reached for his pocket and pulled out a worn leather wallet from which he withdrew two photos and handed them to me. One was a family portrait: Frank, his wife, and their baby. "That's me 'n' Terri and Meghan a few years ago. You remember Terri, right?" Without waiting for me to answer, he continued, "And here's one of Meghan last year." He pointed to the second photo, a portrait of a freckled five-year-old with pigtails and a familiar twinkle in her eye.

"She's adorable," I said, returning the photos to him.

"Yup, she's awesome," he said with a note of genuine awe in his voice as he reinserted the snapshots in his wallet. "Looks just like her mom. But Professor B, I got to ask you about this student of yours, this Belinda Judd." Frank paused and leafed through some papers on a clipboard he had put down when he came in. He pulled out a copy of the sign Betty and I had seen downstairs and placed it on my desk where the pictures of his family had been just a moment ago.

"Of course, Frank. I'm glad you're working on her case. I've been very worried about her. I called her aunt on Saturday when she didn't show up for a Kayaking Club meeting. How can I help?" I asked, wondering if, under the circumstances, it would be a breach of confidentiality to say anything to Frank about Jason.

"Well, Professor Barrett, when did you last see Belinda Judd?" Frank asked, posing this predictable question with all the gravitas of a veteran investigator. Hearing him, I felt another sudden chill spasm through my upper body.

"She had a conference with me at four o'clock on Friday," I said, pointing to my desk

115

blotter-cum-calendar so he could see for him-self where Belinda's name had been written in and then crossed off.

"And when did she leave?" he pressed.

"Around half an hour later. I'm not exactly sure." Before he articulated his next question, I volunteered. "When Belinda left, she said, 'See you tomorrow,' and when she didn't show up the next morning, that's when I started to worry and so I called her house," I explained. "Belinda usually lets me know when she's going to miss a commitment."

"Yeah, not like some students you've taught," said Frank with a wink, obviously re-ferring to his own erratic attendance when he had been at RECC. "Do you know where she was going? Did she say?"

"She didn't say, but she was wearing her uniform, so I assumed she was going to work. She had just gotten a part-time job as a security guard at the Outlets."

"Yeah. Her aunt said that. Good old GuardNJ. I did time with that outfit too for a while," Frank said. "A lot of off-duty cops moonlight there. We were all pretty tight, and I made a lot of good contacts. It was like joining a fraternity almost. A dude I met there helped me get onto the force. We went out for a brew every night after work. Man, Terri was ready to have me whacked," he re-called, grinning.

"Belinda says it's still like that, very

friendly. She feels very accepted there," I said.

"I already talked to a couple of them including her supervisor and they didn't see her that night. She never made it to work," Frank said, frowning. "But her aunt said she belonged to some club here at RECC and that you were the faculty sponsor. She said it was a kayaking club?" Frank's intonation made it clear that he didn't give much credence to the idea of me advising a kayaking club. He leaned back in his chair waiting for me to deny something that so challenged his perception of me.

"It's true, Frank. RECC has an Urban Kayaking Club and I'm the faculty adviser this semester," I said, taking real pleasure in seeing his eyes widen in surprise. "We kayak at the Meadowlands in the Hackensack River and Mill Creek," I added.

Now his eyes threatened to displace his eyebrows, but he said only, "Well, you always did more than you had to for students, but kayaking on the Hack . . . man, that's the supreme sacrifice. I heard —" Frank caught himself before he launched into the familiar song-and-dance about how polluted the Hackensack River is. He coughed and said, "Anyway, I got the names of the students in the club from the dean for student affairs this morning while you were in class. I figure maybe one of them might know something.

But I only got to talk to two of them so far." At this point Frank consulted his clipboard. Looking up, he continued, "Deatra Cain and Jason Carillo.

"You know, Professor B, it was almost funny. The Cain girl said how Belinda Judd had a side thing going with one of the guys in the club, this dude Jason. She sounded absolutely positive and she seems like a serious, straight-up chick."

"Frank, if you forget everything else I ever taught you, kindly remember that females over fifteen are no longer girls and were never poultry." I cut him off in a huff. I was relieved that Deatra had exposed Belinda and Jason's romance. Now at least I didn't have to worry about violating Belinda's confidence.

Frank reddened as he said, "Sorry, Professor B. Okay, Deatra Cain sounded like a serious and straight-up young woman," he recited dutifully although with a barely perceptible twinge of impatience. "So like I was telling you, I caught up with Jason Carillo right after his class, introduced myself, showed him my badge, and asked him when he had last seen Belinda Judd just like I asked you. He said he hadn't seen her since the previous Saturday morning at the club meeting." Frank reached up and scratched his head in a classic gesture of puzzlement. I was confused too. According to Belinda, she and Jason had gone "bird-watching" the very next day at Jason's house. Had the lovestruck teen been wishful thinking or had she been telling the truth?

"Damn," I said. "I was hoping she was with him. I thought she'd had a date with him. Now I'm really worried about her."

"Well, maybe she did," said Frank. "It's just his word against Deatra's. He's probably got a steady girl, so he's not going to let on if he saw Belinda." Of course. I recalled Wendy saying she thought Jason had a girl-friend. Most likely he hadn't mentioned his aborted "bird-watching" date with Belinda so his girl wouldn't find out. I nodded at Frank's wisdom as he continued. "Don't worry yet, Professor B. I still got a lot of people to talk to. Her aunt says Belinda's got a boyfriend she sometimes stays with so I went looking for him at his job. He works in the meat department at Pathmark, and when I went over there yesterday he was cleaning the freezer." Frank grinned and added, "He said he hadn't seen her, but I didn't feature giving him the third-degree then. Man, it must have been three degrees in there! So I'm going to talk to him again later." I knew Frank would persist in his efforts to track down someone in Belinda's life who knew where she'd gone off to, and this was reas-suring.

Leaning forward in Wendy's chair, Frank handed me a card and said, "Listen, Professor B, I know you're no slouch yourself when it comes to finding stuff out." He looked me in the eye for a few seconds while shaking his head from side to side. I knew he was remembering how I'd determined who killed Dr. Altagracia Garcia. He'd been my student at the time and had been astounded when he learned I'd done a bit of sleuthing on the side. But then students were always shocked to learn that their profs did normal stuff like shop for groceries or take out trash, let alone track down killers. When Frank spoke again, he said, "So if you hear anything . . . Here's my beeper number. Stay in touch." By the time I had stashed Frank's card in my wallet, he was gone.

Chapter 12

To: Bbarrett@circle.com,
    Eramsey@NJ.RECC.edu
From: IgutierrezPI@juno.com
Re: the big day
Date: 05/01/01 09:08:04

Chiquitas, so you'll stop bothering me, I scheduled my lumpectomy. Actually I had some help from Elena, the woman who does the scheduling. She's a former client. After she divorced her husband for spousal abuse, he tried to get custody of their two-year-old. She was fighting that and trying to prevent his having unsupervised visitation when he kidnapped the child and took her to Mexico. We traced them and helped get the kid back to her mom. So when Elena saw my name on her list, she called me and said I could have that surgery pretty much whenever I wanted. She'd work me in. Since now I can't put it off, I really want to get it over with. I picked Tuesday, May 8, at 9 a.m. Raoul and Lourdes are going with me. Happy?

Illuminada

It was reassuring to get Illuminada's e-mail and to know that, with a little nudge from Elena, she was moving forward and doing what she had to do. I felt relieved on that front. But by Wednesday evening when Belinda did not show up for class, I was no longer able to stave off my anxiety on her behalf. Surely if she were with Jason or her boyfriend or a girlfriend, she'd have surfaced somewhere by now. Maybe she'd been with Jason and he'd dumped her and she'd felt so rejected she had — No, I reasoned. Suicide wasn't Belinda's style. But where the hell was she?

Given the nontraditional students' tradition of erratic attendance, no one in her section of Basic English remarked on Belinda's absence. If they had connected the bouncy blond in their class with the waif pictured on the poster in the lobby, they didn't say so. There were often notices about missing persons on the bulletin boards at RECC, so this one had attracted no special attention. When Frank O'Leary got around to questioning them, they would take her absence more seriously. I was taking it pretty seriously already. When the seat Belinda usually occupied was still empty halfway through the class, I felt my heart constrict in my chest. *Where could she be? What could have happened to her?*

This time I called her home during the ten-minute break I allowed my students to do whatever they had to do to make it through a three-hour evening class. Most of them made calls, and as I dialed, I heard one young woman singing to her little girl. "Hello, this is Professor Bel Barrett. May I please speak with Belinda?" I said to the woman who picked up the phone before it had completed the first ring, the same woman I had spoken to when I'd called before. I was not happy to note that the chirp had gone from her voice. She sounded frantic.

"Professor Barrett?" she repeated with an urgency that transformed the syllables of my name into a desperate plea. I pictured her seated by the phone all week hoping for a call from Belinda or from someone with information about Belinda. I regretted that I had no good news for her.

"Belinda missed class again tonight. I just wanted to see if there was any news of her," I said, hoping to establish my credentials as a caring academic.

"Didn't you see the posters? Belinda's disappeared. I figured maybe you know where she is. The cop who was here says you were the last person to see her before she disappeared." Every time she repeated the word *disappeared*, I distinctly heard her swallow a sob.

"No, I'm sorry. I was hoping she'd have come home by now," I said, genuinely contrite. Again I was disturbed to have been the last person known to have connected with Belinda before . . . before she vanished. "I hope Belinda is okay and that she comes home soon." Belinda's aunt responded with barely muffled sobs and I heard our phone connection end with a clunk and a click as the poor woman struggled to replace the phone.

By Saturday when I went off to join the remaining kayakers at Laurel Hill Park, I no longer expected to see Belinda. Unlike the students in her class, these kids, who had by then all been questioned by Frank, were very aware of Belinda's absence. Deatra said, "I was hopin' she be here today. She a nice girl, dat one. Very friendly. A cop came by my house askin' 'bout her." Deatra spoke to me while Basil was getting into their kayak. And Jason kept looking over his shoulder in the direction of the parking lot where the bus usually dropped off those kayakers, including Belinda, who didn't drive or own a car.

The Sharma cousins had both been distraught by the appearance of a police officer at their homes. "My father, he always tink *I* did something bad," explained Sandeep.

"The police at my house was very embarrassing for my family," echoed Vekash solemnly. "But we explain to our parents about how our friend is missing and dey understand."

"It's very upsetting," I said, raising my voice a little to be heard over the din of the dirt bikers who had just roared into the park. I wanted to add my two cents to this discussion. "But it's so important that the police are helping to look for her and that we cooperate fully with them. One of us may know something that helps them find her, something we're not even aware we know. Of course, her family is terribly worried," I said. I watched Jason's face intently to see how he was taking this information. I thought he winced, but in milliseconds his features smoothed, and he ran his fingers through his hair and tossed his head. "Oh man, I hope she's okay. Shisele could do the log until Belinda gets back," he said, half to himself. Then he turned abruptly and approached Shisele. In the manner of executives everywhere, Jason was delegating responsibility. Shisele assumed he wanted her to kayak with him, so after agreeing to take notes, she looked pleased when the handsome young man jerked his head in the direction of the closest empty kayak. She followed him, and together they maneuvered it into the water.

Deatra called, "Yo, Basil. Go by yourself today. I'm goin' wid de professor again. You don't mind my company, Professor B?" she asked with an engaging smile.

"Of course not. If Basil can spare you, I'll be glad of your company," I answered and I meant it. The idea of spending three hours paddling alone through the canals bordered by tall phragmites and worrying about Belinda was not appealing. Deatra's company would be a welcome distraction.

At my request, we waited until all the other kayaks were launched and then pushed ourselves off. Deatra was not taking pictures today, so we each paddled in silence until we were midstream and heading for the first of the old railroad bridges. "Tide's in. Head down," Deatra reminded me sharply, just in time for me to duck so I didn't hit my head on the two-century-old timbers. Although these bridges were still in use, I was grateful that no train rushed by just then. There was no sunshine to temper the view of reeds, turnpike span, and power lines. Snake Hill was behind us now. Clouds obscured the towers of Manhattan. "See dat?" Deatra asked.

"What?" I replied, my eyes following the paddle she'd hoisted out of the water to use as an oversized pointer. I focused on two earthen mounds, one about the size of Snake Hill and the other much smaller.

"Dat's Mount Garbagio and the little one next to it, dat's Mount Trashmore," she informed me. "Dey old landfills. Basil and Jason found dat out from de guy at de Environment Center."

I smiled at this bit of local lore, trying to

126

focus on something besides my worry over Belinda. "Boy, those two are certainly spending a lot of time at that Environment Center. I'm glad they're so interested in the Meadowlands," I said as we finally reached the relative calm of Mill Creek. "I hear Jason is doing a lot of bird-watching," I added. The words came out of my mouth automatically, before I even realized that I was pumping Deatra to see if she knew something about Belinda's alleged bird-watching expedition with Jason last Sunday.

"Dat ain't all he doin'," Deatra replied half under her breath. Then, looking around her at the tall phragmites, the calm water, the gray sky, she said, "You know, Jason and Basil, dey go way back. Dey grew up together. And Jason tol' Basil somethin' and it weighed on Basil, so he tol' me." Then Deatra flashed me one of her knowing smiles, saying, "And now I guess it be weighin' on me, so I'm tellin' you." She glanced back at me to see if I was willing to receive this confidence.

I was pretty sure I knew what it was already, but being insatiably curious (*nosy* is an ugly word) and eager to see if it confirmed Belinda's account of her Sunday morning with Jason, I said agreeably, "Okay."

Deatra stopped paddling and twisted her upper body around so that her profile was visible to me. "I tellin' you dis 'cause I don' know if I should tell dat cop. I'll see what you got to say about it first. Jason tol' Basil last week dat he hooked up wid Belinda on Sunday morning at his house. His girlfriend Luisa was on de island dat whole week seein' to her auntie's funeral." When I looked puzzled, Deatra explained. "Puerto Rico. She got family dere. Dat fool Jason, he figured Luisa never know. He figure it was a onetime ting wid Belinda. But den Belinda, dat girl innocent, jus' like a chile." Deatra shook her head at Belinda's naiveté. "She want to be wid him alla time . . ." Now Deatra twisted her torso, stretched, and resumed paddling while I registered this confirmation of Belinda's account of her Sunday morning tryst with Jason.

Before I could decide how to respond, Deatra turned around again and answered her own question. "Basil, he be done wid me if I tell de cop. But someday I gonna be a cop myself. And Basil," here her voice was indulgent and scornful at the same time — "he pretty all right, but he not my forever man anyway. He jus' my for now man."

Chapter 13

RECC COED FATALLY BEATEN BIKERS FIND BODY AT LAUREL HILL

Sean Malloy spotted something large and light blue partly hidden in the tall reeds on the perimeter of Laurel Hill Park while he, Joe Couzo, and Jose Guzman were dirt biking there Monday. "It was back in that off-road triangle. You know, between Snake Hill (recently renamed Laurel Hill), the turnpike, and the river. I figured maybe some dude threw something out of a car, you know, like they do sometimes, so I rode up close to see what it was," Malloy told police. It was the blue shirt on the badly bruised body of eighteen-year-old Belinda Judd. A student at River Edge Community College and a security guard employed by GuardNJ, Inc. and assigned to the Secaucus Outlets, Judd had been reported missing a week ago by her aunt, Mary Waters. Judd's death is under investigation.

This article appeared in the paper the same

day that Illuminada was having her lumpec-tomy. Betty and I along with Vic and Sol planned to bring dinner to the hospital that evening to share with Illuminada and Raoul. We had no plans to talk before dinner, so I was surprised when Betty called very early Tuesday morning. When I heard her voice, I couldn't imagine what she wanted. She began, "Bel . . ." and hesitated. It was too early for any news about Illuminada. The lumpectomy wasn't scheduled until nine. I figured she had forgotten the dinner menu and the division of labor we'd agreed on. To jog her memory, I began reciting the data on the Post-it I had plastered on our fridge. "Sol and I are stopping at Balducci's and picking up chicken and bread on our way to the hospital. We'll look for a dessert too, something portable. You and Vic are driving in and bringing an asparagus salad, paper goods, and a bottle of vino," I rattled off, pleased to be the efficient one for a change. "We're meeting in her room at seven."

"I know," Betty said, her voice unusually low. "That's not why I'm calling."

"Did something happen to Illuminada? It's too early . . ." I said, all the assurance gone from my voice.

"No. But I guess you didn't see the paper yet. Bel, they found Belinda Judd. She's dead. I'm sorry . . ." She paused, waiting to see how I would take this unwelcome news.

"Oh no! Oh my God! What happened?" I sank to the stool near the phone port and pictured Belinda's eager smile and bright eyes, her heart-shaped face. Once again I heard her voice, full of romance, hope, and grit. My eyes filled. Sol heard my exclamation as he was pouring OJ into my glass. He looked at me inquiringly. Still holding on to the receiver, still technically talking to Betty, I said to him, "Belinda Judd is dead. Betty saw it in the paper. Did you bring in the paper yet?"

He handed me the *Jersey City Herald*, the plastic wrapper not yet removed. I spoke into the receiver. "Thanks for telling me. Sol just put the paper in front of me. I'll read about it. I'll see you tonight." I was eager to get off the phone. "Yes, I'll see you tonight," I repeated, putting the receiver back in its charger. I'd apologize later to Betty for my abruptness, but I needed to read for myself the brief article bearing news of Belinda's death. Then I needed to let it sink in, to let this abrasive reality displace from my mind the denial I'd been fostering for over a week. As I sat there, the newspaper in my hand, Sol said, "I'm sorry, Bel. I know you were fond of her."

He was only trying to comfort me, but when I shrugged out from under the arm he put around my shoulders, he said quietly, "Okay, Bel. I guess you want to suffer in solitude for now."

131

And I was suffering. Belinda was dead. *That poor kid. Why would anybody want to kill her?* I sat there for a few more minutes and then went off to work snuffling, trying not to think about Illuminada or Belinda or, for that matter, the other young woman who had died in the Meadowlands, the Colombian woman. Instead, I tried to focus on helping students prepare for upcoming finals, research papers, and speeches. I was somewhat relieved by a call from Raoul, who reported that Illuminada's lumpectomy was over and that she was in the recovery room. Then I dutifully attended a meeting of the Tenure Review Committee, where we spent over an hour discussing whether Sheetrocking the basement of one's church was a substitute for scholarship in one's discipline and RECC committee work.

"I'm sorry. I caught you off-guard this morning" were Betty's first words that evening when we met in the lobby of the hospital. Betty and Vic were chatting with Lourdes Gutierrez, Illuminada and Raoul's daughter, who appeared to be leaving the building.

"Your news was bad and I just needed a few minutes to digest it," I said, giving her a hug with the arm that wasn't holding a bag of groceries. I gave Lourdes a hug too.

"Sure you don't want to grab a bite with us before you go to work?" Vic was saying to Lourdes. But Lourdes was so much like her

132

mother. She looked at her watch, blew us all kisses, and, murmuring thank-yous, raced off. Vic Vallone led us to the elevator. Vic had fallen hard for Betty, whom he met while we were investigating the murder of his brother Vinny. Also hit by cupid's arrow, Betty had abandoned celibacy and tables for one in favor of sharing her life with Vic, the last guy I would have thought would appeal to her because he was so much like her. As Sol teased them, "Together you two will rule the world."

At the door to Illuminada's room we stood back to let a volunteer carrying out two huge bouquets of tulips, lilacs, and hyacinths pass. "Just put those in the children's ward, please," Illuminada was saying. The room was a double but the other bed was empty. Sitting in a chair by the window, our Illuminada looked pale and tired. A voluminous crimson silk robe with matching slippers set off her sleek black hair. Tonight her blunt cut made an austere frame for her pinched face. I noticed that her fingernails were painted the exact same shade of crimson as her robe. She wore no makeup. But she didn't need it because the grin she flashed at us when we trooped in with our offerings brightened her face. Raoul looked pretty glad to see us too.

"*Caramba,* what took you so long? I thought I would starve to death! Look at this

133

stuff they brought me for dinner." She pointed at an untouched tray where pools of multicolored glop had congealed in assorted saucers and bowls. Raoul removed the tray from its stand and left the room with it. Vic and I began setting out the goodies we'd brought while Betty smoothed Illuminada's bedclothes and put fresh ice in her glass. Raoul returned with another chair.

"It's a good thing you guys got here. I swear I thought she was going to eat those damn flowers," he said, flashing a grin of his own. He too looked drawn, but his eyes were clear and his movements casual and easy. Things must have gone well. "She'll be discharged tomorrow morning," he announced.

"*Si,* they're just keeping me here tonight so my drugs can wear off. And I can go back to work whenever I feel up to it," said Illuminada, looking defiant. "My mother will drive me crazy if I stay home." Nobody bothered to contradict her. "We had to tell her I was having the lumpectomy. She didn't say too much. But how much do you want to bet she went to see her obeah woman today?"

"Whatever works," I said, thinking it can't be easy to learn that your daughter has cancer, and feeling more than a little compassion for Milagros Santos.

"Yes, she's got to do whatever she can to get through this," Betty echoed. Illuminada snorted, not about to give an inch on the subject of her mother.

"So tell us about your operation," I inquired, knowing full well that one of the perks of undergoing surgery was the right to chronicle your ordeal to your friends and loved ones.

Sol poured wine into paper cups, surprised when Illuminada covered hers with her hand, saying, "Not tonight. I'm still seriously drugged. I'll just go with water." Illuminada's refusal did not prevent the rest of us from lifting our glasses and toasting her before we attacked the food. "The surgery was nothing, really," Illuminada said, almost apologetically. "The worst part was I couldn't eat last night after eight. Then we had to get up so early to get here by nine because Senor Worrywart over there" — she pointed a stalk of asparagus at Raoul before continuing — "he wanted to be sure to miss the rush-hour traffic, so we left the house before seven. You should have seen Lourdes. She worked late at the bar last night but she met us here this morning. She was in the lobby when we walked in." Illuminada shook her head, marveling at her daughter's love. I couldn't blame her. It is indeed miraculous when a sulky and rebellious teenager who had previously preferred death or dismemberment to making a public appearance with a parent grows into the joys of filial piety. "We were here an hour and a half early, waiting for

\text{}

them to take me up. We spent more time waiting than the whole procedure took." Illuminada spoke between mouthfuls of chicken. "This is so good," she said. "You remembered to get lots of dark meat too."

"So then what happened?" I asked, handing her another drumstick.

"The anesthesiologist came in and started an IV. He was talking to Raoul and when Raoul said he was a CPA, this guy started talking about his taxes. I think Raoul picked up a client," she said seriously. "Then they brought me downstairs and I said goodbye to Raoul and Lourdes. Lourdes looked a little teary, but I told Raoul to take her out for breakfast and some father-daughter bonding." Illuminada helped herself to more asparagus and a slice of crusty French bread. Even though her underarm had to be sore from the removal of several lymph nodes, she was managing to put away her share of dinner.

"*Dios mio,* it's a good thing she came with me. You know, I left the house this morning without any cash. Not even a credit card. I can't believe it. I went to pay for breakfast and I had *nada.*" Raoul laughed. "You'd have thought Mina was having another kid," he added, jerking his head in the direction of his wife, whose eyes brightened as he recounted this joke on himself. "That's how nervous I was. We had used Mina's EZ Pass to get through the tunnel, so I didn't even notice that I had no money. Lourdes had to pay for breakfast. Then she had to go to a cash machine to get more money to give me so I would be able to get the car out of the parking garage when I leave tonight. She really took care of her poor *papi*." Raoul grinned, clearly amused at the notion of his own un-CPA-like fiscal foul-up.

Sol and Vic began tossing used paper plates, cups, and utensils into the bag they came in. "Hey, let's go get some Starbucks to go with those cookies. I'll take orders," said Vic. "Come on. It'll just take a few minutes. I noticed one a couple of blocks away. The walk will feel good." Just as Betty whipped out a pad to record people's preferences, a nurse walked in. "We're making a Starbucks run. What can we bring you?" asked Vic genially.

"Nothing. Thanks though. How's the arm?" As the men filed out, the nurse continued speaking, directing her singsong litany of remarks to Illuminada. "I see they took the IV away. That's good. Tomorrow morning before you go home we'll change that dressing. Those incisions may pinch a little later on, so you want to take this and get a good night's sleep." She handed Illuminada a cup with a pill in it and the paper cup of ice water. Illuminada dutifully popped the pill into her mouth and chased it down with a gulp of the proffered water. "And I want to get your temp and pressure," added the nurse, deftly inserting a thermometer into Illuminada's un-affected armpit. The nurse removed the instrument almost instantly, glanced at it, and paused at the end of the bed to record the results on Illuminada's computerized chart. Then she took her blood pressure, nodding while recording those numbers. "Anything I can get you?" she asked, almost rhetorically, in view of the fact that Betty and I were standing by. "Just push the button if you need something after your visitors leave." And she was gone.

The minute she left, Illuminada said, "Bel, Raoul brought the paper. I read about that student of yours. I'm so sorry. I know you were fond of her. I know you're going to get involved."

"I'm already involved," I said. "I keep thinking I could have done something to help her, to prevent . . ." I saw Betty and Illuminada exchange glances. Betty rolled her eyes.

"*Dios mio*, Bel, that's crazy talk," Illuminada went on, "but tomorrow when I get home, maybe I —"

"I thought you'd never offer," I quipped. I mean, here was Illuminada barely out of the recovery room already offering to help me finger Belinda's killer.

"And what am I? Chopped liver? Isn't that what you always say when you feel left out,

138

Bel?" asked Betty. "Illuminada, if you can find out if they've finished the autopsy and what other leads they have, that would be a big help. Then Bel can . . ." It was reassuring how, even in that hospital room, we quickly assumed our familiar roles, Betty giving orders, Illuminada finding things out, and me, well, the whole thing was all my fault.

By the time the guys returned from Starbucks, we each had a list of things to do, people to see, questions to answer. The men entered the room laughing and bantering, and handed us each a small decaf mochachino. In spite of the fact that her underarm and chest throbbed a little, Illuminada now had some color in her cheeks that had not been there before. "So, Bel, Sol says your granddaughter is coming for a visit. That must float your boat." Sometimes Vic had a real way with words, a veritable silver tongue.

"Yes. I can't believe I didn't tell you. Rebecca has to go to a conference in D.C., so she's leaving Abbie J with Sol and me. I get to play grandma for five whole days."

"Imagine traveling three thousand miles to drop a kid off at Grandma's house. Whatever happened to 'over the meadow and through the woods'?" Vic asked. Until his mother's death, at least two generations of his family had always lived within a few blocks of one another in Jersey City.

"I drive two hours to baby-sit for my granddaughter, and I think that's nutsy," said Sol. "Now Abbie J is jetting across the country so we can sit for her. Am I crazy or is that a little bizarre?"

"It's bizarre, but Rebecca's always been out there, hasn't she?" I said with more than a note of maternal pride. Sol was muttering something about an acorn and a tree when I continued, "I'm glad motherhood hasn't dulled her edges. Besides, I'll be so happy to see Abbie J that I don't care if Rebecca decides to parachute her in."

In the early nineties, my daughter and Keith, her boyfriend, had joined the latest wagon train of young people heading west. There in the frontier city that gave us Bill Gates, Jimi Hendrix, Starbucks, and Chai latte, Rebecca and Keith had respectively temped and Sheetrocked their way to adulthood. Keith is now the super-concierge-manager of a new luxury apartment and hotel on First Avenue near Pioneer Square, where he and Rebecca live rent-free. To relax, he runs, swims, and bikes in punishing Ironman competitions. Rebecca is earning a master's in physical therapy at the university and waiting tables. In the Northwest they had made good friends, conceived Abigail Jane, orchestrated a wedding, and learned to do everything in the rain. They were not coming back.

"Yeah, you could use a little diversion. It'll be good to have her here for a few days," Sol said, making a veiled reference to my on-going concern for Illuminada and my sadness about Belinda.

"And Sadie will be overjoyed," Raoul added. That was for sure. My mother would be thrilled to have her great-granddaughter within cuddling distance. "But I still think it's bizarre that Rebecca is airlifting the kid three thousand miles for child care." That was easy for him to say since his mother-in-law lived upstairs from him.

Before Sol could even begin to sound off on the pros and cons of long-distance grandparenting in the twenty-first century, a common topic in our household, I said, "It's the first time we've had her without Rebecca. I'm a little nervous. But we're saving yogurt containers for her to play with, and planning activities. I just hope I can get my grades in before she gets here and —" I didn't finish the sentence, but Betty and Illuminada knew what I meant. I wanted Belinda's killer behind bars before my granddaughter arrived.

Chapter 14

To: Bbarrett@circle.com
From: Grannyonthego-go@juno.com
Re: When Mom's away
Date: 05/08/01 06:11:56

Dear Bel,

You asked for advice as you plan for that first solo run with your grandchild. You might as well learn from my experience. My daughter Charmaine lives in Butte, Montana, and she had a business trip to Chicago lined up while her husband was going to be away on business himself. Charmaine decided to drop my grandbaby off with me here in Austin. Well, Perry's not such a baby these days, more of a toddler, like your Abbie J. Just like you, I was so excited because I don't get to see that much of her. I even took a week off from work. And just like you're doing now, I stocked up on Pampers. I tell you, going down that aisle in the supermarket again took me back in time to when Charmaine and her sister were both in diapers. Remember when they came out with the pinless version, the ones with the tapes? Pampers were what women's lib was all about for me. Anyway, I bought enough Pampers to change Perry every fifteen minutes.

So what happened? When the plane landed, I was waiting at the gate. At first I couldn't find them because Charmaine was carrying so much stuff her face was hidden behind it. She had asked a total stranger to carry Perry. Bel, half of what she was carrying was diapers. Let me tell you right now, diapers ain't what they used to be. They now have "cloth diaper systems" and "gel-free," "environmentally friendly" disposable diapers which, by the way, are also "perfume free" (remember that nice Pampers smell?).

Of course, I knew my Charmaine wouldn't use disposables at home, but I figured while Perry was here, she would. Silly me! My Charmaine never met an alternative product she didn't like, and, in case you wondered, she is personally responsible for protecting the environment from little Perry and Perry from the environment. Charmaine's blood runs pure green. Even her tampons are organic and biodegradable, but that's another story. My daughter only buys 100 percent unbleached organic cotton (read washable) diaper systems from Sweden that she orders on-line. She carried about a thousand of them with her.

So, Bel, my advice is talk to your daughter about diapers and if she's like my Charmaine, maybe you can take those unopened boxes of Pampers right back to the supermarket and get a refund just like I did.

Good luck! Enjoy Abbie J. Simone (Grandma Simmy)

P.S. While Perry was here, I toilet trained her!

Surfing the Net for advice from other grannies in preparation for Abbie J's visit was infinitely preferable to tossing and turning in bed. Belinda's seemingly senseless death haunted me at night. I lay awake wondering what the autopsy would reveal and trying to attribute motives to shadowy figures in Belinda's life. But even my cyberspace pen pals couldn't prevent me from focusing on how to set up a conversation with Jason. He was the one I wanted to talk to first.

It wasn't going to be easy to arrange a casual chat with him either. That's why the next day I was shocked to find Jason standing alone at the door to my office, alternately combing his hair with the fingers of his right hand and looking at his watch, his book bag on the floor beside him. "Hi Jason. You looking for me?" I struggled to keep the tension and surprise his presence evoked out of my voice.

"Yeah, I am, Professor B. You got time? Or you want me to make an appointment?" he asked, picking up his bag and following me into my small sanctuary. From his tone, it was clear that the idea of having to make an appointment did not sit well with him.

"I have a few minutes now as long as you don't mind if I eat my lunch while we talk," I said, gesturing at the brown bag on my desk. "I have another class soon, so I need to eat before it starts."

"That's cool," he said magnanimously, taking a seat in Wendy's chair. As I glanced at Wendy's pile of accumulating mail, I realized with a flash of panic that I had yet to let Wendy know about Belinda's death. But there was no rush, I reassured myself. After all, there was nothing Wendy could do, and she did have her own troubles. "I got a problem," Jason said as soon as he had seated himself and run his fingers through his hair at least three more times. I noted the signature head toss that customarily followed this gesture was missing. Jason, usually so smooth and confident, looked decidedly ill-at-ease. I was a bit on edge myself, hoping that whatever he had come to say would shed some light on who killed Belinda.

"Well, Professor B, you know Belinda Judd is . . . like she's dead, right?" Jason sounded very unsure about Belinda's death. Perhaps he too had not fully accepted it. I nodded, a mouthful of tuna fish sandwich sparing me from having to reply in more detail. "Last week, before they . . . before they . . . found her, this cop from JCPD came around asking me when I seen her last," Jason recounted as if this were a bizarre line of questioning instead of SOP. "So I told him it was Saturday, you know, when she came to the UKC. Then this week after . . ." He paused, looking for words with which to say the unspeakable. "After they found her," he said gruffly, "a different cop came by my house and asked me when I last seen Belinda Judd." Now Jason shook his head while running his fingers through his hair, exasperated by those cops who were clearly making a nuisance of themselves.

"I told him the same thing I told the other one. But man, somebody else told him I seen her," he said, speaking fast in the manner of someone who is not used to explaining himself. "The problem is," Jason continued with a worried scowl, "I had seen her. It was the next day, Sunday, just for a couple of hours." Jason was speaking even faster now as if to minimize the importance of the time he had spent with Belinda. "Man, that chick Belinda, she could run her mouth, and she must've

146

told somebody, probably some girlfriend, about me seeing her that Sunday. And, man, whatever motor mouth she told must've told one of them cops." Here Jason shook his head yet again, this time incredulous at the very idea of anyone ratting on him.

"So because of that, the second cop thinks I was lying, man." He continued to shake his head, now perhaps at the absurdity of anyone doubting his word. When he spoke next, his eyes were lowered, his head facing the door. "But, Professor B, I did hook up with Belinda. You know she liked me, and Luisa was away," he explained, raising his eyes heavenward as if powerless against the effects of his charm. "It was just for a few hours, man." Jason paused and raised his eyes to meet mine. "But I didn't kill her," he said, his voice still low but steady. I remained silent, waiting.

Correctly interpreting my silence as an invitation to continue, Jason explained, "See, I already got a girl, Luisa. She's a nature lover like me. She really came on to me at the Laurel Hill Park dedication. She was there with this group she started, SSGNJ, State Students for a Greener New Jersey." He paused, perhaps remembering his pleasure at being singled out of the pack by such a worthy young woman. Then, realizing he had digressed, he continued, "Luisa and me, we been together over a year now, and, trust me,

147

she definitely does not understand when I see other chicks even if they don't mean nothin'." Jason shook his head yet again, this time at what he clearly perceived as Luisa's patent unreasonableness. I thought his summary of Luisa's attitude merited another nod. Then looking at the young man in front of me, a denim-clad composite of arrogance and anxiety, I fought a sudden urge to curse him for his narcissistic and cavalier attitude toward women foolish enough to favor him. But even as I wanted to berate him, I believed him.

"Why are you telling me all this, Jason?" I asked, suddenly aware of the clock.

"That second cop, man, he's talking about indicting me and having me go before a grand jury and I'm hoping to transfer to Rutgers. I can't have a record, do time, not for something I didn't do . . . I'm getting a public defender. I had to tell my father. I live with him. He just got out of the VA hospital again. He's a 'Nam vet and, man, he already got stomach problems." At the thought of his dad's ill health, Jason's hand found its way to his hair again. As if fortified by this familiar gesture, he looked up and said, "Professor B, everybody knows you're good at figuring stuff like this out. I didn't kill Belinda. Somebody did. I figure maybe you could help me out . . ."

I decided not to tell Jason that I was already on the case, so to speak. What I said when I stood up was, "Well, Jason, I'll have to think about it. And you should also do a little thinking about how you got into this mess in the first place. I was very fond of Belinda, and if I do decide to look into who murdered her, it will be to have her killer put in jail, not to keep you out. I'll get back to you after I've made up my mind." The look that Jason shot me as he departed was not pretty. If he was a killer, I knew that my self-righteous and judgmental pronouncement would have put me at the top of his hit list.

After my Intro to Lit class, I beeped Frank O'Leary, who called me back from a phone in his car. I could hear horns honking and brakes squealing in the background as we talked. "Hi, Professor B. What can I do for my favorite slave driver?" I had to smile. When he teased, Frank had always reminded me of my son Mark. I was happy that Frank's good humor remained intact despite the fact that he was obviously busy. I tried to speak quickly so he would not end up as one of those statistics cited by legislators to support banning cell phone use while driving.

"Frank, I know you're off the Belinda Judd case, but —" I began.

"Yeah. I was gonna call you. County Homicide's got that one now. I'm sorry to hear what happened to her," he said. "But you know, I was right about that dude Jason.

Deatra Cain called me and told me she had heard that Jason was with Belinda one morning when his girl was away." Frank was obviously proud of his ability to read a situation. I didn't mention that I'd already heard all that from Jason himself.

"Good work, Frank," I said, and I meant it. Then I cut to the chase. "Listen, Frank, did you ever talk to her boyfriend? The one who works in Pathmark?" I asked. "I just wondered if you had his name."

"He wasn't around when I got back there, but his name's Andy Dawes, and the aunt is Mary Waters," Frank answered before I had even clicked open my pen. For a moment I was dazzled by Frank's instant recall of these names. Shortly after blowing out those fifty fatal candles, as if on cue, my friends and I had all lost our ability to remember names. We had learned not to ask one another people's names and developed elaborate ruses to avoid introducing one another in public. We had begun to appreciate events requiring name tags.

Recovering quickly, I jotted down the two names. "Thanks, Frank."

"But listen up, Professor B." Frank surprised me by continuing the conversation. "I asked you for help when Belinda Judd was missing. Now she's dead, murdered, it looks like. So you better leave this to the professionals, to County Homicide, okay?"

"I hear you, Frank." I forgave him his somewhat patronizing tone because I knew he spoke out of concern for my safety and respect for the competence of his colleagues on the County Homicide squad, not out of a desire to put me down. "Thanks for the advice." I said goodbye quickly. I had a little grocery shopping to do before I went home.

Chapter 15

To: Bbarrett@circle.com
From: ShiseleN@juno.com
Re: Doing something
Date: 05/09/01 10:02:10

Dear Professor B,

I feel so bad about what happened to Belinda Judd. I can't really believe something like that could happen to a girl like her. She weren't no gang girl or nothing. Anyway me and Deatra were talking and we was wondering if there's going to be a funeral or something. We was thinking of going to pay our respects and say good-bye. The paper didn't say nothing about that. We figured you might know. If you do, would you e-mail me back?

Thank you.
Shisele Norman

Shisele's inquiry was waiting for me when I checked my e-mail later that night. I was pleased to get it because Shisele raised a point I hadn't considered at all. If Belinda's family was having a funeral, I too wanted to go, not only to pay my respects and say goodbye, but also to see if I could learn anything there about who had wanted Belinda dead. I made a Post-it note to call Belinda's aunt, Mary Waters, the next day. As I wrote, I hoped that perhaps she would agree to meet with me. She herself might have some ideas about who had killed her niece and why.

My visit to Pathmark had been wrenching, but not, in my opinion, very helpful. When I arrived at the meat department, I asked for Andrew Dawes and was directed to a large young man hunkered over the display case setting out cellophane-wrapped Styrofoam trays of pork chops. Andy Dawes, Belinda's boyfriend, was a handsome blond fellow about six feet tall with a beefy build befitting a butcher. He wore a white blood-splattered apron and a white coat that made him look even bigger. Andy's lips seemed fixed in a sad, sweet smile and his gray eyes were focused on something far away. Looking at him I suddenly flashed on Lenny in Steinbeck's *Of Mice and Men*.

"Andrew Dawes? I'm Professor Bel Barrett. I was Belinda Judd's English prof at RECC. I was very upset to learn of her death, her murder." The smile stayed. His eyes remained distant. I might have been talking about the weather rather than the murder of his girl. I shuddered involuntarily, recalling the Steinbeck character's fatal caresses. I persisted. "I was very fond of Belinda. I wonder if I could talk with you for a few minutes? Can I buy you a cup of coffee across the street?" After what Frank had said about Andy not keeping their appointment, I was not expecting an interview, but I was wrong. Like many young people, Andy had found talking to cops less than rewarding.

"Yes, ma'am. I got a meal break comin' up. I'll take it now. I'll be with you in just a minute." Andy's almost excessive politeness struck me as studied, perhaps a carefully cultivated way of dealing with a bewildering and intrusive world. He disappeared behind the counter and into the butchering room behind the glass partition. In a few minutes he returned minus his white coat and bloody apron. He wore jeans and a navy blue open-collared short-sleeved knit shirt. Together we crossed the street and settled into one of the two booths at the coffee shop, where the matronly looking waitress smiled familiarly at Andy and gave me a frankly measuring look.

"Glad to see you back, Andy. It's terrible what happened to Belinda," she said, patting him on his shoulder as she handed us menus. "I'm so sorry." Andy put his hand over hers for a moment and then glanced at the menu.

"I'll just have a cup of decaf tea," I said. "Andy, do you want supper now? This is

154

your dinner break, right?" At the thought that this sad young man might miss a meal, my inner Jewish mother leaped out unbidden. "Eat, Andy, please, eat something."

Andy consulted his watch, and said, "Thank you, ma'am." Then turning his head to the waitress, he ordered. "The usual please, Lucy." The way he managed to look at things and people who were close up without losing that faraway look in his eyes was starting to be a little eerie. I was surprised when, without benefit of a leading question, he began to speak. "Belinda." That was all he said for about a minute that seemed like an hour as I forced myself to wait in silence for the rest of his thoughts. I was richly rewarded for my patience. "Belinda," he repeated like a monk intoning a mantra. "I loved her. We been in the same class since eighth grade." The pauses between his short statements gave me plenty of time to picture the two blond pubescent youngsters bonding in a Jersey City public school special ed classroom.

"She loved me too. We did everything together in high school. We went to the prom." At this point, Andy reached into his back pocket and pulled out his wallet. I braced myself for what I knew was coming. There it was, a photo of him and Belinda in full prom regalia. He looked dashing in a black tux, she radiant in a cloud of lilac tulle. "We were

155

going to get married. But then she went to college. And that's when she started changing. She stopped loving me." I decided against interrupting this young man to tell him that it was not uncommon for romances to sour when one member of the couple went on to college and the other didn't. "She studied all the time. She started joining clubs, meeting different people. She got a different job. She used to work at Pathmark, shelving stock. She was a stock girl," he added kindly as if I needed that explanation.

"She said she didn't love me anymore," Andy added simply, without changing his tone of voice. He did square his shoulders though as if to better bear the burden of this rejection. "She gave me back the necklace. I gave it to her for her eighteenth birthday. It had her birthstone. It had an opal. See?" To my amazement, Andy now reached into the front pocket of his jeans and pulled out a gold chain with a small opal at its center. Then I saw that the smile had left his lips, his formerly faraway eyes were squeezed shut, and his big shoulders heaved as he sobbed silent, wrenching sobs. He brought the necklace to his lips. From across the table I had a front-row seat at this highly personal psychodrama and I felt like an invader, a voyeur. The waitress, approaching from behind Andy with his meat loaf special, observed his state, and signaled to me over his shoulder that she

156

would hold the order.

In a few minutes, Andy had regained control of himself, blown his nose, and repocketed the necklace. "I'm sorry," he said. "I wish she was back here now." He spoke as if Belinda had merely taken a trip. "Even if she didn't love me anymore. I just wish she was here."

"I know you do, Andy. And so do I. Believe me, so do I." I reached across the table and patted his forearm. "Andy, I just wondered, since you were so close to Belinda for so long, do you know of anybody who didn't like her? Who was angry with her? Somebody at Pathmark maybe? Or a relative or a friend from high school?"

"Belinda was voted friendliest in our school. At Pathmark everybody liked her. She was always helping everybody. And her family . . . no." Andy summarily vetoed the very idea that any of Belinda's relatives might have harbored a grudge. To emphasize that point, he added, "Her cousin and her aunt loved her a lot. Even her aunt's boyfriend liked her. Belinda didn't like him that much though," Andy added. Then hastily he repeated, "But he still liked her."

Repressing a second urge to lecture Andy, this time on the complexity of intergenerational familial relationships in today's fragmented families, I signaled the waitress and said, "Andy, here's your dinner." As the

157

young man attacked his meat loaf and mashed potatoes, I noted that grief had not robbed him of his appetite.

That evening, I fixed myself a cup of Soothing Moments herbal tea, welcomed my black cat, Virginia Woolf, onto my lap, and called Wendy in Florida. It would not do for the overactive RECC grapevine to transmit news to Wendy before I did that a member of the UKC had been found beaten to death not far from our launch site. Wendy's reaction was typical, "Bel, are you making this up to distract me from thinking about why my mother doesn't want to do her physical therapy exercises or how I missed my granddaughter's first gymnastics demonstration and Grandparents' Day at Brendan's kindergarten?"

"No. I wish I were. And I'm sorry about your mom. Maybe a different PT?" I said, trying to be helpful.

"We're on the third PT. Never mind. Oh my God. Poor Belinda. Who killed her? Why would anybody kill her?" Wendy asked. "She seemed so sweet."

"County Homicide is working on it, and they think maybe . . ." I hesitated. Wendy was not going to be happy that a member of her precious UKC was a prime suspect in this murder. The funding agency would not look kindly on renewing a grant for a club

158

whose president had fatally assaulted the organization's recording secretary. "Well, Jason told me they've been questioning him," I explained reluctantly. "He lied to them at first about when he saw her last. Didn't want his girlfriend to know."

"Know what?" asked Wendy. "Don't tell me he and Belinda . . ."

"You got it, Wendy. He spent a couple of hot and heavy hours with Belinda one Sunday morning while his girl was out of town. Figured his girlfriend would never know. Figured sex with Belinda was just a slam-bam-thank-you-ma'am deal, kind of like the D.C. intern of the week. He couldn't care less about her. Meanwhile Belinda broke up with her longtime boyfriend . . ." I added, picturing Andy Dawes sobbing in the coffee shop.

"Jesus, Bel. Do you really think Jason killed her?" Wendy asked, the sordid details coloring her view of Jason just as they had caused the cops to rethink his role in the murder.

"No. Of course, his lying made the cops even more suspicious of him. But I still don't think he did it," I added quickly. "Anyway, that's my gut reaction after talking to him. I think he's a narcissistic macho man whose ego outweighs his brain, but I don't think he's a killer."

"Oh God, I can see the headlines now,"

Wendy said, sounding resigned. "There goes my grant renewal." That's why I was surprised when her next words came out in a rush. "But listen, Bel, I don't think Jason would kill anybody. He wants to transfer to a four-year school," she added, as if the wish to acquire a bachelor's degree, that precious passport to the middle class, somehow exempted Jason from homicidal impulses.

"That's what he told me," I said with a smile Wendy couldn't see. "That kid's so narcissistic he can't see beyond his own petty stuff. It's like Belinda meant nothing to him, so her death doesn't mean much either except he realizes that a murder rap is not exactly a transcript enhancer. He really made me mad," I said, relieved to vent my feelings to Wendy.

"Oh God, I hear my mother calling. I have to go. I'll call you. Bel, you know I've never been in favor of your sleuthing activities before, but if you could absolve Jason and save the grant, we're talking Belgian chocolate. Just be careful."

Chapter 16

To: Bbarrett@circle.com
From: Gram1@hotmail.com
Re: Separation anxiety
Date: 05/10/01 07:10:19

Dear Bel,

Now you just relax. Your little Abbie J may shed a few tears when her mama says goodbye, but she'll recover and you all are gonna have a wonderful time. I had the same concerns the first time my only grandbaby, Zoe (actually, she's near two now, but she's still my baby), came from Minneapolis to stay with me and Big Buzz here in Atlanta while her daddy was having surgery. Kim, that's Zoe's mom, wanted to be able to go back and forth to the hospital to see Little Buzz, without worrying about who was taking care of Zoe. Kim is a wonderful mom, but she goes just a tad overboard sometimes. Zoe's never had a paid baby-sitter!

See, Kim and Little Buzz are into "attachment parenting." Sounds like your daughter and her hubby are attachment parents too. That's probably why she said never mind about borrowing the Portacrib. See, Zoe sleeps right there in the bed with Kim and Little Buzz. Actually it's a miracle that Little Buzz only fell out of bed once. And the doctor says this operation's going to fix his collarbone right up. Well, anyway, Big Buzz wasn't too sure about having Zoe in our bed at first, but he adjusted. It was that or the couch for a week. I couldn't believe how Zoe could sleep through Big Buzz's snoring, but that child is amazing, let me tell you.

Remember how we used to carry our kids in backpacks? Well, Kim and Little Buzz don't carry Zoe. They "wear" her. They use these over-the-shoulder slings just like the moms in Africa and South America do when they wear their babies while they pick crops and gather at their village well. Kim says "baby wearing" keeps Zoe in intimate contact with Mom or Dad and gives her a sense of security and lots of stimulation. But like I said, Zoe is nearly two and she's a good eater. So Big Buzz wore her more than I did. Now that Zoe's back home, the chiropractor has really helped Big Buzz a lot and he says he misses wearing his love bundle.

Zoe took to us pretty fast, so don't worry about separation anxiety. These kids are being raised to attach, and, who knows, maybe they'll make the world a better place.

Enjoy Abbie J's visit. Good luck!

Sue

Fantasies of showing off Abbie J while I ran errands in Hoboken lifted my spirits as I cruised the Heights, Mary Waters's Jersey City neighborhood, in search of a parking place. I passed newly renovated one-family houses trimmed in the yuppie palette of pastels and contrasting colors named after vegetables sharing street space with clapboard two- and three-family homes and an occasional apartment building. The area takes its name from the palisades on which it sits overlooking Hoboken and the Manhattan skyline. Actually the skyline is visible only to a well-situated few. Residential streets arc sandwiched between the area's old commercial spine, Central Avenue, and the palisades.

After I finally lucked into a parking spot, I strode rapidly to Mary's house on Webster Street a block or so before the park that edges the neighborhood on the north. By the time I reached it, I had banished all thoughts of Abbie J and even of Illuminada from my mind and was focusing once again on finding Belinda's killer. After all, that was why I had

163

called Mary Waters and set up this meeting. Mary lived in a three-family house fronted by a flight of stairs bordered on either side by a slightly overgrown lawn. At the front door, I pushed the buzzer for the second floor as Mary had instructed on the phone, and then waited.

The woman who answered the door after only a minute or two was about Belinda's height, but there the resemblance ended. Mary Waters had short dark brown hair spiked with gray. Her eyes, behind metal-framed glasses, were dark brown also. She wore no jewelry and was still dressed in a light blue two-piece uniform. In one hand she held an unlit cigarette. She extended her other hand to me. "Hello, Professor. Thanks for coming." Her voice was muted now, her handshake tentative. *There is not a trace of chirp left in this poor soul,* I thought as we shook hands and I followed her up the carefully maintained and well-lit flight of stairs.

Standing aside at the top, she motioned for me to precede her into her railroad flat. "Coffee? Tea? A beer?" she offered, gesturing for me to take a seat. I quickly scoped out the small front room in which the smell of cigarette smoke mingled with the cloying aroma of pine-scented air freshener. There was a dark blue sofa spanning the wall beneath the windows, and across from it a television. Against the wall opposite the doorway were two easy chairs, each with a swath of blue-flowered material neatly draped and tucked over it, perhaps camouflaging worn upholstery. I headed for one of these and sat down, saying, "Tea would be fine. Decaf or herbal if you have it. Otherwise regular." I hated myself for being fussy, but if I could avoid lying awake half the night, I wanted to. Mary disappeared for a minute.

While she was gone, I noticed a photo atop the TV set. Belinda smiled out at me flanked by Mary Waters and a uniformed young man I didn't recognize who appeared to be in his early twenties. Andy Dawes stood behind Belinda, his arms circling her waist like a human belt. On the table between the chairs there was another photo, a black and white picture of a smiling Mary Waters without her glasses but with a tall handsome man of forty-something. He wore a dark suit and she a light colored, slinky sheath. They faced the camera with the skyline at their backs. It looked as if the photo had been taken on the Weehawken palisades. Next to this photo was an ashtray with a couple of butts in it. On an end table beside the sofa a philodendron overflowed its clay pot, sending streams of heart-shaped leaves cascading down. An oval hooked rug partially covered dull, worn hardwood floors. The many shades of blue in the rug coordinated with the colors and patterns of the furniture. Clearly this was a room in which someone took pride. Mary soon returned with two mugs of hot water and a small dish of assorted tea bags. I was relieved to find several without caffeine and helped myself.

There was an awkward silence that I allowed to continue for a minute or two while I sipped my fruity brew and studied Belinda's aunt. Behind her glasses, Mary Waters's eyes were red-rimmed and her prematurely lined face bore no trace of makeup. Her hands were also red, her unpolished nails short, and her cuticles ragged as if she chewed them. Beneath her uniform, I could make out a skinny frame, with only the slightest suggestion of breasts and hips. What had happened to the sexy woman smiling up at the handsome man in the photo? "I'm just so sorry about Belinda's death," I said, finally, not wanting to add to this woman's misery by subjecting her to an uncomfortable silence but hating to speak of her terrible loss.

"Thanks. Thanks for coming, Professor," she said, her voice still low. "Mind if I smoke?" Mary asked, speaking so softly now that I had to lean forward to catch her words.

"No. Of course not," I lied. "Mary, Belinda told me you raised her . . ." I paused, waiting for the back-story I knew was there.

Mary took a tiny lighter out of her uniform pocket and ignited her cigarette, inhaling deeply. "Belinda was my brother Gary's daughter," Mary began, her voice slightly more audible now. "Him and his wife Karen, they had her when they was just outta high school. No, actually Karen quit school to have her. They were livin' with me and my husband." Mary sighed as if she were tired of repeating this familiar sad story. Taking another deep drag of her cigarette, she went on. "Then one Saturday when Belinda was just a few months old, they left her with me and went to look at an apartment over in Union City. They figured they could afford their own place 'cause Gary was makin' good money doin' construction," Mary explained. "On the way home they was hit by a drunk driver and Karen got hurt pretty bad." I nodded sympathetically, not wanting to interrupt Mary's outpouring. "Some creep was drivin' drunk in the middle of the afternoon," she said, shaking her head at the absurdity of this. "She died on the way to the hospital. Then six months later, Gary fell off one of them high buildings he was workin' on over in Fort Lee. He fell thirty stories and they scraped him off the sidewalk," Mary said, making no effort to hide her bitterness. "Gary and I were always close as kids. He always took my part with our folks and he helped me out with money when Joey wasn't workin'."

"Joey?" I asked, pointing at the photo on

the table. "Your husband?"

"That's not Joey," Mary said quickly, reddening almost imperceptibly. "Joey was my husband, but after our son, Carl, was born and Gary died, Joey left," she said without inflection as if noting the departure of a total stranger. "That's Carl there," she said with some pride, pointing to the young man in the picture with Belinda and Andy Dawes.

"You've had so many losses." I pitied the fragile-looking woman grinding the remains of her cigarette into the ashtray. "Thank goodness you still have Carl," I added, hoping that he was a source of comfort to his mother.

"Well, I'll have him soon," she said. "He's in the service at Fort Bragg. He came home last week when I called him. He couldn't believe his cousin was dead. He had to go right back after two days, but he'll be home for good in a couple a weeks. We decided to wait until then to plan some kinda memorial service for Belinda. It's just me 'n' him 'n' Andy." She pointed at the group photo, but before her finger had settled on Andy, the tears silently coursing down her cheeks forced her to reach into her uniform pocket and fish out a Kleenex.

"Actually Belinda's friends from the Kayaking Club want to know about your plans for Belinda's funeral," I interjected, thinking that this sign of concern on the part of Belinda's friends might be comforting to Mary.

"I'll let you know," she said as the only acknowledgment of my remark. When she spoke further, it was of Andy Dawes. "Andy was Belinda's boyfriend since forever," she finally said, lighting another cigarette.

"He must be terribly upset too," I said, deciding not to mention just yet that I'd met Andy.

"Yeah, he is. They were gonna get married. They were in the same class in school. Andy Dawes was the best thing that ever happened to Belinda in that damn special ed class they put her in. That's him there," she said, again pointing to the photo. "Belinda said she broke up with Andy, that she had outgrown him. Get that!" Mary snorted softly. "A good-lookin' guy like Andy with a steady job who'd do anything for her. She got a little nuts when she went to college, my Belinda did." Now that she had shed a few tears, Mary seemed to welcome the opportunity to talk. She lit another cigarette. Her mug of tea sat neglected on the table beside her.

"What do you mean?" I asked.

"Well, like you know, she started actin' like a real teenager, like on TV, doin' nutsy things. She'd been helping me out with the bills for years. She was always good that way. But after she started college she up and quit her job at Pathmark. Got herself a job way out in Secaucus, where she had to take the bus at all hours. She started stayin' out late at the job, comin' home smellin' like beer even though she was just eighteen. What could I do? And she joined that canoe club of yours. No offense, Professor, but Belinda never was in a boat like that in her life," Mary said, clearly convinced that trying something new was in itself evidence of lunacy. "And she would study all afternoon," Mary added, as if describing the ultimate aberration from normal behavior. A bit taken aback, I stifled the urge to say something to the effect that studying is what college students are supposed to do. Instead I listened. "You know, even with her, you know, her little reading problem, Belinda got very good grades in high school. She said college was real hard."

I couldn't control myself any longer. "You know, Belinda was really amazing. At RECC her dyslexia made it difficult for her to keep up with the other students, but she kept plugging away. Perhaps her high school classes weren't as challenging," I speculated, picturing the notorious urban special ed class in which the teacher considered it a good day's work when the students filled in a few worksheets and didn't kill each other. "At RECC Belinda was in precollege classes preparing herself to do college-level work." I wanted Mary to appreciate Belinda's desire to study hard. "Belinda very much wanted to earn her associate's degree, but her reading problem made that very hard work. I really admired her determination," I added.

Suddenly I realized that my posthumous defense of Belinda's study habits was somewhere between overkill and ridiculous, so I shifted gears. "And you know, she really enjoyed our kayaking trips and her new job too. She threw herself into all these activities with such energy and enthusiasm. She was meeting new people all the time, making new friends . . ." I hesitated, waiting to see if Mary would mention Jason. She didn't. I tried again. "She certainly wasn't the first girl to dump her high school boyfriend when she went to college . . ." I put down my now empty teacup.

"No, I guess not. But poor Andy. He's like family. And he's just lost without her," Mary said softly. "We both are. I keep waitin' up for her to come in at night . . ." she said, arms crossed over her chest, hands gripping her thin shoulders as if literally holding herself together. She began slowly rocking back and forth in her chair, new tears welling behind her glasses. "I keep buyin' the kind of ice cream she liked, Ben & Jerry's Coffee Heath Bar Crunch. And I still gotta go through her stuff." Mary sighed at the depressing prospect of sorting through Belinda's possessions. "And Gary. I keep thinkin' about

Gary. He wanted a better life for her." She began rocking harder. "I'm sorry," she said between sobs. "I'm just tired of talking to cops. They just didn't know my Belinda." I went over to the sofa and sat beside her and put my arm around her. Still sobbing, she spoke into my shoulder. "Belinda was the daughter I never had. I can't believe she's gone." Finally, with a touch of defiance amplifying her voice, she lifted her head and said, "And I can't believe that somebody killed her. Maybe she couldn't read so good, but she was smart and Belinda never hurt anyone in her whole life."

"That's the way I saw her. She was a very, very sweet girl," I replied. "But, Mary, somebody did kill her. And I'm trying to figure out how that might have happened." Mary took in this piece of information without responding. For all she knew, professors routinely involved themselves in solving murders. Since she asked no questions, I continued my line of inquiry. "Mary, I was wondering if you knew of anybody who didn't feel the way we did about Belinda. Maybe somebody who was jealous or who held a grudge? A relative, perhaps? A high school friend or a friend from her old job or, for that matter, her new one?" I was pressing now and Mary pulled away from me a little abruptly, I thought. She fished out another Kleenex, swabbed at her eyes, lit a cigarette, and said, "No, Professor. Like I said, my Belinda would never hurt anyone."

I couldn't help picturing Andy Dawes sobbing in the coffee shop. I reminded myself that Belinda hadn't set out to hurt him. Of that I was sure. She'd just made the mistake of falling in love with someone else. Had this turned out to be a fatal error?

Chapter 17

How to Find a Breast Cancer Support Group

For women and their families, a diagnosis of breast cancer can be overwhelming. Support groups can provide a confidential and supportive arena where the many challenges of living with cancer can be shared with others with similar experiences. There are various types of support groups, including groups that target specific populations or women with a particular stage of breast cancer diagnosis. In addition, groups can be facilitated either by peers who are cancer survivors or by professionally trained social workers or counselors. There are also many support groups now available on the Internet. Since every support group is different, it is often helpful to visit several groups to see where you feel most comfortable.

I was looking forward to a brief respite from thinking about Belinda's violent death. Betty and I had arranged to take Illuminada out to lunch when her lumpectomy was over.

Betty had made us reservations at Casa Dante, a venerable and posh Italian eatery near RECC frequented at noon by Jersey City's better-heeled movers and shakers and by the same cast of characters with their families at night. We rarely went because it was a bit on the pricey side, but this was, after all, a special occasion. Casa Dante was also one of the few places in town where you could get lunch late and linger over it all afternoon if you liked.

I got there first, tired from a morning spent reading exams. Betty and Illuminada came in just as I was debating whether to order champagne. One look at Illuminada's face banished that thought and prompted me to blurt out, "My God, Illuminada, what's wrong? You look awful." Dark circles beneath her eyes bore witness to sleepless nights and new sharp lines accentuated her cheekbones. She had looked better in the hospital.

"Thanks, Bel. You really know how to make a girl feel good about herself," snapped Illuminada as she took her seat, shook out the enormous snow white napkin folded into a pyramid at her place, and spread it across her lap. Before I even had a chance to apologize, she continued, "Yesterday the oncologist told me I had no affected lymph nodes, but I still have to have chemo and radiation. 'Cancer has become more aggressive, so we have to treat it more aggressively,'" she said

with an edge to her voice, obviously par-
roting her doctor's rationale for further treatment. "Chemo starts in about a month."

"But we assumed that you would do that.
That's the way to play it safe," said Betty
reasonably. "We knew the lumpectomy was
just the first step."

"*Caramba!* Maybe you knew it. But I was
hoping . . ." Illuminada's voice faded. Then,
squaring her shoulders and lifting her head,
she resumed. "I was hoping to avoid at least
one of them. The chemo takes three months.
I have to have four treatments, one every
three weeks. That's twelve weeks. Count 'em.
Dios mio, we're talking about three months.
And then the radiation takes another month.
There goes my life." She sighed wearily. "It's
not enough that they took a chunk the size
of one of Bel's M&M's out of my boob. Now
they want to radiate me and shoot me full of
chemicals till I throw up and lose my hair."

While Illuminada was talking, I reached
into my purse and handed her a sheaf of
printouts from the National Association of
Breast Cancer Organizations listing area
breast cancer support groups as well as on-
line groups. "Here, take this. It's all the info
you need to find a support group so you can
communicate with other people going
through the same thing."

Illuminada barely scanned the first page of
the printouts before giving me an utterly

scathing look and thrusting the papers back at me, saying, *"Como mierda,* Bel, you're the queen of the cyber groupies, not me. You can't even go to the bathroom without joining an on-line support group. I would never e-mail a lot of strangers about my personal business. And who wants to listen to a bunch of other miserable women whining about their problems? Not me, thank you very much. Did you really think those would help?" she asked, gesturing dismissively at the printouts and looking at me as if I had suggested she stand on her head naked while reciting the Communist Manifesto in Times Square.

Tears stung my eyes as I told myself that Illuminada's angry diatribe was not a personal attack on me so much as a way for her to vent, but I still felt hurt and at a loss to respond. I was relieved when Betty broke what was rapidly becoming a long silence to say, "I'm taking the rest of the afternoon off, so I'd like some wine. Should I order a bottle for us to share or just ask for a glass for myself?"

We agreed on a bottle of Casa Dante's most affordable Chianti and placed our food orders as well. That done, we sat again in uncharacteristic and uncomfortable silence. I was beginning to regret instigating this supposedly celebratory get-together. But then for the second time in five minutes, Betty salvaged our civility level and raised our spirits. She mustered up a grin and turned to Illuminada, saying, "Well, girlfriend, you trashed Bel for just suggesting you consider a support group, so I guess I'm taking my life in my hands by giving you this." She handed Illuminada a newspaper clipping and explained, "I found it in the *New York Times* a couple of weeks ago, and since I did assume you were going to have chemo, I saved it for you." Having said this, she put her hands palms out in front of her face as if to fend off a blow.

Illuminada actually smiled for a nanosecond before she spoke. "So, *chiquitas*, you think I don't have enough to read, enough to do? Don't make me read this whole article. Just tell me what it's about," said Illuminada, returning the clipping to Betty. "Brief me like you do President Woodman." Betty had often regaled us with hilarious stories of summarizing letters and articles for her boss.

She was quick to oblige. "It's about an American Cancer Society–sponsored program called Look Good . . . Feel Better. They help you deal with the effects of surgery and chemo. I don't think they mean effects like nausea because they give you antinausea drugs now. But I was hoping they'd tell you where to get a glamorous turban or a funky hat. Because, frankly, I don't particularly want to have to look at your bald head either, girl-

178

friend," said Betty with another grin.

Illuminada stuffed the clipping into her purse and then reached across the table for the printouts I had tried to foist on her and added them to her cache. I sat there marveling at how Betty had managed to get Illuminada to at least consider our well-meant suggestions and at the same time to restore a modicum of good humor to what was, after all, supposed to be a festive meal. I reminded myself that, unlike me, Betty seldom lost her temper with her ex-husband no matter how outrageously he behaved. "He's still Randy's father," she'd say when I questioned her restraint. "The marriage is over, but the family goes on."

We raised our glasses to Illuminada in a wordless toast. As we helped ourselves to portions of fried calamari, I abandoned my resolve not to bring up the subject of Belinda. "Well, actually, now that you mention it, Illuminada, I don't think you have enough to do, so I need your help with something. I've had two opportunities to chat with Jason Carillo."

"Oh, what did you do, follow him into the men's room?" asked Betty facetiously. She sometimes made fun of my persistence in these matters.

"No. I didn't have to. He actually came to my office and asked me to help him. Are you ready for this one?" I leaned forward and lowered my voice. "He claims he's innocent and he doesn't want a murder rap on his transcript." I sat back waiting for the guffaws I knew this information would inspire. I was not disappointed. "He admitted that he lied to the cops at first by saying he hadn't seen Belinda that Sunday, but then he got caught in that lie, which, of course, made him a serious suspect. He claims he lied because he didn't want his girlfriend to know about the time he spent with Belinda."

"Sounds a little narcissistic, if you ask me," remarked Betty.

"A little?" echoed Illuminada. "He sounds like the original macho man."

"Well, I guess that's one way of looking at it," I said. "I saw him again last Saturday when the UKC met. He was slightly less *moi*-centered. Shisele and Deatra had called him and said that the UKC should do something to honor Belinda's memory, so right before we launched the kayaks, we all walked over to the spot where they found her body. Deatra propped up a framed photo of a vibrant, smiling Belinda that she had taken at one of the earlier kayaking sessions. Shisele put a bouquet of daisies in a vase of water next to it and asked us all to join hands for a minute right there. Counting Basil and the Sharma cousins and a couple of bikers who came over to pay their respects, there were nine of us in a small circle around the improvised shrine. Then Shisele asked us to sign a condolence card that she was going to mail to Belinda's family. It was very sad." I swallowed hard, hoping to fend off tears at the memory of the makeshift memorial and the dead girl it honored.

"What did Jason do?" asked Illuminada. "You implied that he had changed his attitude a little, maybe become sensitive to the fact that his out-of-bounds cuddle had become a corpse."

"When he saw the photo, he did a kind of double take. I remember when Deatra snapped that picture, and I think he did too. In the picture, Belinda was smiling adoringly up at him. After he saw it, Jason didn't say much, but he did seem to have gotten the idea that something awful had happened to a real person," I said, remembering how Jason had kayaked alone that day for the first time.

"I don't know, Bel," said Betty, wresting a clam from its shell atop the bowl of linguini with white clam sauce she had ordered. "He could just be putting on."

"He sure could," I said. "Because when we got back to the park a little before noon, there was a tall, thin reincarnation of Cher in a State T-shirt standing next to a convertible in the parking lot. He beached his boat and walked over to her and kissed her. I assume she's his girlfriend Luisa."

"I bet he didn't show her the shrine," said

Illuminada.

"No, you're right. He didn't. In fact, he quickly introduced her to the others and before anybody else could mention it, he hustled her into the car and drove away. But you know what else happened?" I asked rhetorically.

"Out with it, *chiquita*. Now that I'm committing the next segment of my life to exorcising mythical cancer cells from my body, I have even less patience for your slow-as-forever narrative style. What else happened?" Illuminada was picking at her sole Française as she made this inquiry.

"Don't look now," said Betty softly, "but Senator Maldonado just walked in with a couple of cronies." I raised my eyes and stared across the room where, indeed, I saw the distinctively rotund senator and two other men entering in the wake of the maitre d'. They paused at several tables to shake hands and exchange a few words. As they came closer, I recognized one of the men as Morris Dickman, a prominent local attorney whose firm represented RECC. The other one was not familiar.

When Senator Maldonado approached us, he paused and bent over to give Betty a peck on the cheek and a hand squeeze. She controlled access to RECC President Woodman and so was on kissing terms with lots of powerful people. I was impressed. Even

Morris Dickman acknowledged her presence with a nod and his best effort at a smile. The resulting toothy grimace made him resemble a shark with indigestion. "Senora Gutierrez," purred Senator Maldonado, bending over Illuminada to plant a kiss on her tiny, exquisitely manicured hand, which, I was amused to see, she had regally extended. As a member in very good standing of the Cuban-American community that had launched his political career, Illuminada had herself become something of a force. In fact, several prominent people had suggested that she run for local office.

"Senator, meet RECC English professor Bel Barrett," said Betty. "Bel, Senator Maldonado."

"Ah yes, Professor Barrett," the senator responded gallantly as he shook my hand. In turn he presented us by name to the unknown companion, "Larry Janko, Professor Barrett, Betty Ramsey, and Illuminada Gutierrcz." Larry smiled a greeting. Morris Dickman acknowledged us with a barely perceptible nod. It was all I could do not to stick my tongue out at him as the procession advanced to greet the senator's constituents at the next table.

"Now that our celebrity sighting is over, Bel, finish your damn story, please," said Illuminada, winding a forkful of pasta into the bowl of a spoon.

"Okay, so Deatra approached me, asking if

183

I would kayak with her again, and since Shisele and Basil had already teamed up and the Sharma cousins were still joined at the hip, of course, I said yes. We launched our boat last, and set out. It was cloudy, cool, and the air was kind of heavy —"

"Bel," Illuminada warned, rotating one fist around the other as if cranking up a machine. "Spare us the weather report, please."

"We both paddled and she told me she had applied for and gotten Belinda's job. She gave notice at her other job, where she was a home attendant for an elderly man. She said Belinda's job has more to do with her major and would give her valuable experience," I said, not mentioning the fact that it had taken a while for Deatra to explain all this. "She started working security at the Outlets this week."

"Interesting, but hardly surprising," said Illuminada. "After all, Deatra is a criminal justice major and security work will give her relevant experience and a perspective that she couldn't get doing home health care."

"I realize all that. It just struck me as a little ghoulish to hear that somebody you know has died and then you go and apply for their job." I paused, remembering how surprised I had been at Deatra's news.

"*Dios mio,* Bel, as I recall, Deatra Cain was sending money back to her sister and her mother in the Caribbean every month and

184

going to school and paying her own rent up here . . . A job opening is a job opening, after all," said Illuminada.

"I'll drink to that," said Betty, raising her glass. This oblique remark was the first reference she'd made in ages to Randy's ongoing job search. But she didn't pursue it. Instead she said, "Poor folks can't afford to stand on ceremony, Bel."

"Deatra struck me as very ambitious too. And I advise all criminal justice majors to get jobs in a related area if they can, so she's just making a good career move," added Illuminada. Both my friends were explaining Deatra's behavior to me as if I had not had decades of experience with community college students in all majors. How quickly Illuminada had forgotten that I had been her mentor when she first began adjuncting in the RECC criminal justice department. I focused on winding pasta around the tines of my fork. The action felt mechanical. Since Illuminada's diagnosis, I had lost most of my enthusiasm for eating, and even Casa Dante's flawless linguini carbonara had not restored my appetite. Nor did it distract me from my pique at Illuminada.

Before I got too annoyed, I changed the subject. "I've talked to Belinda's aunt, who is very sweet. She doesn't seem to know about Jason. I think she herself has a boyfriend. Could you find out if anybody else lived at this address with her and Belinda over the last eighteen years?" I asked, handing Illuminada a Post-it with Mary Waters's name and address scrawled on it.

"I've talked to Belinda's childhood sweetheart, the one she dumped. He mentioned a boyfriend of Mary's whom Belinda didn't like. That sounds worth checking out. And there's still a cousin to talk to, but he's out of town. And, of course, there are the people from her job." I paused. "So I think we should go shopping." I looked up to see if Illuminada and Betty were on track.

"I do need a new pair of sandals. Soon it'll be too warm for pantyhose," said Illuminada innocently.

"Come to think of it, I wouldn't mind a new dress to wear to Vic's cousin's wedding next month," said Betty, a twinkle brightening her eye. "I'm so tired of wearing that beige linen thing every time I have to get dressed up. And I want a pair of black patent leather open-toe and open-heeled pumps or maybe slingbacks. I told you, I've taken the rest of the afternoon off."

"I hear there's a sale at Eileen Fisher in Secaucus," I added.

Chapter 18

To: Bbarrett@circle.com
From: Alice@juno.com
Re: Childproofing
Date: 05/15/01 14:22:01

Bel honey,

I know how excited you must be over your granddaughter's upcoming visit. I was like that when my oldest girl, Tamarind, left little Jeffrey here for the first time when he was about two. Like you, I thought I'd do some basic childproofing, you know, put the knicknacks, medicines, and cleaning supplies out of reach, buy a few outlet covers, and borrow one of those accordion gates for the stairs. That's more than I did when I was raising Tammy and her sisters, Thyme and Turmeric, but that was another time. See, back when the girls were toddlers, Harry and me lived in a commune in Vermont. A whole mess of us built a geodesic dome up there in God's country, and we farmed and raised our kids together. There was never a safety problem 'cause there were always at least one or two adults around, but, like Tammy's always saying, "Mom, that commune scene is old. Besides, Grandma says practically everybody there was stoned all the time anyway."

The week before little Jeff's visit began, the FedEx man dropped off a carton full of gadgets, a present from Jeff's dad, George. George said we should use the stuff he sent to "create a safe and child-friendly environment." George gets all these ideas from a fathers' support group he joined. Do you know, Bel, that man sent special pads to cushion the corners of tables and the spigots and even the drain in the tub? He sent doodads to keep the drawers from closing on Jeff's fingers, and, I swear, even something to keep the toilet cover closed so the little devil wouldn't fall in. And, Bel, Tammy and George not only said the accordion gate I'd borrowed was not acceptable, but they ixnayed the rails I was going to put up on the side of his little bed too. Said he could get his head caught.

Well, it took Harry and me the better part of two days to install all the stuff George sent, but we didn't use it much. The day after he arrived, we took him tent camping, and wow, did he have a blast. The thunder and lightning didn't bother him at all and every time he spotted a bear he'd say, "Pooh! Pooh!" I'm telling you, Bel, he's just adorable. Enjoy your little visitor!

Peace and love,
Alice the (ex-)hippie

The rows of uncurtained cubicles that constituted the Eileen Fisher fitting room afforded us uninterrupted views of one another, making it easy to get and give feedback. Unfortunately, other women en route to their own cubicles could also eyeball us, but I tried to ignore them. "That is just not you, *chiquita*," said Illuminada as she wriggled effortlessly into a sleek white sleeveless sheath and adjusted the gauzy overdress that seemed *de rigueur* this spring. The silky fabric clung in the bodice where it should and floated down around her hips. She looked like an X-rated angel. Unfortunately, I had tried on a larger version of the same thing in gray. Even before Illuminada had said anything, I was fully aware that in this get-up I looked like an elephant shrouded in mosquito netting. Eileen could now join the ranks of such designer luminaries as Anne, Donna, and Gloria who had not had my size 16–18 body in mind when they dreamed up their spring and summer lines.

"Let's go to the Burlington Coat Factory. They've got more stuff for Bel and me."

Once again I appreciated Betty's tact. She wore a size 12–14, and it was generous of her to lump us together. "And they've got a petite section for you too, girl. But take that. It looks great on you." Betty's tone was imperious.

But Illuminada wasn't about to be bullied into making a purchase she didn't want. "*Dios mio,* where the hell am I going to wear something dressy like this? To chemo?" I was glad to see that our late afternoon shopping spree had revitalized Illuminada's sense of humor as well as her energy level. *If they could give her chemo at the Outlets, she might not even notice it,* I thought, smiling at the sight of my shopaholic friend swirling before the mirror. I wondered how long it would take her to dream up an excuse to buy the dress. Not long, as it turned out. "On second thought, the state chapter of Raoul's CPA association of which he is treasurer is having its annual awards dinner-dance in a couple of weeks. I wanted to get out of going, but Raoul is getting an award, so . . . I'll take it." Illuminada slid out of the gossamer garments and folded them carefully before she dressed.

As we left the fitting room, we almost bumped smack into Deatra Cain, who was in uniform standing beside the counter giving directions to a woman clutching several shopping bags and eager now to make her way back to the highway with her spoils. As soon as the woman walked away, Illuminada approached her former student. "Deatra, how good to see you. How are you?" Illuminada did not hug Deatra as I often did when encountering my ubiquitous former students. Rather, she extended her hand and the two women shook hands.

Deatra's smile made it quite clear that, hug or no hug, she was delighted to see Illuminada again. "Professor Gutierrez. How you doin'? Buyin' yourself a pretty dress, I see. Hello, Professor Barrett, no dress for you? Dis here wouldn't work out so good in a kayak, right?" She fingered Illuminada's sheer dress.

Before I could introduce Betty, Illuminada said, "Deatra Cain, meet Betty Ramsey, President Woodman's executive assistant." Betty smiled and there was more handshaking. "Deatra was in my criminal justice class a few semesters ago," Illuminada said. "She was an excellent student. You must be nearly ready to graduate, right?"

"Yes. I got one more semester to go. I still got a 3.8 GPA too." Again Deatra grinned.

"I'm not surprised," said Illuminada. "You must be getting some good experience here and meeting lots of moonlighting cops and security executives."

"Yeah. We got a few of both." Turning to me, Deatra asked, "Dey find the dude who killed Belinda yet, Professor B?" Before I could formulate a reply, she pointed to the left as if giving us directions, and said, "Well, very nice to see you, Professors, Ms. Ramsey. Gotta be goin'." And she walked away. Over Illuminada's shoulder I spotted the reason for Deatra's abrupt leavetaking and non sequitur gesture. A short uniformed man had just entered the store and was standing at the doorway, scanning the selling area. He looked vaguely familiar. As Illuminada paid for her purchase, Deatra approached the man, nodding deferentially. He jerked his head toward the outside, indicating that she was to exit the store, but he did not move out of the doorway as she did so. I saw her raise her head and suck in her gut as she squeezed through the doorway. In spite of her effort to avoid touching him, her breasts grazed his chin. He turned and followed her outside.

They were nowhere in sight by the time we left the store. "What was that all about?" asked Betty once we were in the car en route to the next stop on our impromptu exercise in surveillance as shopping.

"Yeah, what was that all about?" said Illuminada.

"That girl seemed so together and then she started making with the sign language and disappeared. Did she dis us or what? And what was with that other guard, the macho pygmy who copped a feel with his chin when she left? That kinky bastard. Why didn't she just shove him out of her way? Who the hell does he think he is?" Betty was never one to mince words when she was mad.

"He's probably her boss," I ventured. "I think I've seen him before. But I know I never taught him." People in my world fell into one of three categories: current students, former students, and everybody else. I thought for a minute or two. As we were getting out of the car, it came to me. "He must be the boyfriend of the Latina woman, the one they found dead in the parking lot. I remember seeing his picture in the paper. He's a security guard here. He must have been Belinda's boss too," I said. The thought was not a happy one. "I'll have to ask Deatra about him tomorrow," I said. "He's a piece of work."

At Burlington Coat Factory Betty and Illuminada cruised the racks and checked into the back-to-basics fitting room, carrying armfuls of clothes. Not tempted by anything on the racks in my size, I followed a security guard who appeared to be discreetly tailing a couple of leggy, ponytailed adolescent girls rifling through rotating carousels of lingerie. It wasn't clear to me if he was following them because they were attractive or because he suspected them of shoplifting. Before I discovered his motive, I returned to the dressing room to weigh in with an opinion should one be wanted. Betty had fallen in love with a gray and silver embossed silk mandarin-collared sheath that subtracted inches from her hips and added them to her height. It would be perfect for the wedding and, thanks to several reductions, was surprisingly afford-able. She didn't need me to tell her to snap it up. Illuminada had found two summer suits, one black and the other pale green. They fit beautifully. *Of course,* I said to my-self without resentment, *everything fits her beautifully*. "They're perfect for work," she said, not referring to the fact that she already owned enough suits to stock a boutique.

As we stood in line at the counter waiting for a free cashier, I noticed the security guard and the same two teenage girls. Now they flanked him, smirking defiantly while looking around, as if in search of an escape route. As they walked, the guard was talking into his cell phone and propelling them to-ward a door behind the long counter with the word *Security* printed on it. While I tried to imagine Belinda apprehending shoplifters, the door opened and another guard stepped aside to let the group enter.

I glanced up at the blurry image of myself on the ubiquitous TV screens that monitor the aisles and probably even the dressing rooms and marveled that people would even attempt to shoplift given the array of technology dedicated to exposing them in the age of Big Brother. As the door closed behind the trio, Illuminada followed my glance and read my mind. "All this hardware's not just for customers with sticky fingers. Sometimes it prevents employee pilferage. That's a big problem today," she said, handing over her credit card. "It's a little harder to pocket a twenty when you're on TV."

We were all pretty tired by the time we got to His 'n' Hers Shoes, so we walked slowly through the huge store's busy parking lot. Now that the workday was over, a different crowd of shoppers was starting to arrive. "Over there's where Gina says they found that Colombian girl," Betty said, pointing to a corner of the lot behind the loading dock not readily visible to those entering and leaving the large one-story square building. Recalling the pretty girl whose photo I'd seen in the newspaper, I was unprepared for Betty's non sequitur, "so maybe I should look for white silk shoes and have them dyed gray."

"*Dios mio,* Betty, you don't want to look like a dove. Why not get a pair of sexy stiletto sandals? Something in a really bright color? And a bag to coordinate with them." Illuminada was the Imelda Marcos of Union City, with a closet full of sexy, impractical, once-worn shoes in a rainbow of vibrant colors.

"NOT," I said. "Just get the black patent slingbacks you wanted in the first place. They'll look really classy with that dress and you can wear them with your standby beige one too. And if you don't have a black patent leather bag, my mother has one. It's a smart little clutch from 1957 that's back in style. She'd love to lend it to you."

By this time I was a little tired of shopping, not having found anything I really coveted as much as I coveted a handheld organizer that I was convinced would simplify my life, improve my memory, and save me writing a million Post-it notes a day. I felt quite virtuous because I had not spent a dime since lunch. After all, the only special event on my calendar was the arrival of Abbie J, and that certainly did not require a new dress. Then, about halfway down the first aisle of shoes, I spotted a pair of soft brown leather flats with a strap, and cutouts in front. They looked like Mary Janes with attitude. They had my name on them. There was a pair in my size. I bought them. They would be perfect for taking Abbie J to the park.

Chapter 19

To: Bbarrett@circle.com
From: Gram2@hotmail.com
Re: Pumping and dumping
Date: 05/19/01 16:23:12

Dear Bel,

I can't believe you never heard about "pumping and dumping"! My two girls, Emmilee and Maribel, they pump and dump damn near every weekend. That's because they have a couple of glasses of wine or a cosmopolitan when they go out and they don't want their babies to take in that booze with their milk. So before they bring the little angels to my house where I baby-sit them most Saturday nights, Emmilee and Maribel pump and freeze breast milk. Then they carry some of it here with them in special plastic bags for the kids to have when they're at Grandma's house. After Emmilee and Maribel get done partying, they pump the milk that's been contaminated with alcohol and dump it down the drain. That's pretty SOP for today's breastfeeding mom who wants to have a drink or two every now and then. Sounds like your Rebecca is planning to party hearty in Washington! Go Rebecca!

Emmilee's little Sarah is two and Maribel's Jennifer is almost four. I hope Maribel's planning to wean Jenny before college, but I don't say a word. I breastfed my babies for three months, but it was very hard after I went back to work, so I stopped. Now they sell "breastfeeding systems" and my girls have "lactation consultants" and belong to breastfeeding support groups. All I had was Jim's mother standing over me saying how I was starving little Maribel to death.

And now it's legal to breastfeed in most public settings. I remember getting thrown out of a restaurant when I tried to nurse Maribel in a booth. And expressing breast milk at work? Forget it. I tried to do it in the restroom, but my manager didn't approve. Now Maribel expresses in the "lactation lounge" at her office, can you imagine? She's got herself a double electric pump, so she can pump both breasts at once and save a little time that way. For Christmas last year I got Jenny a set of nursing mother and baby dolls. The mama doll has breasts with Velcro nipples and the baby has Velcro lips. Jenny loves them.

I hope you and Rebecca and Abbie J all have a great weekend!

Good luck.
Jean

Sunday morning, after making a note to clean out the freezer so there would be room for a five-day supply of breast milk, I headed for the dining room table where I had spread out all my end-of-semester paperwork. It was crunch time, and I was, as usual, struggling to get all my students' research papers and final exams read, evaluated, graded, and final grades turned in by the date the registrar had established. At times like this, Sol did more than his share of the housework so I could concentrate on schoolwork, and I always felt guilty even though I thought the exercise was good for him. After we had both been working for a couple of hours, he turned off the vacuum cleaner, came downstairs, and stood behind me kneading my shoulders. "I'm taking a tea break. Want some?" he asked.

"I'd love a mug of Earl Grey decaf." When I heard the microwave buzz, I pushed my papers and grade book aside, making room for my tea. It was good to see Sol. He had spent a few days baby-sitting for his toddler granddaughter, who, he said, was thriving on a diet made up largely of chocolate milk, Oreos, and frozen fried fish sticks. He'd arrived home late the night before to find me slogging through the familiar arduous ritual of bringing closure to the semester. "So catch me up. Any word from Mark? How's Illuminada doing?"

A thumbs-down sufficed to cover his first question. My son, globetrotting English-as-a-foreign-language teacher that he was, apparently had no time to e-mail his mother from Buenos Aires. I sighed the sigh of a practiced martyr and addressed Sol's next line of inquiry. "Illuminada's still pretty bummed out that she has to have both chemo and radiation as precautionary measures even though her lymph nodes are clear," I said, sipping my tea.

"Don't tell me she's not going to have both treatments." The beginnings of a frown working across his forehead, Sol sat down across from me, a mug of tea in his hand.

"No. She'll do what she has to do. She's just really mad. Nasty too," I said with a mock shudder. "She near about took my head off when I brought her some support-group literature."

"Well, of course. You and Betty are her support group. Illuminada's not going to sit around unloading on a bunch of women she's never seen before," Sol said. "You might, but she won't." He was always so reasonable that sometimes I had to struggle not to hold it against him. "Just hang in there with her."

"We are," I said with a sigh. "I asked her to find out about Belinda's aunt's boyfriend."

"Oh? Her aunt had a beau?" said Sol. I smiled at his quaint wording. "I don't remember hearing about him."

"No, Mary didn't mention him but Andy Dawes did. Said he liked Belinda but Belinda didn't like him. There was a photo in Mary's apartment of Mary with some guy. She said he wasn't her husband but she never did say who he was. They looked like lovers in the snapshot." I recalled the sparks in Mary's eyes in that photo. "So Illuminada's going to check him out. And you know, I think I'll ask her to see what she can find out about Mary Waters's ex-husband while she's at it. I forgot all about him. I think he left when Belinda was a baby, but I'm not sure. He might know something about the family . . ." I was musing out loud as I reached for the phone.

After I had left Illuminada a message, Sol said, "So you're just abandoning that kid in the Kayaking Club as a suspect? I forget his name — you know who I mean — the one Belinda had the hots for?"

"Well, not exactly, but I really don't think Jason did it, and the police are all over him anyway. Last week at the UKC meeting he seemed more aware of the fact that Belinda had been a real person and that now she is dead. The other kids made a little shrine for her and when he saw her photo there, he seemed to finally get it," I said, recalling Jason kayaking off alone. "His girl, Luisa, picked him up after we got back, and he rushed her out of there before anybody could say anything to her about Belinda. Luisa must have found out about Belinda by now, but she seems to have forgiven him," I added, recalling the kiss they had exchanged.

"Maybe she knew all along. Maybe somebody told her that her boyfriend was double dipping and she killed the competition." I had known it was only a matter of time before Sol suggested jealousy as a motive for Belinda's murder.

"Sol, you live in a soap opera world, I swear," I said, laughing. "You're always trying to convince me that there's a homicidal jealous lover lurking behind every tree. Now you want me to believe that Luisa, a Cher look-alike who must weigh all of twelve pounds soaking wet, beat up Belinda, who was pretty sturdy . . ." I paused a moment remembering Belinda's surprising strength when she had paddled us to safety that first day on the river. Returning to the present, I completed the scenario, "Then you want me to believe that Luisa dragged Belinda's body into a car and unloaded it at Snake Hill?"

"I'm only reminding you that 'Hell hath no fury like a woman scorned,' and this Luisa might have found out that Jason was seeing

Belinda and gotten mad. And who knows, she may have had help, a brother, a cousin . . ." Sol leaned back in his chair, envisioning his own version of Belinda's death at the hands of an enraged Luisa and her posse of equally enraged relatives ready to kill to avenge her betrayal by Jason. "You can laugh all you want, Bel, but if I were you, I'd check her out," said Sol. "And for that matter, I wouldn't write off Belinda's boyfriend either. Just because his lights aren't all on doesn't mean he can't blow a fuse." That sorry bit of wordplay masquerading as advice was Sol's last admonition before he rose, nuzzled my neck, and returned to his vacuuming. I've never been one to argue with a man doing the vacuuming, so I made myself a Post-it note to see what I could learn about Luisa. I wrote down Andy's name too, followed by an oversized question mark.

It was hard to return to my papers, but after making yet another note to remind Illuminada to get the autopsy report, I did. By five-thirty I had finished all but one section, which I was too drained to tackle. It would have to wait until Monday morning when, after what I hoped would be a good night's sleep, I could think clearly again. That would work because grades weren't due until Monday at five. I'd even have time to run a few suspect papers through a computer check for plagiarism at turnitin.com, a special program faculty members use to search for a match among ready-made papers for sale on the Net. The term paper business was getting more sophisticated every semester, and now mediocre or poor writers were able to order and get mediocre or poor term papers in the hope of passing these sorry documents off as their own sorry work. Shaking my head at the absurdity and pathos of it all, I clipped each pile of papers together, placed them in appropriate folders, and stuffed the whole lot of them into my book bag.

By three on Monday I had turned in my grades. With a relieved sigh, I postponed thoughts of the weeks ahead when, uninterrupted by a summer teaching assignment, I hoped to spend long days polishing my doctoral dissertation and preparing to defend it. Instead, I drove the few miles to State, parked, and approached the public relations office, a cubicle in the Department of Development and Planning. I devised a game plan as I walked.

"Bel Barrett. I freelance for the *Jersey City Herald*," I said, extending my hand to the young African-American man I found at the computer. "We're doing a feature on green women at the grass-roots level." Looking dumbfounded, he shook my hand. I refined my script. "Young women active in the environmental movement. I hear you have an environmental organization here, Students Making New Jersey Greener or something like that." I paused, cursing my failure to remember the exact name of the group Jason had credited Luisa with spearheading.

The man appeared to be listening intently. "Alekem Smith here, assistant director of public relations. Pleased to meet you," he said formally. Then he typed a few words into his PC and a column of phrases leaped onto the screen, presumably a list of clubs and activities. Running the cursor down the list, he said, "Ah, I see. You mean State Students for a Greener New Jersey. They have a new website. Let's see." Obligingly, he keyed in the URL and up popped a logo. "Here, I'll print that out," he said, still obliging. "You're in luck. The president of that group's a woman, Luisa Cortez. Why don't you start with her? See, here's the contact information." He pointed to an e-mail address on the printout, looking quite pleased with himself for having managed so easily to provide me with what I ostensibly wanted.

"Thank you very much," I said. "You've just saved me a lot of legwork." Actually I was annoyed that I hadn't thought to do the same thing from the comfort of my own office and saved myself the drive across town. I was always happy to use a computer, but sometimes I completely forgot about the damn things and their potential for saving me time and energy. When that happened, I regressed to operating as I had in the days when legwork was actually done by legs, not fingers.

Feeling rather sheepish, I wandered over to a bench and read the printout. According to the organization's website, members of State Students for a Greener New Jersey planned to rally Friday night at Laurel Hill Park. I read no further. Pulling out my cell phone, I punched in the one digit that would instantly connect me to the private line of my old friend Sarah Wolf, managing editor of the *Jersey City Herald*. "Sarah," I spoke into her voice mail. "Sarah, it's Bel. Want to go with me to a rally some greenies at State are staging Friday night at Laurel Hill Park? Dinner later at Laico's? Please." Accompanied by Sarah posing as a photographer I occasionally researched freelance articles for the *Herald*. This activity provided me with an excellent cover and good company while I nosed around people and places I might not otherwise visit. I put away the phone and once again wished I had a handheld device that would enable me to e-mail Luisa Cortez and arrange an interview. Annoyed not to have spoken with Sarah and not to have portable e-mail access, I scribbled out a Post-it note reminding myself to e-mail Luisa. Then I walked to the car, slapped the Post-it on the dashboard with all the others, and drove home.

By the time I got there Sarah had left a message on my answering machine saying, "Sorry, Bel. Friday night's no good. I've got an anniversary party. But I bet I know what you're up to, and I hate to miss out on the action. If you get a story, we'll run it. Let's do dinner soon." Disappointed, I resolved to invite Sol. He'd welcome a chance to interact with a new generation of environmental activists. I e-mailed Luisa, explaining that I was doing a piece on women active in environmental causes and requesting an interview with her after the rally.

Sol promised he'd meet me at Laurel Hill Park that Friday night after his scheduled root canal if he felt up to it. I drove there alone, noting for the first time the county pre-release jail complex that formed the unofficial gateway to the area. As darkness threatened, my overwrought imagination conjured up images of modern-day Magwiches prowling the marshes in search not of victuals but of victims, young women like Maria Mejia and Belinda Judd. Before I wrote off this Dickensian scenario, I resolved to determine if there had been any escapes lately, all the while telling myself that a prisoner due to be released soon would hardly be motivated to stage a breakout. The small parking lot was nearly empty, not a good sign for a rally that should have started half an hour ago.

Silhouetted against the setting sun, Snake Hill rose like a monumental and monolithic gravestone above the spot where the bikers had found Belinda's body. I snapped a photo of it with the camera I had brought.

A scant thirty people stood near the gazebo at the water's edge listening to a speaker. As I walked past the launching bay, the wind rose off the river. I pulled my ruana around me and prayed that the chilly breeze would discourage the infamous Jersey mosquitoes from attending this rally. I recognized Luisa on the top step of the gazebo exhorting her constituents to contact their legislators and make known their opposition to the proposed office-tower complex. I could just picture Goliath developers like Hartz Mountain quivering in their corporate boots at this slender David aiming her slingshot at them. As I got closer, I could make out her passionate plea, repeated over and over, "Let your legislator know you care. Vote with your cell phone, your e-mail, your pen, and your feet. Visit your legislator here and in Trenton!" Students cheered, but the sound of their voices wafted out over the darkening river, muting the effect.

As Luisa spoke, a familiar figure handed out leaflets to the young people milling around. It was Jason, not himself the president here but instead a lackey in the service of the chief executive. Luisa may have looked like Cher, but she sounded like Hillary stumping for senator with Jason playing the postpresidential Bill, a contrite and decidedly background figure. Jason was such a big fish in the smaller less competitive RECC pond, but he looked decidedly diminished that night among the State students.

Damn! I probably wouldn't get to talk with Luisa alone unless I could get Jason out of the way. Where the hell was Sol? He could distract Jason, leaving Luisa unattended for a few minutes so I could chat her up. I thought fast and then turned around and strode back to the car. Unlocking the door, I buried my camera under the front seat on the passenger side behind a semester's worth of Styrofoam teacups and empty M&M's bags. Then I locked the car and took the ignition key off the chain with my house key and attached it to my other chain, the one holding the key to my office at RECC. I headed back to the gazebo where Luisa stood, bidding farewell to the faithful.

After she finished conferring with a ponytailed young man carrying a hand-lettered poster reading "Keep the Meadow in the Meadowlands," I approached her. Extending my hand, I said, "Luisa Cortez? I'm Bel Barrett, the *Jersey City Herald* reporter doing the piece on women active in environmental causes. I e-mailed you about a short interview, remember?"

"Hi. Sure, I do. Cool." We shook hands as she spoke.

"Professor B? What are you doing here?" It was Jason, taking what he obviously felt was his rightful place beside Luisa. "Man, you must really like this place. You gonna sleep here or something?" he asked, attempting a humorous reference to the rather disturbing fact that, indeed, I would be back at Laurel Hill Park in the morning for the UKC's final meeting. He seemed to harbor no hard feelings about the way I had chastised him for his callous indifference to Belinda.

"I freelance for the *Jersey City Herald*," I explained. I took a tiny tape recorder out of my shoulder bag. "I'm doing a feature story on women active in environmental causes," I repeated for his benefit. "Luisa's name was given to me by the assistant director of public relations at State." Jason nodded and encircled her with his arm. I would not have been surprised had they burst into a chorus of "I Got You, Babe."

"Luisa, I thought I might just get a little bit of information about your background and a quote and, of course, a photo. I could probably use a photo of both of you just so we get a little PR for RECC in there too," I added, gratified to see Jason's eyes gleam at the prospect of being photographed for the newspaper. Like most good-looking people, he did not automatically recoil at the pros-

210

pect of posing. Luisa in turn responded sensibly by pointing to a bench along one side of the gazebo.

We sat and I made a pretense of fumbling around in my bag. "Damn!" I muttered. Then, looking up, I said, "I seem to have left my camera in the car. Jason, would you mind terribly?" Ferreting around once more in my apparently bottomless purse, I dug out a key ring and handed it to Jason. "My car is the white Toyota parked near the Porta John. I must have left the camera there."

"No problem. I'll be right back." Pocketing the key ring, Jason took off.

"Thanks so much. Just ignore the mess in my car," I called after him. I was determined to make the most of the few minutes I'd contrived to spend alone with Luisa, so my opener was calculated. "Luisa, I really admire the work you're doing, so, off the record, I hope this recent mess with Jason hasn't interfered with your campus organizing." Luisa stiffened, confirming my sense that I had caught her off-guard. "Damn, I'm still trying to get this thing going. I hope the battery didn't die on me," I said, pushing buttons on my tape recorder and finally pocketing it with a disgusted shrug. I suspected I'd get a more candid response if it were crystal clear that whatever she said next really was off the record. When she still didn't respond, I added, "Women activists sometimes have family and relationship responsibilities that can limit their involvement." Silently I begged forgiveness of my feminist forebears for this heresy. When Luisa continued to maintain her silence, I persisted, adding all the bait I had and then some. "I mean it must be extremely stressful waiting to see if your fiancé is going to be indicted for murdering his lover."

"Jason never had another lover," Luisa said, finally breaking her silence. "And anyway, we're not engaged. Not yet anyway." Her tone was neutral, but the quick, almost furtive glance she cast down at her still ringless hand told me that she anticipated the day Jason would propose. "He never had another lover," she repeated. "Why would he want one?" She smiled at the absurd notion that any man of hers would ever feel inclined to stray. "He just doesn't do very good by himself, you know, and I was on the island for a few days." Luisa uttered this explanation in a voice full of conviction, the same voice she had used to urge her constituents to vote with their feet. "I'm sorry that poor girl is dead, but Jason didn't kill her. He'd never kill anybody. He works so hard at raising the consciousness of those kids at RECC about the environment." Her voice dripped with condescension when she mentioned the "kids at RECC." It was dark now except for a few lights along the road leading into and out of the park, so Luisa's stand-by-my-man speech floated toward me, a disembodied stream of words.

"Sorry, Professor B, but are you sure this is the right key? It don't work and it don't look like a car key either," Jason said, sounding annoyed as he handed me the key I had given him.

"Let's see," I said feigning curiosity and trying to make out the key in the dark. "Oh my goodness, you're right. I'm so sorry. That's my house key. Let me look for the car key." I dug into my purse again and, after a convincing interval, produced the other key ring. Jason took it and trotted off again.

"You seem very understanding of his weakness for women." I pressed her now, trying to see if her loyalty resulted from denial or pragmatism.

"Jason doesn't have a weakness for women. He just can't handle being alone," said Luisa.

Before I could reply, Jason returned with the camera. "Here you go, Professor B. I found it under the seat," he said, handing me the key ring.

"Thanks, Jason," I said. "I hope these photos come out. I haven't used this camera much in the dark. Luisa, let me get a head shot of you since the scenery won't show up." The lovely young woman smiled obligingly while I snapped several pictures, the flash temporarily blinding us. "And now let me get a couple of you both. Jason, sit next to Luisa, please, and smile." Once I put my camera away, I took out a notebook and said, "So, Luisa, what I really want to know is how you got interested in environmental activism."

"You ever been to Puerto Rico?" she asked, now turning the tables on me by posing her own question. When I shook my head, she said, "Well, it would blow you away, it's so beautiful there on my island. And every time I visited even when I was young I wished I lived back there with all that beauty. Then I saw *Erin Brockovich*, you know, the movie?" I nodded. "That woman was just so cool the way she stood up to everybody and did all that research and proved her case. Awesome. So I decided to start an environmental organization at State to get students to work to keep what little green we have left in New Jersey. Protesting this new development in the Meadowlands is our first project," she added with more than a tinge of pride in her voice.

"That's the quote I need, what you said about Erin Brockovich and keeping the green in New Jersey. That's really straightforward and moving. I guess she's been a role model for you," I said, writing furiously.

"Yes. Like I said, she's totally awesome. We're trying to get the real Erin Brockovich to speak at graduation next year. I'm on the

214

committee," said Luisa.

After a few more questions, the three of us headed for the now deserted parking lot. As we walked, Jason only glanced once in the direction of the small shrine memorializing Belinda. Sol had never shown up, so I drove down County Road past the darkened prison wondering about Luisa. She denied Jason's propensity for infidelity by passing it off as an inability to deal with her absence. Would she kill to preserve this egocentric illusion?

Chapter 20

To: Bbarrett@circle.com
From: IgutierrezPI@juno.com
Re: Mary's boyfriend
Date: 05/28/01 13:20:42

Chiquita,

Lyle Hendricks used to live at the Webster Street address you gave me for Mary Waters. He moved out in '97. Now he's at a Union City address, 456 Summit Avenue. He works in the food service department at St. Mary's. He's active in their union. Holler if you need help.

Illuminada

Why would I need help? St. Mary's Hospital was literally around the corner from the brick row house in downtown Hoboken that Sol and I called home. And classes were over for the semester, so I was free to amble over there anytime I wanted. Still savoring my hard-won summer freedom, I showered, forcing myself to carefully palpate each soapy boob in search of unfamiliar nodules or masses. Illuminada's diagnosis had been all the wake-up call I needed to remind me to do regular breast checks even though, like most women, I dreaded what I might find. As usual, I was relieved to feel nothing untoward.

Just to make sure Lyle Hendricks was working that day, I called St. Mary's office of facilities and maintenance and, representing myself as a loan officer, asked to speak to him. After a bit of a wait on hold, I was told he had a midmorning break in another twenty minutes at which time, if I left my number, and if he chose, he might call me back. Relieved that he was, in fact, working that day, I left a phony number and hightailed it over to the hospital. On the way, I decided not to use a cover but to tell him my real reason for seeking him out.

In the hospital cafeteria, bantering green-garbed workers holding plastic trays were lined up for the fortification that only coffee and muffins provide. Pallid, slightly wild-eyed visitors, the ones who had been there all night or whose dear ones had just been wheeled off to the OR, nursed cups of coffee at tables scattered throughout the room. I made my way among them to the counter where I approached one of the line servers. Decades of teaching enabled me to cajole with an air of command, as if I expected my request to be gratified. "Please tell Lyle Hendricks there's someone to see him. If necessary, I can wait a few minutes until his break."

The young woman frowned for a millisecond and looked me over quickly before smiling obligingly and disappearing into the kitchen. When she returned, she said, "He'll meet you at ten-thirty over by there." Still smiling, she pointed to a table near the wall. "Coffee?" she asked, pointing to the urns and towers of Styrofoam cups at the nearby beverage station. "Eggs? Toast?" She continued pointing to the inevitable container of glutinous scrambled eggs dehydrating in the stainless steel tray between us. They had probably been quite good an hour ago, but now . . .

"Yes, thank you. I mean, no, no eggs. Just tea. I'll fix it while I wait." I quickly poured some hot water in a cup, plopped in a decaf tea bag from the nearby basket, paid for it, and took a seat at the table the young woman had indicated. At exactly ten-thirty a slightly weathered version of the man in Mary's photo walked through the door from the kitchen carrying a cup of coffee. Glancing in my direction, he smiled the smile the photographer had captured and made his way over to where I sat.

"Lyle Hendricks. You lookin' for me?" he asked amiably, pulling out a chair and sitting down.

"Bel Barrett. Yes, I wanted to talk to you for a minute or two about Belinda Judd." I scrutinized his face as I uttered the dead girl's name. Did his eyes blink, one corner of his mouth twitch? We shook hands.

"You a friend of hers?" he asked, still amiable, but now decidedly guarded. "How is little Belinda?"

Could it be that he didn't know? Didn't he read the paper? Of course not, I reminded myself. *Hardly anybody reads the paper anymore. Or is he feigning ignorance of her death to cover up his role in it?* "Belinda Judd is dead, Mr. Hendricks. I'm sorry. I thought you knew."

There was no missing the twitching of Lyle Hendricks's mouth now. "Jesus. No. I ain't seen her in years. Her aunt and me, we were together, but that ended and I moved on. Ain't seen none of them in" — he stroked his chin below the still moving lips — "I guess it's been about three years. I made a clean break, you know . . ." His voice trailed off as he continued to stroke his chin. I waited for him to ask how she had died.

When he didn't, I said, "Mr. Hendricks, Belinda was murdered."

He put his coffee cup down and I saw his fist tighten. "Why that lousy —" He stopped himself midsentence. His veneer of easy amiability faded completely.

I waited for him to complete his sentence. When again nothing was forthcoming, I said,

"Mr. Hendricks, I taught Belinda at River Edge Community College. I was very fond of her. I'm trying to figure out who killed her, and I just thought that since you once lived with the Waters family, you might remember something that would help. Was there anybody who didn't like her?"

"What about the police? Last I heard they were still supposed to solve murders." Now he sounded hostile. I could see him as a union rep, fueling worker dissatisfaction and firing up the rank-and-file to demand better working conditions and pay. I could see what Mary Waters saw in him too. This tall rangy guy with the aquiline nose and fiery temper was an eagle to her wren.

"They have a suspect, but I'm just checking into a few things on my own," I said.

He glanced up at the clock. "Well, somebody better check on cousin Carl. When I saw what was going on with him and Belinda right under Mary's eyes without her doin' nothin' about it, that's when I split. I'm not a religious man, but them two was first cousins, more like brother and sister. Mary raised them both. It just wasn't right. He took advantage of that girl. Now, you gotta excuse me. I gotta get back." He tapped his watch to signify that his break was over, stood, and with a perfunctory nod of his head, strode back to the kitchen.

My head was reeling as I walked the few blocks home. I wanted to retreat to the privacy of my yard where the May sunshine had coaxed out a few tulips. The squirrels hadn't demolished all of them yet, and there was a dwarf lilac that ought to be blooming right about now. Lyle Hendricks's revelation had astounded me, and I needed time to reconsider Belinda's death in this new and shocking light. In fact, I needed to reconsider her life as well, to factor in the possibility that Belinda had been romantically and possibly sexually involved with her cousin Carl.

Armed with a rake and a few plastic lawn and leaf bags, I headed out the back door determined to clear the yard of winter's legacy of leaves and twigs that were the price we paid for the shade afforded by a neighbor's tree. I raked and bagged until the bricks that paved most of the yard and the border garden were cleared of debris. The order I brought to our little enclosure was a small but real compensation for the complete chaos that still reigned in my head when I contemplated Lyle Hendricks's bombshell.

After all, the Belinda I knew had been challenged by college, bored by Andy, dazzled and taken in by Jason. Would she have been so taken in by Jason if she were already intimate with Carl? Wouldn't Andy Dawes have sensed something amiss if Belinda had been involved with someone else all along?

He wasn't a genius, true, but he wasn't brain dead. He had certainly noticed her interest in him waning when she got to college. And what about Belinda's aunt? Wouldn't Mary Waters have recoiled at the notion of her son and her niece connecting romantically? And would she have let Lyle leave rather than intervene in Belinda and Carl's relationship?

Hungry for a little lunch, I went inside and reflexively checked my answering machine. There were three phone messages. "Bel, I'm hoping for an update. Is the UKC dead in the water, no pun intended, or have you saved the grant? Call me." In spite of Wendy's totally tasteless humor, I resolved to call her and recorded that resolve on the obligatory Post-it.

"Sibyl, remember our appointment for our mother-daughter pedicure is tomorrow. I'm just reminding you. We're taking you girls to lunch afterward." It was Ma. I'm trying to solve a murder that is becoming more complex and weird by the minute and my mother wants me to get a pedicure. And if I don't, I'm a Bad Daughter, unlike Sofia Dellafemina's daughter Marie, who is, I must admit, a Fabulous Daughter.

Sofia and Ma met and bonded for life in the ladies' room at the Grand Street Senior Citizens' Center. Sol and I call it the Miracle on Grand Street because they've been housemates for years now, two widows with a weakness for the casinos, alternately bickering and commiserating in one of the apartments in Sofia's two-family house in Hoboken. I love Sofia. And I even love Marie, who helped Sol and me wrest the car keys from the Odd Couple, as we call Sofia and Ma. Marie makes as many supermarket runs and doctors' visits with them as we do. Ma is a frequent and welcome guest at Marie's summer place on Long Beach Island. Marie is always dreaming up activities for the Odd Couple. I'm sure this most recent outing was her idea. Last winter she orchestrated the mother-daughter facial that, I must admit, was lovely.

As I was reliving the facial and writing out a Post-it, a familiar voice intruded. "Professor Barrett, this is Mary Waters. Carl is home and we've set a date for Belinda's memorial service. It's Wednesday, June 6 at ten a.m. at St. Paul's. Please tell anyone at the community college who might be interested in comin'. And, Professor, at the service, me and Carl would like you to say a few words about Belinda, if you don't mind. Please let me know. Goodbye."

I'd like to say a few words all right, but I didn't think Carl would want me to say them in public. I certainly intended to confront him, and Mary too, for that matter, with Lyle Hendricks's accusation. I knew what Sol would say, and for once it didn't seem too

far off. If Carl and Belinda were sexually involved, and Belinda was going to marry Andy
Dawes, Carl might have killed Belinda rather
than lose her permanently to Andy. And
what might Carl have done in a fit of jealous
rage if he'd found out about Belinda's tryst
with Jason? I scrawled a Post-it reminding
myself to ask Illuminada to find out if Carl
Waters had been on base the night Belinda
was murdered. Then I punched in Mary's
number.

Chapter 21

To-Do List

Ask IG if CW on base night B was killed.
Remind IG to get results of autopsy.
Pedicure & lunch with OC and Marie
10 a.m.–2
Mary & Carl Waters — 8 p.m.
Call Wendy.
Childproof house and yard.

"You have such good feet, Bel," crooned Marie, staring down at my very ordinary feet, soaking in the warm and scented mini whirlpool bath. I struggled to respond civilly to what seemed like an inane compliment. Civility was not easy after a night's sleep interrupted by the mild but still hard to ignore hot flashes that had resumed since I'd decreased the amount of estrogen and progesterone I took. I'd cut down on my dose in response to ongoing controversy about whether the stuff was killing me or curing me.

Ma saved me the trouble of responding to Marie at all by claiming the compliment for herself. "Sibyl has my feet. Look." Ma lifted her right foot out of the swirling water, gracefully extended her leg, and twirled her ankle, at the end of which was a delicate, perfectly proportioned foot. "She has my legs too, good legs. She should wear heels more often and show them off." Whenever Ma spoke of me in the third person in my presence, I had to fight a temptation to strangle her that was at odds with the spirit of mother-daughter bonding this outing was intended to foster.

"What color are you getting, Sadie?" asked Sofia, interrupting my matricidal fantasy. She was addressing Ma, but the young women charged with reclaiming our feet from the ravages of winter dryness and transforming our blank toenails into digital art said, "Choose from these or these." She handed us each a palette with an array of colors including some, like black and green, that, quite frankly, I wasn't ready for.

Once upon a time in another life, before I'd married and had kids, I'd painted my own teenage toenails a bright crimson and been pleased with the glamorous effect. Then, during the years when I rushed from classroom to carriage, sandbox, or PTA meeting, there was simply no time at all. In fact, for whole decades I rarely thought about my toenails. What's more, I began to view women who devoted time, energy, and money to tinkering with their toenails as frivolous consumers of a decidedly unfeminist bent. Then, last year, Sol and I were invited to a wedding and my own decidedly coquettish inner consumer clawed her way out of the depths of my psyche. I bought some deep red polish. It was my hope that if I jazzed up my perfectly proportioned feet, they would distract viewers from the less perfectly proportioned rest of me. But how far away my feet seemed as I bent down to embellish them. Even though I wore my reading glasses, the resulting "toe job" appeared to have been inspired by Jackson Pollack, and I resolved not to try again without doing an hour of yoga first so I could bend lower for longer.

"Bel, I hear Abbie J is coming," said Maric, undaunted by my silence. "You must be so excited. I know Sadie is counting the days, right, Sadie?"

"You can bet on it," said Ma, who tended to express herself in terms of her passion for gaming. "Sofia, Bel, and I are going to take her to the center. Everybody wants to meet her," Ma said. "I know Bel won't mind." I smiled, my crankiness dissipating at the mention of my granddaughter. I also knew Ma wanted to show off her utterly adorable great-grandchild and I understood that impulse. I had a few plans for showcasing the kid myself. Lots of people I worked with at RECC wanted to meet her.

"Do you need anything, Bel?" When I looked quizzical, Marie said, "I mean for Abbie J when she's here. There's no point in your buying all that childproofing stuff for just a few days. I've got it all and we don't use it anymore. Why don't I drop it off with Sadie next time I'm there and you can take a look at it?" This was typical Marie, thoughtful, generous, and kind. She was a stay-at-home grandma with untold hours to devote to keeping her stunningly renovated brownstone clean, baking cookies, tending to her mother, and baby-sitting on a regular basis for her numerous and nearby grandchildren. I tried hard not to hold any of this against her, especially when Ma sang her praises.

By two that afternoon, we all had designer toes, the soft pumiced heels and soles of pampered princesses, and that lazy I-ate-too-much-but-boy-was-it-good feeling. Marie had sealed her triumph over my resentment by admiring Abbie J in all my photographs and sharing an order of flourless chocolate cake with me. I had long ago discovered that the best people to share dessert with were those who, like Marie, wear size 6. After I dropped off the Odd Couple and Marie, I drove home. I knew that Ma and Sofia would nap for a while, and it occurred to me that now that classes were over, I too could enjoy one of my rare naps.

Feeling positively guilty, I slunk upstairs with a half-finished crossword puzzle and stretched out on the bed. Before I could even begin to figure out a four-letter word for what brings traffic to a standstill or a fifteen-letter word for a typical dervish, I was asleep. That turned out to be a mistake. Instead of waking up an hour later refreshed and re-newed, I awakened an hour later groggy, sweaty, and scared after a nightmare in which Belinda appeared in my office to tell me something, and every time she tried to speak, all that came out of her mouth was a scream.

I wish I'd had a chance to confer with Betty and Illuminada or Sol before visiting Mary and Carl Waters, but although I was free from teaching for the summer, Illuminada and Betty were hard at work. And Sol was on a retreat in the Poconos with the board of his precious Citizens Committee to Preserve the Waterfront. It took me a full half hour to find someone pulling out of a parking space in the Heights, so it was dark by the time I had locked the car and walked the several blocks to the Waters's house. This time a young man with black eyes and a black crewcut wearing a black T-shirt and chinos answered my ring. Even out of uni-form, I recognized Carl Waters from the photo I'd seen on my earlier visit.

"Carl Waters?" I asked, extending my hand. "Bel Barrett. Belinda's professor. We spoke on the phone." In fact, when I'd returned Mary's call, Carl had answered and accepted my condolences on the death of his cousin before calling his mother to the phone.

"Yes, ma'am. Come in." Carl smiled a smile that was an eerie echo of Belinda's and stood aside as I passed ahead of him into the stairwell. "My mom's not here yet. She gets off work late tonight. She ought to be back soon." This was not good news. I was acutely aware of the fact that the young man climbing the stairs behind me cut off my access to the front door. With every step we took up the stairs, I was coming closer to being trapped in a deserted apartment blocks away from my car with a possible killer. I fumbled in my purse for my cell phone, fondling its familiar and reassuring plastic surface.

"I'm sorry. I could have come later or tomorrow," I said. Actually I wasn't at all sorry to have a chance to grill Carl about Lyle Hendricks's accusation, but I was really nervous about being there alone with him and curious as to why Mary had scheduled our appointment for a time she couldn't make. "Mary didn't mention anything on the phone about working late," I said.

"It just came up today." As soon as we entered the apartment, Carl lit a cigarette and then as an afterthought offered me one. He leaned over and turned down the sound of the television show he had been watching, leaving several young men running around the screen shooting at each other in total silence. Now at least if I screamed and if somebody was home downstairs or next door, they might hear me.

"No, thanks," I said.

"Somebody was out, so Mom got to do a little overtime. She just called a few minutes ago to tell me. Said I should tell you about the service we put together for Lindy and by then she'd probably be here." Carl looked down when he spoke his cousin's name, or rather the name he called her. "You want a beer or somethin'? I could make coffee."

"No, thanks," I said, wondering if there was a back door or a fire escape. "But do you mind if I use the bathroom?"

Carl shook his head and pointed toward the hall leading from the living room to the rest of this fairly typical railroad flat. I walked down the passageway until I came to the still steamy bathroom. A wet bath towel was draped over the edge of the tub, an open shampoo bottle perched on the corner of the tub enclosure, and an open can of shaving cream crowned with a blob of foam sat on the shelf over the sink. I had to smile, recalling the joys of sharing a bathroom with one's adult kids who come home to regress. Climbing into the tub, I peered out the small open window, but all I could see was the

231

house next door. This made sense. After all, a fire escape or a back door would be in the rear of the house, not on the side. Wiping my footprints out of the tub with toilet paper, I flushed the paper away and washed my hands. All I had learned was that young men returning to the nest do not always pick up after themselves in the bathroom, and I already knew that.

Carl had turned up the sound on the TV while I was gone and dutifully turned it down when I returned. "I'm honored that you and your aunt want me to speak at the service you're planning for Belinda. As I told you yesterday, I was very fond of her and I'm very upset about . . . about . . . what happened to her," I said.

"Me too. You better believe it, me too. We was close, very close. She was like a kid sister to me." My stomach tightened as I saw him sitting there, clenching and unclenching his fists. For the first time, I noticed his sculpted biceps, the muscles bulging in his neck. Trying to recall my limited repertoire of self-defense tactics, I almost missed his next words. "Don't say nothin' to my mom, Professor, but I know who killed Lindy, and I'm gonna get him if it's the last thing I do." When the meaning of this vow finally registered, I stifled a gasp.

"I'm trying to figure out who killed her myself, Carl. Who do you think did it?" I asked, struggling to keep my face from revealing how surprised I was by his outburst. I completely forgot how scared I was to be alone with him.

"I don't think. I know. It's him. There's the SOB that killed her." My eyes followed Carl's pointing finger and I found myself staring once again at the photo of Lyle Hendricks and Mary Waters, posed like lovers at the Weehawken waterfront.

"Who is he?" I asked, playing dumb.

"He used to be my mom's boyfriend. She met him when she was on the picket line at the hospital where she works. She's on the line in the cafeteria. He's some honcho in the food service workers' union and he came down to support the strikers. Next thing I know he's movin' in here, givin' orders, actin' like he owns the place," Carl said, lighting a cigarette and taking a deep drag.

"Gee, Andy Dawes told me your mom's boyfriend liked Belinda. I still don't see why he'd kill her," I said.

"Poor Andy. He's got a heart for a brain. He just didn't get it because he's too dumb. And lovesick. Like my mom." Carl winced. "And you don't get it because you're too smart. Ol' Lyle did like her. Everybody liked Lindy." Carl's twisted smile was painful to see. "He was always touchin' her, pattin' her. Dancin' with her even. I tried to tell Mom it wasn't right, and Lindy even said something once or twice, but Mom didn't want to hear it." Carl brought his fist down on the arm of his easy chair and sat there in silence for a moment that seemed like an hour.

I was surprised how low his voice was when, staring at the rug, he finally spoke. "See, I work nights. I'm an EMT, you know. So this one night, must be three years ago now, I came home from work. I thought everybody was asleep. Lindy used to like to go to sleep listening to Phish. So I used to go into her room and turn off the CD player. Once in a while she'd be up and we'd talk, but most of the time, she was asleep with that damn thing on." He brushed his hand across his eyes as if the memory of Belinda's nighttime ritual had moved him. When he made this gesture, my last vestige of fear evaporated. It was hard to sustain fear of a man who was on the verge of tears.

"So this one night I hear Phish so I go in Lindy's room and there's this SOB naked and ready for action pullin' down the comforter and Lindy is strugglin'. She couldn't scream 'cause he had his hand over her mouth. Jesus Christ, she just turned fifteen the week before." My stomach churned and I was afraid I was going to be sick. The image of Belinda, beleaguered on all sides by predatory pedophiles so that she was not even safe in her own bed, was profoundly disturbing. I swallowed hard and the feeling passed. Carl had lowered his head into his hands.

Neither of us had heard the key turn in the lock, so neither of us was prepared to greet Mary Waters as she entered. I wondered if she had overheard Carl's shocking story, but her weary eyes and polite greeting gave me no reason to believe that she had. Fleetingly I wondered if she had ever heard this story. "Oh, Professor Barrett. I'm so sorry to keep you waiting. I worked a little overtime, and the first bus that came by didn't stop," she said. She walked over to Carl and tousled his hair. "Carl, didn't you fix the professor any tea?" Shedding her sweater, she headed into the hall leading to the kitchen.

"She didn't want nothin'," said Carl. "I asked her. She just got here."

"He's right. I'm fine," I said. "I just want to find out about what you have planned for the service, what you want me to say." Mary returned, lighting a cigarette, and sank down into the chair next to Carl's.

"You want a beer, Mom?" said Carl, taking pity on his mother, whose wrinkled uniform hung loosely on her thin frame and whose entire posture spoke of fatigue.

"Yeah. That would be nice, Carl. Thanks." Carl left the room. "He's a good boy, that one," said Mary. "Thank God he's home now."

When Carl returned with two beers and a

glass, he looked at me and said, "Sure you don't want nothin', Professor?"

"I'm sure, Carl. Thanks. If you two will just explain what you have in mind for the service and where I fit in, I'll leave you to get some rest." I wasn't going to get anything more out of Carl now that his mother was home, and I wanted very much to be on my way so I could think about what he had already said.

"It's very easy. Father Santos is going to do a service, say Mass, actually for Belinda. Then Carl is gonna read the Twenty-third Psalm. And Andy's gonna sing a hymn." When my eyes widened, Mary said, "He's got a beautiful voice, that Andy. He sings in our church choir." I nodded, inordinately pleased to learn of Andy's gift. "And we just thought since you were so good to Belinda and she liked you so much, you'd say a word or two about her. You know, like you were saying the other day, how hard she worked, how enthusiastic she was, you know, Professor . . . It don't have to be long, just from the heart."

"Of course," I agreed.

Chapter 22

To: Bbarrett@circle.com
From: Mbarrett@hotmail.com
Re: Miss you
Date: 05/29/01 08:19:45

Buenos dias, Mamacita, it's your long-lost wandering boy checking in. Can only afford a few more minutes at this rip-off cyber café computer, but wanted to let you know that everything's still cool here in beautiful Buenos Aires. I'm working hard, eating well, improving my Spanish, and making music once in a while. Met a totally awesome girl named Heidi from — would you believe? — New Jersey. But she's got an apartment in Manhattan now. Ran into her right here while she was e-mailing her mom. She's on holiday, staying in one of the posh hotels. But we met for coffee a few times. She has a totally happening career. She's a clutter consultant. She's met lots of cool people. They fly her all over the country to consult. Well, gotta go. Still not sure about the backpacking trip. But don't worry about us visiting Colombia. It's cool. Hi to Sol. I hear my awesome niece is coming to stay for a while . . . enjoy.

Love,
Mark

When I got home from the Waters's, in addition to Mark's e-mail, there was a second message from Wendy on my answering machine. I printed out Mark's latest missive to worry about later, left urgent summonses for Illuminada and Betty, and called Wendy at her mom's apartment in Fort Lauderdale. While I waited for her to pick up, I poured myself a glass of cold ginger ale. I hoped it would settle my stomach, still soured by Carl Waters's disturbing story. When I heard her voice, I said, "Hello, Wendy. It's me. Sorry I couldn't get back to you sooner. I've been a little busy. How's your mom?" I settled into the sofa and extended my feet onto the coffee table.

"Slightly better. Walking with a walker. Slowly getting used to the idea that she should move back to Jersey." Wendy sounded tired. "Why're you so busy? You've turned in your grades, right?" I thought she sounded a little wistful. Was it possible that she missed reading papers and grading students?

"Yes. I turned them in last Monday, two hours before the deadline. I've been running around trying to save your grant," I said.

Seeing me on the sofa, Virginia Woolf seized the opportunity to get her head scratched and jumped onto my lap. I obliged.

"That's what I wanted to find out about. Any progress? Do they still suspect Jason?" Wendy asked.

"Yes. In fact, I think he's going to be indicted soon. At least that's what he told me on Saturday. We shared a kayak," I said between sips of ginger ale.

"Bel, tell me, why would you share a kayak with a murder suspect? Are you crazy?" Wendy's voice squeaked as it always did when she questioned my sanity.

"Remember, I don't think Jason killed Belinda," I said. "I'd seen him the night before at a rally his girlfriend staged. I was checking her out as a possible suspect." Actually, alone in the kayak with Jason while a gray spring rain flattened the phragmites and rippled the water around us, I had briefly entertained the notion that he could easily hit me on the head with the paddle and flip me overboard to swim with the fishes. Instead, he had chosen to talk about the inaccessibility of his court-appointed attorney and his dread of the pending indictment.

"Is she a viable suspect? That would be so great," said Wendy, with a real lift to her voice. It was clear that to Wendy any suspect who was not a member of the UKC was a better suspect than Jason.

"She might be. She denies Jason's woman-izing. Maybe she needed to get rid of the competition to preserve her illusion that there was none," I said. "And I've come up with a couple of other suspects, a cousin and Belinda's aunt's ex-boyfriend."

"Tell me more." Wendy sounded intrigued. She wasn't going to like my response.

"I will but not until I've checked out their sordid and depressing stories. You'll have to slake your thirst for sensational gossip else-where for a while." I was unwilling to discuss Belinda's troubled home life with Wendy until I had more information.

"Okay, okay. So tell me, how did the last meeting go?" Relieved that I had come up with some new suspects, Wendy was willing to let me off the hook on the details.

"It went fairly well, considering." I had to add the qualifier.

"Considering what? That one member of the club has been murdered, perhaps by the club president?" said Wendy, with more than the customary edge to her voice. And I'd thought we'd put that topic to rest.

"Well, that too, but I meant the weather. It was raining a little. But everybody showed up and we actually kayaked for over two hours in the rain. It wasn't an electrical storm, so it was okay. But we had to have our final picnic in the gazebo." I repositioned Virginia Woolf so that the claws on her kneading forefeet would not leave permanent scars on my thighs.

"What final picnic?" Wendy asked.

"Weeks ago Shisele and Deatra suggested that we have a picnic on our last day, and we did. Everybody brought something." Actually, only Shisele, the Sharmas, and I had remembered to bring food, so we had a rather lopsided and cold meal of barbecued wings, vegetable samosas, and brownies. Not only had Deatra forgotten to bring something to eat, she had also forgotten her camera and her photos. She had looked tired and preoccupied as she and Basil paddled off together.

"How was it?" Wendy sounded a little wistful again.

"Actually, it was kind of pitiful in the aftermath of Belinda's death, and the rain didn't help, but at least we marked the end of the season," I said, recalling the ritual exchanging of e-mail addresses and phone numbers. "And Shisele put the log in a class-A binder for you and gave it to me." Wendy and I often joked about the faith RECC students had in the power of a fancy binder to compensate for an inadequate paper. Long ago we had categorized binders into classes A, B, and C, class A being the most elaborate and expensive. "Everybody signed it. Deatra said she had photos to illustrate it, but she forgot them. She swore she'd put them in my mailbox at RECC."

"That's so sweet of them," said Wendy. By the time we hung up, we both felt a little better. Wendy was optimistic about my prospects of pinning Belinda's murder on a suspect who was not a member of the UKC and I was able to draw a line through *Call Wendy* on my to-do list.

In response to my urgent summons, Betty and Illuminada arrived the next night. Since I was not teaching, I had scrubbed the cobwebs out of my kitchen and prepared a perfect spring meal, my favorite creamless asparagus soup, spinach pie, and salad. After a labor-intensive afternoon peeling asparagus and folding fragile sheets of filo dough, I remembered why I had all but retired as chef in residence. For dessert we would have to make do with Dove Bars.

"Raoul dropped us off," said Illuminada when she and Betty arrived looking tired after a long day's work. "He made me an offer I couldn't refuse. I just didn't have the energy to look for a parking place in this town tonight. He said he'd come back later." Since Illuminada's diagnosis, the ever-attentive Raoul had doubled his efforts to drive, shop, and run other errands. He was a one-man cancer-support group.

"Maybe Vic can pick us up. He's working late tonight. There's a big wake," said Betty, wrinkling her nose and sniffing. "What's for dinner? Oh my God, Bel's had a Martha Stewart moment!"

"Hell, I've had a whole Martha Stewart afternoon." I pointed at the printout of Mark's e-mail on the table next to the wine and wineglasses and went into the kitchen to get the soup. "After you pour the wine, check out Mark's latest e-mail and tell me, if you can, what the hell a clutter consultant does."

"*Chiquita,* a clutter consultant is someone you pay to help you clean your closets, you know, organize them, throw stuff out," said Illuminada after we had settled around the table. "This soup is delicious, Bel."

"Do you mean to tell me that my bright, sensitive, articulate, musical son is in love with a closet cleaner-outer?" I asked, taking a sip of wine.

"Could be. God, Illuminada's right, Bel. This is really good soup. You ought to slave over a hot stove more often. The *spanitokopita* is great too, better than what we get from our Greek place, even," said Betty, helping herself to another square. "Listen, you should worry a lot about Mark marrying the clutter consultant because that will take your mind off him backpacking through Colombia, where they kidnap American tourists and have them for breakfast."

"She's right. Besides, I read somewhere that those clutter consultants make big bucks.

243

And if he's going to teach, his wife at least should have a paying job." Illuminada smiled. "So, *chiquita,* did you get us over here because of this?" Illuminada picked up the printout as she spoke. "Or did you need tasters to practice on? Or have you found out something new about the Judd killing?"

"Yes, I've found out several things, in fact. As I see it now, there are five suspects: Jason Carillo; his girlfriend, Luisa Cortez; Belinda's boyfriend, Andy Dawes; her cousin, Carl Waters; and Mary Waters's former boyfriend, Lyle Hendricks. We've talked about Jason and Andy, but I haven't seen you since I checked out Luisa Cortez." I paused and poured another round of Chardonnay. "Luisa doesn't acknowledge Jason's infidelity as anything other than an inability to get along by himself. She just might have killed Belinda to preserve her illusion that there had been no other women."

Betty reacted at once. "She wouldn't be the first or the last to do that. Does she have an alibi?"

I shrugged.

"And does she have the strength?" Illuminada spoke while removing a folder from the briefcase at her feet. "According to the autopsy report which I just got, Belinda Judd was killed by a blow to the head with a blunt object after a scuffle during which she was badly beaten and kicked." She tossed the folder onto the table.

"Oh no!" I had not allowed myself to picture Belinda's final moments as an agony.

"She was probably unconscious when she died," said Illuminada, perhaps in deference to the tears welling in my eyes. I hoped she was right. "Could Luisa Cortez have inflicted that kind of damage?"

"I don't think so. Not without help." I took several deep breaths, not wanting to say more until I was sure I could speak without crying. "She's thin as a rail, a Cher look-alike. But let me tell you about the other two, okay?" I noticed that Betty had put her now-empty plate aside and snapped open her Palm Pilot. In a second she'd be taking notes.

"There's Carl Waters, Mary Waters's son and Belinda's first cousin." I tried not to speak too fast so Betty could get the names and relationships straight. "He's in his early twenties. Just out of the service. Lyle Hendricks, the mother's onetime boyfriend, fingered him, implying that he and Belinda had been sexually and romantically involved and that when he pointed this out to Mary, she had refused to believe or to stop it. Lyle claims that's why he left Mary and moved out three years ago."

"If Carl was involved with Belinda, why would he kill her?" asked Betty, automatically collecting our plates and flatware and piling them at the end of the table, demonstrating her formidable ability to multitask.

"Same reason her boyfriend Andy might have done it," I said, with a silent bow to Sol. "Jealousy. Fear of losing her to Andy, whom she had planned to marry, or to Jason, a new rival. Maybe she tried to break off with him and he got angry."

"*Dios mio,* I thought you said she was a sweet, naive kid," said Illuminada, shaking her head. "She sounds to me like a piece of work. What about the last guy?"

"Well, that's what really got to me. Lyle Hendricks is a food service worker at St. Mary's, a union rep, who met Mary when she was on strike and later moved in with her. Carl claims Lyle was always groping Belinda and that even when he and Belinda mentioned it to Mary, she didn't want to hear it. Carl also claims that he caught Lyle Hendricks in his birthday suit about to climb into bed with Belinda one night when she was asleep," I said, glad to have finally come to the end of this sad litany of suspects.

"Whew, girl, you've been busy," said Betty. "I'm telling you, you should quit teaching and go to work with Illuminada full-time. You get stuff out of folks it would take Dick Tracy years to find out."

"Any time, Bel," said Illuminada. Before I had time to fully savor their compliments, Illuminada went on. "But right now, what about this Lyle Hendricks? What I don't get is why would he now, out of the blue, kill Belinda? He's been out of that house for years and presumably he hasn't seen her since he left. He's probably got another teenager lined up by this time." Illuminada shuddered.

"Maybe the dude ran across her someplace by accident. Maybe he's been stalking her all along. Maybe he heard about her getting married and lost it. What do you think, Bel?" Betty turned to me.

"The thing I remember is Andy Dawes saying this guy liked Belinda but she didn't like him. That makes sense, especially if Belinda complained to Andy about Lyle's attention and how she didn't like it." I spoke slowly, recalling the look the young counter worker at St. Mary's had given me when I'd asked for Lyle. Had he been groping her too? "It also makes sense that Mary Waters would have fallen for Lyle. He would seem quite charismatic to her."

"Yes, and if she didn't want to believe he was groping her niece, well, she wouldn't be the first woman to deny that kind of thing either," said Illuminada with a sigh.

"Oh, I almost forgot," I said. "Carl said he planned to 'get' Lyle. I suppose I have to worry about that too."

"*Caramba,*" said Illuminada. "You'll probably have to go to the police with that piece of it. Otherwise if —"

"I know, I know," I said, not wanting to think just yet about being responsible for preventing another murder. "But I just can't believe what a complicated life poor Belinda had. And I thought her biggest problem was that she didn't read well."

"Bel, at the risk of seeming rude, isn't there any dessert? All this depressing stuff calls for a little medicine. Didn't you whip up something sweet for us today, girlfriend?" Betty was trying her best to sound like a plaintive child and doing a good job of it.

"I didn't whip up anything, but I did *not* forget dessert. Will you settle for a dark-chocolate-covered Dove Bar?" It was a rhetorical question. I rose from the table and headed for the fridge. "It's going to be a long night."

Chapter 23

Belinda Judd
Basic english 1
Professor barret
April 23 2001
Jurnal

The job I got is so cool. I like it a lot. I tell peoeple were things are and look out for shop lifters. I spotted one the other day and I told the boss and he got her. I get to talk to a lot of peoeple, the time goes reel fast. I reely like the boss and I have a lot of frends there. Every nite a big groop of us goes out, its so cool. I don't always get everthing they say like the blu mall of license or fucking (sorry, Professor B) more so I just lisen. Sooner or later I'll figur *it out. Evrybody takes turns paying for beer even the boss. last nite I paid. And I'll still finish reading the House on Wango St befor the test . . .*

In search of inspiration for the right words to say at Belinda's memorial service, I had gone to my office to retrieve her Basic English I folder. Flipping through her assignments, I recalled the dream I'd had about Belinda trying to tell me something. As I scanned each paper, I wondered how I had ever managed to make sense out of the alphabet soup that, unfortunately, had represented her best effort to express herself in written English. Out of respect and affection for the dead girl, I struggled anew to translate her convoluted spelling. Then in one of her notes to me, a phrase caught my eye, and then another and another. *Blu mall of license. Fucking more. The House on Wango St.* I stared at this seeming gibberish and repeated each string of letters aloud. Oh my God! Belinda *was* speaking to me from the grave. Why hadn't I picked up on this right away? Belinda might be alive today if only I had cracked her code sooner.

With shaking hands, I reached for the phone to call Betty and then Illuminada and then I left for home in a sweat that, for a change, had nothing to do with my hormones. I was trembling by the time I reached the house. Sol was back from the retreat, and I didn't waste any time making him party to my revelation. I pulled Belinda's journal out of my book bag where I had stashed her folder. "Look," I said, giving him a cursory peck on the ear. "Belinda wrote this." I shoved it in his face as he stood at the stove rotating a saucepan. "I think she was hanging out with people who knew something about that murder. Will you look?" My voice was pleading as, still brandishing the paper, I followed him to the sink island.

"Easy, Bel," said Sol, maneuvering around me with a plate on which he'd just turned out a perfect omelet. He placed it on the island and motioned me to sit. It was only after he had made himself one and put out a warm brick-oven-baked baguette and a stick of butter that he picked up Belinda's note and skimmed it. "How the hell are you supposed to do college work with somebody performing at this level? This poor kid was only marginally literate. What the hell was she trying to write about?"

"Sol, listen," I said, trying not to lose it over his seeming unwillingness to hear what I was saying. "Remember when I showed you an article in the *Jersey City Herald* about a woman who was murdered at His 'n' Hers

Shoes? Remember?"

"Yeah, vaguely. But you said you didn't know her." Sol ripped off a chunk of bread, slathered it with butter, and handed it to me. In spite of his obtuseness at the moment, it was good to have him home.

"I didn't know that victim. But remember I told you about Belinda's dyslexia? Remember when she signed up for the Urban Kayaking Club because she thought it was the Urban Kickboxing Club?" I persisted, trying to convey a sense of the urgency I felt.

"Well, I don't know if I told you, but shortly before she was killed, Belinda took a job as a security guard at the Outlets and she started going out for a beer with the other guards after work. So now I think she over-heard them saying something about that murder. Look." I pointed to the lines as I read. *"Blue mall of license.* See, that probably means *blue wall of silence.* Sometimes she mixes up *W*'s and *M*'s. Dyslexics sometimes confuse letters that are mirror images of each other. The other guards were probably talking about a blue wall of silence. You know, that's what the cops call it when they don't rat on each other. And here she wrote *fucking more.*" I moved my finger along be-neath the next fractured phrase. "See, that could be *fucking whore.* Belinda said she didn't know what they were talking about, but when they realized how naive she was

252

and what a Chatty Cathy besides, and that they had said all this in front of her . . ." My voice trailed off.

"That's pretty far out there, even for you," said Sol, finally attuned to what I was talking about. "Aren't you going to have your soup? C'mon, Bel. Jesus, what are you crying about?"

"Sol, if I'd figured out what she was saying sooner, maybe . . ." Tears spilled into my soup as I recalled how quickly I'd read Belinda's note, how appalled I'd been by her spelling. Talk about missing the forest for the trees. Now I felt responsible for her death. If I had paid more attention to her note when I first got it . . . If I had been more effective in communicating with her, warned her about the dangers of being too trusting . . . Instead I had gone on at her about her damn spelling and sent her to a tutor. "I feel like it's my fault she's dead, Sol."

"Bel, don't even go there." Sol was not unfamiliar with my propensity for guilt. A half an hour and many Kleenexes later, he still had not completely convinced me that I had not somehow contributed to Belinda's death. "Okay, Bel. I give up. But you really need to accept the fact that you and your actions just aren't so important in the overall scheme of things. There are events that take place regardless of what you do or don't do. The universe does not revolve around Bel Barrett.

253

And even if you had never read that assignment or even if she had never written it, that girl would be dead today. Don't you get it?" I nodded, but I didn't totally believe him.

"Bel, if you're right about what she wrote, and I'm still not sure that you are, it's a miracle that you managed to make any sense at all out of that mumbo-jumbo." Sol cast a disparaging glance at Belinda's note. "Whoever murdered her is responsible for her death, not you. For once in your life, don't buy a ticket for that guilt trip."

Sol's somewhat skeptical response made me eager to see Betty and Illuminada, so I was relieved when we assembled the next morning at the RIP. "So, girlfriend, what brings you out so early now that the semester is over? Nostalgia for the sound of the alarm clock? Sympathy with the working classes? You sounded so hyper on my machine, I thought about calling 911." Betty was smiling in spite of the hour.

"Lose your estrogen patch in the shower again, *chiquita?*" Illuminada pulled out her chair, sat down, and picked up the grimy plastic menu, holding it between her thumb and index finger as if it were a long-dead fish someone had put on her placemat as a joke.

I ignored their good-natured barbs, passing them off as the ramblings of caffeine-deprived individuals who were really glad to see each other. "Look at this. It's one of Belinda's assignments." I put the all-important paper on the table. They glanced at it briefly and then at me. Before Illuminada's eyes could blaze with the impatience that my somewhat digressive narrative style frequently inspired, I rushed on. "I think this note says that Belinda overheard a conversation about the other murder in the Meadowlands, the one at His 'n' Hers Shoes last month. The one that Gina told you about, Betty. Remember?"

Although I directed the last part of my question to Betty, I looked from one to the other of my friends to see if their faces revealed their recollection of our long-ago conversation. Betty's eyes gleamed first, and in another second, Illuminada, suddenly attentive, checked in, saying, "Yes. Gina was pulling out of the parking lot and somebody found a corpse, right? A Colombian girl."

I nodded before I resumed my tale. "Remember, I told you that Belinda was dyslexic and a bit naive? Well, she wrote this right after she started working at the Outlets." Now Betty and Illuminada put their heads together to examine the piece of paper as I continued speaking. "I think she's saying that she went out for a beer after work with the other security guards and something was said about a blue wall of silence and about a fucking whore. See?" As I had when I showed the note to Sol, I underlined the critical phrases with my finger to highlight them for Betty and Illuminada. "Belinda's spelling may be confused, especially the *M*'s and *W*'s, but her message is clear. Her new friends, including her boss, might have known something about the fatal stabbing of the woman found in the parking lot. They might have babbled their bloody secrets into their beer in Belinda's presence. And just maybe, one of them realized that Belinda, an innocent in so many ways, was more capable of inadvertently repeating their conversation than she was of understanding it." I looked across the table at my friends, waiting for a reaction.

The arrival of the waitress with our breakfast postponed any discussion until she left. In between bites of English muffin, Illuminada pushed Belinda's paper back across the table to me, saying only, "Here. Put this away so we don't get any grease on it." She wiped her lips daintily with her napkin and spoke again, her voice low, her brow furrowed, "*Dios mio,* Bel, you know, I think you just might be right. I think she might very well have heard something she shouldn't have. That doesn't necessarily mean that the other guards saw her as dangerous and did away with her. But . . ." She hesitated for a moment before continuing. "I wouldn't rule it out. What do you think, *chiquita?*"

Betty had polished off most of her egg sandwich while Illuminada was speaking. She held the last bite in her hand when she answered, "I agree. This is probably the group that provided the alibi to Hector what's-his-name, that poor woman's boyfriend. It said in the paper that he was drinking with his buddies at the time of her death, remember?" Betty took a sip of coffee and rested her head against the back of the booth for a minute. Then, facing us again, she asked, "So now what do we do?" It was so unlike Betty to ask for direction instead of giving it that Illuminada and I exchanged a glance.

"We have to take the note to whoever is handling the Colombian girl's murder at the Hudson County Homicide Squad," Illuminada said promptly.

"Will you stop calling her the 'Colombian girl'?" I snapped. "Her name was Maria something-or-other and she's a woman."

"Okay. I forgot about your fanatic politically correct streak. Far be it from this Cubana to violate your gringo sensibility, especially at this hour. Forgive me. I just couldn't remember the poor woman's name. Now we can call her Maria something-or-other if that makes you happy." Illuminada managed a trace of her usual grin that took the sting out of her words.

"Before we turn this over to the cops, you have to discuss it with the RECC attorney, and before you do that, you'll have to get the go-ahead from President Woodman." Betty

257

spoke in a singsong rhythm, taking me completely by surprise. In response to my puzzled stare, she continued. "Hello, Bel. You taught the young woman who wrote this and you are the adviser of a college-sponsored activity in which she participated." Betty's clipped words and strident tone made it easy to understand why she had been nicknamed Ramrod Ramsey. No wonder Gina and the rest of the president's staff, even, it was rumored, Dr. Woodman himself, jumped when Betty said jump. I stifled the urge to thumb my nose at her.

Instead, recognizing the truth of what she said and forgiving the abrasive way she put it, I answered, "Damn. You're right. I guess I do have to jump through those hoops. Thanks for reminding me. I'm so upset that I forgot my sacred duty to the college. Silly me." Toward the end of that speech my words were edged with irony, and I placed my hand over my heart as I said them.

"*Dios mio,* yes. Betty certainly is right. You have to cover yourself and RECC," echoed Illuminada, looking pensive.

"Cover *myself? Moi?* What for? What have *I* done?" I asked, turning from one friend to the other, familiar tears welling in my eyes. "It's what I didn't do. If I had spent a little more time reading this, maybe I would have figured it out sooner, and maybe Belinda would still be . . ."

Illuminada rolled her eyes. "Bel, let's not go there just yet." This expression, an echo of Sol's response, never failed to impress me with its blatant evasiveness. Her next words were further indication of her lack of interest in my self-castigation. "We don't have time this morning to talk you through your current guilt trip. Just go ahead and make an appointment with President Woodman and get clearance to talk with the college attorney. Morris Dickman's office handles RECC's legal stuff now, right, Betty?"

"Right. Tell me when you're free, Bel, and I'll make an appointment with Woodman for you. Then, after he okays it, I'll set you up with Dickman. Just check your calendar." Betty stood over me as I fumbled dutifully in my purse and withdrew my date book, wishing automatically that it was both wireless and handheld. Betty too had no ear for my guilt-ridden recriminations.

"I want to see both of them today," I said, a bit tired of being ordered around by my well-meaning but suddenly overbearing and decidedly unsympathetic friends.

"Be sure and make a copy of that note before you show it to anybody." As she spoke, Illuminada counted out her share of the check. "The cops will keep it."

"I already made copies," I snapped as I threw a five-dollar bill on the table. "Get back to me, okay? I'm outta here."

Chapter 24

RECC STUDENT HELD
FOR MURDER OF COED

Jason Carillo, the nineteen-year-old River Edge Community College student suspected of slaying fellow student Belinda Judd, was arrested today. He is being detained without bail in the county jail pending indictment. A Jersey City resident, the suspect lives with his father, Alonso Carillo, a Vietnam veteran, who told reporters, "He's goin' to college. The kid's an A student. He wants to be somebody. He didn't kill nobody." The accused is represented by a public defender. . . .

Damn. I sure wished I'd paid more attention to Belinda's journal as soon as I got it. I hoped it wasn't too late for my decoding to do Jason some good. He hadn't been honest with the women in his life, true, but if that was a crime, half the population would be behind bars. Besides, I suspected that being falsely accused of murder had taught him a lesson. Attempting to tame my frizzy hair with a few strokes of my hands and making sure I had a copy of Belinda's journal in my purse, I left my office and headed for the elevator. I didn't want to be late for the meeting Betty had orchestrated for me with her boss, RECC's president.

Walking into Dr. Ron Woodman's fourteenth-floor office, I felt as if I had entered a diorama in a millennial museum of urban higher education. Past and present members of the Board of Trustees glared from oversized portraits hanging in two rows above the massive but generic wood desk. With the glittering narrowed eyes that must have been a requirement for board membership, this rogues' gallery of local politicians and business people appeared to be scrutinizing the college president's every move. The American flag and a magenta and gold RECC flag, which, for reasons that have been obscured by history, features a rear view of the Statue of Liberty, flanked the photos. Left of the president's desk, the picture window afforded a panoramic view of the city. From here the scurrying students entering below looked like ambulatory dots.

Against the other wall were two upholstered chairs with a square table between them. On the table were the requisite copies of the *Chronicle of Higher Education*, two or three journals about two-year colleges, and a portfolio of favorable, although slightly misleading, newspaper clippings about RECC. Above the table hung Dr. Woodman's credentials, a dizzying array of degrees in education, business, and the business of education, as well as various awards from organizations whose primary business appeared to be honoring educators. The president's office and the adjacent board meeting room were the only carpeted rooms in the entire college.

Betty, who had ushered me in, smiled and exited, leaving the door slightly open behind her. As I settled myself in a chair, it occurred to me that this office went a long way toward explaining Ron Woodman's tendency to minimize the importance of students and maximize that of the trustees. Ron Woodman, a portly man with a wreath of black hair encircling a bald spot, seated himself behind his oversized desk and began our exchange on a note of cordiality. "Hi, Bel. Hope you had a good semester."

"Hi, Ron," I replied, reminding myself that he was at least ten years younger than I was, that I had tenure, and that these factors as well as his use of my given name more than entitled me to address him by his. Nonetheless, he looked startled and adjusted his collar. "Good to see you too," I said, smiling. "Well, the semester was going well until —"

"Yes. Terrible about that girl. But at least her body wasn't found on campus. The papers did mention that she was a RECC stu-

262

dent, but that's all. So far. I hope they don't uncover anything that links her killing to RECC. We just don't need any bad PR." He glanced behind him at the portraits of the trustees on the wall while I thanked God that he hadn't yet seen the morning paper in which Jason's pending indictment had been trumpeted to the world. "Betty said you had an urgent problem. Let's hear it. I hope I can be of help," he replied, still cordial but just a shade more formal now.

"I hope so too. You see —" I was unprepared for his next interruption.

"By the way, good of you to pitch in with that canoe club. Me, I wouldn't be caught dead on the Hackensack River in a canoe if my own mother begged me," he said with what he obviously thought was an engaging and conspiratorial grin. Then, remembering those who had, in fact, replaced his mother in the driver's seat of his psyche, he stole another anxious glance over his shoulder at the rows of eyes glinting down at him. "That's not a river, that's an industrial cesspool," he pronounced with a shudder.

Sidetracked, I said nothing for a moment, reminding myself that the man was from Nebraska and so could hardly be expected to appreciate that the Hack was now cleaner than it had been in decades. Ron Woodman was still suffering from culture shock. He was also suffering from political shock. New

Jersey bigwigs were making national headlines for tolerating racial profiling by the state police, influence peddling, and just plain graft. Jersey City itself had always had a long and impressive history of patronage politics. No wonder the man kept looking over his shoulder.

When I spoke again, I said, "Well, actually, it was lovely out on the river. The club members and I really enjoyed exploring the Meadowlands." I was surprised to note that I meant what I was saying. Suddenly an image of Belinda appeared in my head, and I caught myself before I could digress into a panegyric on the glories of the local flora and fauna. My God, two young women were dead, Carl Waters was about to kill somebody, an innocent person faced indictment, and I was making small talk. I plunged into an explanation of my visit. "But I'm really worried. Belinda Judd was in my Basic English I class. She was dyslexic and kind of naive. I'm afraid she heard some people talking about a murder. I think they were referring to the killing of that poor woman whose body was found in a parking lot in the Meadowlands at one of the outlets, remember?"

Woodman's brow convulsed and his mouth tightened. I hadn't done a good job of presenting my concern, and I'd caught him off-guard, not generally a sound idea. I hurried to clarify. "Belinda wrote about it in her journal. See? Here it is." I unfolded the paper, leaned forward, and pushed it across the desk. Ron Woodman briefly considered Belinda's scrawled and enigmatic prose. Shaking his head, he shoved back the piece of paper, disdain puckering one corner of his mouth.

"We get some pretty weak students in those basic classes, don't we? I guess you had your work cut out for you with this one," he said in what he probably thought was an empathetic tone. But the fact that he was completely ignoring what I had said did not escape me. I resolved to try again.

My voice was stern this time. "Ron, Belinda Judd, a RECC student who was brutally murdered, communicated in writing to me, her professor, that she heard the people she works with discuss the 'blue wall of silence' and a 'fucking whore.' Dyslexics often reverse letters and sounds. This conversation took place just a short while after the girlfriend of one of the guards she works with was found slashed to death in a parking lot at their workplace." I paused for breath. Woodman rubbed his chin until it reddened. Then he turned around, reflexively looking up at the trustees. I had gotten his attention.

This time I carried Belinda's journal around the desk and stuck it under his nose, hunching over him and pointing at the words on the paper as I spoke them. "See? Here she's written *blu mall of license*. But, like many dyslexics, she sometimes switches mirrored letters like *M* and *W*. So she probably means *blue wall of silence*. Then here, she's got *fucking more*. That's probably *fucking whore*. Belinda was repeating fragments of a conversation that she didn't quite understand." I paused for barely a moment and went on before he could speak. "And a few hours after she wrote this, she was dead." Again I paused to let the import of what I was saying sink in. He was holding his head in his hands now, so I figured he'd grasped the problem. "Ron, I wanted to let you know that I'm taking this note to the authorities who are investigating Belinda's murder and the murder of that other young woman. Maybe they can stop this murderer before he kills again."

"Bel, please." Rubbing his chin with the other hand this time, he turned and cast an imploring look at the trustees as if asking them to consider what he had to put up with. Only then did he address himself again to me. "There will be more press." He announced this as if proclaiming the return of the bubonic plague, his lips now compressed into a crease, and his left eye twitching. I knew he took the heat from the board every time RECC got even a hint of negative publicity, and I was telling him that there was a

266

serial killer on the loose, so he was worried about the press. What was wrong with this picture? I fought the urge to strangle him or at least to treat him to a string of invective.

"Excuse me, Ron. Have you stopped to consider what kind of press there will be if word gets out that RECC is withholding evidence?" I waved Belinda's journal in the air like a banner. "If we keep this from the police much longer, RECC could be accused of exactly that. For that matter, so could I. Furthermore, according to this morning's paper, the cops are about to indict an innocent RECC student for Belinda's murder. So I want your permission to talk to Mo Dickman before I go to the cops. That's why the board retains him. I'm trying to protect the college, not hurt it." Now it was my turn to meet the staring eyes of the trustees. I hoped that by confronting their glances myself, I could convince the worried man in front of me that there was no way out of this one. He was damned if he did and doomed if he didn't. I just wanted him to hurry up and give the okay. My anxiety increased each time I re-read Belinda's journal.

"You know, Bel, I think you *should* run this by Mo Dickman. Let him take a look at that paper, see what he thinks. I'm willing to be guided by his judgment. He got us out of that other situation without any unpleasant leaks." My mind flashed back, as I tried to recall the "situation" he was referring to. There were many choices. The most distasteful one and the one that would have earned us nasty headlines for sure was a suit brought against the college by a former employee discharged after auditors discovered her "misappropriation" of thousands of grant dollars. In retaliation for her dismissal, she had charged the RECC board with racism and sexism. The college had awarded the woman a generous out-of-court settlement to subvert her suit. And who said crime didn't pay? No wonder Ron Woodman was worried.

"And you know what?" he was saying. "You're in luck. Mo's due here any minute for dinner with the board before tonight's meeting. If you have a seat out there, you can catch him. I'll have Betty give him a heads-up. Good to see you, Bel. Keep me posted." Standing now, he pointed to Betty's office, where I knew there were chairs for those awaiting presidential audiences. The poor man appeared relieved to be ending our meeting and passing the latest "situation" on to Mo Dickman. Woodman picked up his phone and said something to Betty about alerting the attorney to the need to have a word with me as soon as he arrived.

Increasingly worried about Carl Waters's next move and impatient with all this bureaucratic nonsense, I looked at my watch. It was getting on toward five. By the time I finished talking with Dickman, it would probably be too late to catch anybody involved in the investigation of the Mejia murder. In spite of my impatience, I was relieved not to have to cross town at rush hour to go to the fancy office Morris Dickman shared with his partners. Their firm, Caputo, Dickman, and O'Reilley, was a stronghold of legal talent currently enjoying favor with those who disbursed lucrative municipal contracts. Where mismanagement was rife, lawyers were busy. With what RECC spent annually on legal fees, the college could have hired three full-time faculty members and had money left over to stock the computer lab with state-of-the-art machines that actually worked.

Betty winked at me as I took a seat opposite her desk to wait for Dickman. The smell of garlic wafted in from the board room, where trustees were already gathering for the traditional pre-meeting feed, catered no doubt by one of their cousins. I recalled other occasions when I had cooled my heels in this aromatic outer circle waiting for an opportunity to address the board. Now I listened to my stomach growl and worried about Carl's next move.

Mo Dickman was not eager to please. He was over an hour late, unapologetic, and talking on his cell phone. He interrupted his call long enough for Betty to reintroduce us. Then she returned to her desk and Dickman resumed his phone conversation. He seemed to think that facing me while saying, "Yeah, yeah" to the caller fulfilled his obligation to meet with me, a mere professor. Mo Dickman negotiated faculty contracts on behalf of the administration, so he knew exactly how much money I didn't make, and therefore he knew exactly how unimportant I really was.

Worried, tired, and now livid, I was in no mood to be ignored by a rude dude in a suit that cost more than I earn in a month. I put my palm on the extended elbow connected to the hand in which he held his cell phone and applied pressure, lowering arm, hand, and phone. His eyebrows jumped at my bold breach of conventional underling behavior. I spoke in the voice I used to admonish students whose beepers go off in class, "Mr. Dickman, I have evidence that Belinda Judd, the RECC student who was murdered, knew something about the murder at the Outlets last month. She wrote about it in an assignment. I'm going to the police . . . ."

Apparently all he heard were the words *RECC student* and *murder* and *assignment*. He applied his own syntax, and, in the current climate of school shootings, these buzzwords caused him to draw a totally erroneous conclusion. "A RECC student's going to murder someone? She wrote that in an assignment? We've got to alert the cops, keep her off campus, maybe close down the college until she's locked up." Woodman had worried about the press. Dickman had his own media-fed fantasies. I shook my head in frustration. Betty motioned us into Wooodman's now empty office, and I entered with Dickman at my heels. Betty snapped on the light and, once again, exited the room, leaving the door slightly ajar.

And once again I explained Belinda's dyslexia, her journal, my certainty that she had been an unwitting participant in a conversation related to the Meadowlands murder. Once again I reminded him that Belinda was dead. Once again I translated Belinda's sad misspellings.

"You've got to go to the cops. Jesus, Professor. We can't have a college employee withholding evidence. Just don't let the press get ahold of this." He pointed to Belinda's journal. "You don't want to have people think RECC students can't write any better than that, do you, Professor? Don't worry about your own liability. That's what you got a union for. Let me know what happens. I don't want to have to read about it in the paper." With this series of directives, Mo Dickman turned and followed his nose into the board meeting.

Chapter 25

To: Bbarrett@circle.com
From: Progranny@hotmail.com
Re: Always a first time
Date: 06/04/01 11:05:15

Dear Bel,

Now you just relax. Your grandbaby is going to have a wonderful time visiting with you and your friend. You asked for some tips, so here's advice from an experienced granny of six who knows how to make the littlest houseguests so happy they don't even notice their parents aren't there.

Forget the yogurt containers. Our kids used to play happily with them for hours, but that was then and this is now. Stash them in the attic with those macramé hanging planters I just know you've got up there. Then go to Toys "R" Us and buy that little girl something you know her parents will disapprove of like a water pistol or anything plastic that makes noise.

From what you wrote about your

daughter, her poor deprived kid is probably on a sugarless diet. As a good grandma, you should be the one to introduce her to chocolate ice cream. Don't think of this as disloyalty to your daughter but rather as bonding with your granddaughter.

Since your daughter works and goes to school, she probably doesn't have time to take the kid on many outings. But since you live near Manhattan, you can take her to the Tisch Children's Zoo in Central Park. They've got a petting zoo with goats, pigs, cows, and other benevolent beasties she can feed and fondle. The staff there wear frog and turtle costumes and your little animal lover will have a wonderful time.

Well, that's it for now. I have to get my grandson at the airport. I'll get back to you if I think of anything else. Have a wonderful visit.

Emily

There was no time to think about entertaining Abbie J because I was eager to turn in my evidence to the cops. "Gotta run. I'm going to turn Belinda's journal over to an investigator. Illuminada's picking me up. She'll drop me back here later." Giving Sol a quick hug, I grabbed my book bag and purse and stepped outside just as Illuminada pulled up in the space in front of the fire hydrant a few doors from our house.

"Now just remember, *chiquita,* you're giving the County Homicide guys a lot to think about and more work. They think they've got two murderers to find, and now you're telling them there's only one." After years of working with, around, and in spite of the local police, Illuminada had come to know their mind-sets pretty well.

"You mean nobody else has connected Belinda's killing with the Mejia murder?" I asked.

"I doubt it. That's why we're here and that's why you're going to try to talk to the detective investigating that murder, Ralph Falco is his name, and let him coordinate with whoever they've got working on Belinda's murder." Illuminada's strategy sounded logical. "But before you go in, give me the *Reader's Digest* version of what happened yesterday when you talked to Mo Dickman."

I had to smile at Illuminada's straightforward effort to avoid one of my attenuated narratives. She didn't want a blow-by-blow replay of the game. She just wanted the score. "He said I should get Belinda's journal to the investigating authorities ASAP so I, and by extension RECC, couldn't be accused of withholding evidence. Neither he nor Woodman wants any more unfavorable press."

After my terse recap, Illuminada nodded and said, "Well, do it. I'll wait here. Then, *Profesora*, I'll let you buy me some breakfast if you have time."

"Deal," I said as I stepped out of the car. Illuminada, who seldom wasted a minute, began punching numbers into her cell phone before I had a chance to slam the car door shut.

Along with all the other citizens seeking access to municipal or county services or themselves serving as jurors, witnesses, clerks, lawyers, judges, cops, or maintenance workers, I submitted to the airport-style security check. Retrieving my bag containing Belinda's all-important journal, I made my way into the elevator and up to the seventh floor where I found a door labeled "Hudson County Homicide Squad." "Detective Ralph Falco," I said to the uniformed young man at the desk. My voice was the one I used to "suggest" to students that they stop writing and turn in their tests. It was a voice that expected to be heeded.

"He know you're coming?" asked the officer, looking up at me. I compressed my lips into a no-nonsense line and glared at him. He turned around and bellowed, "Falco! You got company."

A lanky man in shirtsleeves with gray eyes defined by promising laugh lines emerged from the nether regions of the nondescript office suite, smoothing his thinning crew cut. He looked at me with who-the-hell-are-you-lady? written all over his face. However, what came out of his mouth was "Detective Falco here. What can I do for you, ma'am?" His hand reached for mine and shook it with enough enthusiasm to convey confidence but without breaking any bones either. With my hand still in his, he checked me out, noting my salt and pepper frizz, black jeans, leopard-print shirt, and gold hoop earrings. Even as his wedding ring brushed my palm, I could tell he appreciated what he saw.

Retrieving my hand, I smiled for the first time since entering the building and replied, "You can find us a place to have a private conversation, for starters."

"That's the best offer I've had in a long time," he said jovially. His remark may have been slightly sexist, but it was also flattering. I was not unreceptive to a little flattery, especially from attractive men with promising laugh lines. I followed him through a room where several men and one woman sat in front of computers. He stopped at the door to a cubicle that turned out to be as gray on gray as the rest of the place, but that boasted ceiling-high walls and a door as well as a desk, a couple of chairs, and a window.

"I'm Bel Barrett, Detective Falco. Thanks for your time," I said, attempting, now that I had his ear, to match his civility with a little civility of my own. "I teach English at River Edge Community College." I fished in my wallet for one of my cards and handed it to him.

He put it on his desk without looking at it, instead focusing his attention on me. "Well, I could probably use an English lesson, but I suspect that's not why you're here." He grinned, still working the charm.

"I understand you're investigating the murder of Maria Mejia," I said. Falco nodded and leaned back in his chair, assuming a listening posture. I knew I was in the company of a man who was good at getting people to tell him things. Well, I had something to tell him. "Belinda Judd, a student of mine, was found dead . . ." I began. He was absolutely silent during my entire recitation, and when I pulled out the original copy of Belinda's journal, he hunched over it with me. His eyes followed my fingers as I read it to him. His brow contracted fleetingly as I repeated the key phrases that alluded to the murder and explained how Belinda mixed up her *M*'s and *W*'s. When I finished, I handed him the piece of paper, saying magnanimously, "You may keep this. River Edge Community College and I are not withholding evidence."

Falco grinned a slow, easy grin and said, "No, you certainly are not, Professor. You're bringing it here where we can follow up on it. And, believe me, I am going to do just that, because it's a promising lead." He patted Belinda's journal and then paper-clipped my card to it and placed them both atop the other papers on his desk.

"I think so too. This gives you a basis for questioning Maria Mejia's boyfriend again, doesn't it? I mean, this could blow his alibi, right?" I asked.

"It sure could, Professor," he said. Getting to his feet, he added, "And I really appreciate your taking the time to drop this off. You can be sure I'll check into it along with all the other leads we've got." He made an exaggerated pretense of wiping his forehead. I took the hint and stood. "And, Professor, when you get tired of reading all those books and papers, you got yourself a job offer right here as a detective, remember that." Falco was still smiling engagingly as he showed me through the door and escorted me back past the people busy at their computers to the reception area in the front of the office. "And, again, thanks for taking the time to come in and drop off that piece of paper. We welcome citizen participation." Now we were both smiling.

When I got back to Illuminada's car, I began, "He was charming and attentive —"

"*Caramba*, Bel. This isn't *The Dating Game*. What do I care if he was charming? What did he say about the journal?" Illuminada snapped. I hoped her mood would improve with breakfast.

"He paid real close attention when I explained about Belinda's dyslexia and went over her journal. He got the idea right away. And he said he'd look into it along with all the other leads they have. But he put it on top of his in-box. And he thanked me for bringing it in," I answered.

Perhaps regretting her earlier outburst, Illuminada said, "Good work. Now you deserve a real breakfast. Let's go to the Country Kitchen and then I'll drop you off at home." I was so happy to see Illuminada, who gave new meaning to the word *workaholic*, taking time out for the fresh-squeezed OJ and fabulous pancakes they made at Country Kitchen that I didn't argue with her. She'd begun chemotherapy, and maybe that infusion had already begun to slow her down a little. Besides, I don't usually fight the prospect of a really decent breakfast. My typical breakfast consisted of OJ, no-fat yogurt, and decaf tea. But breakfast with friends, even at the decidedly quotidian RIP Diner, was an excuse to indulge. And I seldom had to be persuaded to indulge myself at the table. I knew others who, like Illuminada, when faced with intimations of mortality in the form of a dreaded diagnosis, had also made room in their busy lives for living.

Over whole-grain pancakes topped with

enough Vermont maple syrup to energize us for a year, Illuminada surprised me by listening to the long version of my interview with the charming Detective Falco. She didn't interrupt once to tell me to speed it up, nor did she glance at her watch the way she often did during my playbacks. When her coffee and my ginger citrus tea arrived, she finally spoke. "*Dios mio,* I'm not surprised he was receptive. That's an intriguing piece of evidence you brought him. But are you sure it was just the evidence he was interested in?"

I stuck my tongue out at her. I was encouraged by Detective Falco's interest in Belinda's journal, but I was still anxious about Jason and Carl. And I still felt guilty about taking so long to uncover the journal's secrets. So, fueled by anxiety, guilt, and good old-fashioned sugar, I resolved to keep on doing whatever I could to nail Belinda's murderer. I just prayed no one else got killed while I was doing it.

Chapter 26

Memorial Service for Slain Student Draws Family, Friends, and Profs

Mourners seeking to come to terms with the death of Belinda Judd, the eighteen-year-old River Edge Community College student found dead in Laurel Hill Park, filed into a memorial service at St. Paul's Church yesterday. Judd is survived by an aunt, Mary Waters, and a cousin, Private First Class Carl Waters, both of Jersey City. The deceased was eulogized by Father Enrique Santos, who praised her hard work at the church's shelter, where she had helped prepare and serve food to the homeless since she was ten. Numerous shelter regulars and staff members were among the mourners. RECC English professor Bel Barrett also shared her memories of the deceased, emphasizing the hard work, determination, enthusiasm, and intelligence she brought to her studies as well as to the extracurricular activities in which she participated. RECC president Ron Woodman, several RECC faculty members, and many students were also present. After Father Santos said Mass, Private Waters led the congregation in a recitation of the Twenty-third Psalm, and Andy Dawes, a close friend of the family and a choir member, sang "Against All Odds."

The reporter failed to mention that a few of Belinda's colleagues from GuardNJ attended her funeral. Shortly after I had delivered my brief tribute to Belinda, my stomach churned as I recognized her supervisor, Hector Ramirez, appropriately dressed in a dark suit. Deatra, who sat with me, pointed out a few others with him. They were sitting near the back, not far from Shisele, the Sharma cousins, Basil, and a pale and tight-lipped Jason. I thought I saw Detective Ralph Falco standing in the back of the chapel, but before I could be sure, Deatra pointed wordlessly to a young woman in the uniform of GuardNJ sitting alone two rows ahead of me on the left. Her face was impassive but just then Andy Dawes began to sing an oddly haunting version of Mariah Carey's "Against All Odds." He hadn't intoned more than the first line when I noticed this woman's profile crumble and her shoulders heave. Tears coursed down the cheek I could see, and she wiped them away with the back of her hand. Aware of my obligation to speak, I had held up pretty well until this stranger's tears invited my own, and I finally wept for Belinda.

When I left the service, drained and sad, I walked to my car and noticed that an urban vandal had snapped my antenna, not a discovery designed to elevate my mood, but not the end of the world either. By the time I got home, I'd almost forgotten about it. "I'm just about cried out," I said to Sol by way of greeting.

"Well, hers was a sad, sad death, tragic in fact. But you did what you had to do."

"I thought I saw Detective Falco there. Maybe he was planning on bringing in Hector Ramirez for further questioning," I speculated, sniffling and emptying my pockets of balled-up Kleenex.

Sol enveloped me in a bear hug. Disentangling himself, he said, "Time will tell. You've got a phone message. I took it. It's on the sink island. A guy from the JCPD wants you to call him. Frank somebody." I picked up the scribbled note and read "Call Frank O'Leary." His number followed, and I punched it into the phone. Maybe Detective Falco had enlisted some help from the JCPD and Frank was back on the case.

"Hi, Professor Barrett, thanks for getting back to me. Sorry to bother you at home, but I'd like to talk to you. It's pretty important. Can we meet somewhere in about half an hour?" Frank sounded oddly formal. Even when he had been my student he had never called me anything but Professor B.

"Sure, half an hour is good." As I spoke, it occurred to me that I could kill two birds with one stone. "How about meeting me at the Rat Trap?" I wanted to check out the old gin mill where the security guards gathered after work every night, and this was as good a time as any. Besides, I knew Frank was familiar with the place from his days with GuardNJ.

"You sure? It's kind of, uh, funky." Once again, Frank's voice was just one in a chorus of traffic noises.

"No problem." I had vowed that I would never utter this ubiquitous and often empty phrase, but it had rolled off my tongue. This was not the time to ponder my linguistic decline, though. "I like funky places, and I have to go there anyway. See you in half an hour." As I replaced the phone in its cradle, I noted that Sol looked disappointed but resigned to the fact that I was running out again. I picked up my purse and headed for the door. "I'm going to check out that bar Belinda used to go to after work. I'm meeting Frank O'Leary there. He wants to talk to me. But it'll be just you and me for dinner tonight, I promise," I said, blowing him a kiss.

If I hadn't been looking for the place, I would have driven right by it. The building was set way back from a busy service road cutting through the Meadowlands north of the Continental Stadium between a used-car lot and a dump. You could hear the whoosh of traffic from the highway behind it while on the other side of the smaller road was a sea of phragmites. Only a small sign saying "Rat Trap" nailed onto the weathered wooden door assured me that I had come to the right place. There was one pickup truck in the scruffy parking lot.

Deciding to wait inside for Frank, I pulled open the door and walked into a diorama in which Davy Crockett meets eBay. Above the old splintery wooden bar across from the door hung a series of rusted metal contraptions. A couple of large wicker baskets nested in one corner of the room, and there were some odd-looking wooden sticks leaning against the wall in another corner. On the walls above the tables were photographs, posters, and yellowed newspaper clippings. Over the spot where there might once have been a fireplace hung an animal pelt, stretched taut by a peg protruding at each paw. I stepped closer to see what was in the frame propped beneath it on the onetime mantel. It was a collection of rather ordinary-looking flatware gleaming incongruously in the dappled late-afternoon light.

Behind the bar, the barkeep looked up. "Lost, ma'am?" We were alone in the empty room.

Blinking as my eyes adjusted to the dimness, I guess I looked lost. "No. I'm meeting someone here. I'll wait. Is there a ladies' room I could use?" In a hurry to meet Frank, I'd rushed out of the house, forgetting that, unlike my hips, my bladder had shrunk of late. I'd resigned myself to exploring ladies' rooms wherever I went. The bartender pointed to the right.

As I recrossed the room, a glass case in which a stuffed muskrat crouched caught my eye. Transfixed by this relic of the lost arts of both trapping and taxidermy, I tripped. I put out my arms to brace my fall and felt a clawlike hand clamp onto each of my wrists. "Easy now, lady. I gotcha. There you go." A wizened gnome who had been seated at a table in the far corner released my wrists from his viselike grip, and I was on my feet again. I had not noticed him until I got tangled up in his outstretched legs. His leathery face, faded brown flannel shirt, and dark khaki trousers rendered him nearly invisible in the shadowy saloon. "Now you go on ahead and do whatcha gotta do," he chortled, obviously pleased with his rescue effort.

There was no arguing with him or with my bladder. Before I tripped, Mother Nature had called. Now she was shouting. I took the remaining few steps to the door marked "Ladies" and groped for the light switch. My appreciation of funky places did not extend to funky bathrooms, and I braced for a toilet-tissue-less, soapless, paper-towel-less, fetid, and vermin-infested experience with possibly fatal consequences. I was wrong. A roll of toilet tissue graced the top of the tank, a functioning and stocked paper-towel dispenser hung next to the mirror, and there was a half-full bottle of liquid soap on the sink. The room was clean and reeked only of Lestoil.

Grateful, I availed myself of the facility and found myself face-to-face with what looked like a century's worth of graffiti. Every woman who had sat there before me seemed to have had the need to leave her mark, and some had actually left more than that. There were short poems extolling the virtues of a current beau as well as prayers, advice, and adages. Scanning the canvas for Belinda's tag, I was not disappointed. There, just above the bottom hinge of the door, was her familiar scrawl. She had written her name and the date followed by a question mark and enclosed this girlish autograph in a clumsily drawn heart. I pictured her sitting where I sat now, two days before her death, and perhaps on the very night she overheard the conversation that had doomed her, trying to decide between the faithful Andy and the dashing Jason. Tears welled anew.

When I emerged, Frank had still not arrived. The gnome was seated where I had left him, now dozing against the wall. The bartender was washing glasses. As I approached, he looked up. "Your friend's not here yet. Can I get you somethin'? A beer? We got wine too," he added after looking me up and down. He was about my age, with the white skin of someone who spent his life indoors. His long brown hair was tied back in a ponytail at the nape of his neck. It looked as if he had tied it there in 1992 and just left it. He wore a burgundy T-shirt with "Rat Trap" emblazoned across the front in big white letters, and I noticed a pile of similar shirts on a shelf.

"Thanks. What I'd really like is a Sprite or a Seven-Up," I said. "This is such an interesting place. I've never been here before. Do you own it?"

"Yeah. I do now. It was my old man's, but when he died I took it over. Beats standin' in that booth all day collectin' tolls." He jerked his head in the direction of the turnpike. "Besides, I like being my own boss, and there's a steady clientele that comes in, regulars." He handed me a can of Sprite and a glass of ice. "Name's Hal," he said. "And you're . . . ?"

"Bel," I said. We shook hands across the bar. "So this is an old place with a lot of history, I bet. Was your dad a muskrat trapper?"

"Yeah, he was a real meadows man, one of the last. He trapped till his arthritis got him.

That's when he opened this place, back in the sixties. All his buddy trappers used to stop in. The place got to be quite a hangout. Lot of those old-timers, they were out settin' traps or bringin' 'em in, you know, like they say now, 24/7. They needed someplace to rest up, have a brew."

"Is that gentleman a former trapper?" I pointed to the gnome. "How old is he?"

Hal smiled an indulgent smile that made him look almost handsome. "George? He's over ninety. Him and my dad, they grew up together out there." His gesture encompassed the phragmites across the road and the area where the stadium now stood. "Trapped in the Meadowlands for a livin', both of 'em right up until the sixties. That was before the stadium was built or the offices or the malls . . . There used to be rats enough out there for everybody. My dad sold the pelts for two bucks apiece. Him and George was real meadows men. But the rats are mostly gone now. And the animal rights people . . ." He shook his head vigorously at the very thought of those who crusaded on behalf of the rights of muskrats. "They even slashed the tires on my truck once . . ."

Perhaps fearing that in the heat of passion he might say something he'd regret, Hal called across the room, "Hey George! George! Wake up! Tell the lady about the rats you caught." The gnome stirred but didn't awaken. "He ain't gonna wake up. He mostly snoozes all day," Hal said, shaking his head. "Don't bother nobody. His grand-daughter drops him off on her way to work and he just sits here. Keeps me company till the regulars come in. It's hard to believe now, but that guy once caught three thousand rats in a year. Used to pull them traps up out of the ice with his bare hands."

"I believe it," I said, recalling the strength in the old man's grip. Hal paused a moment and looked at the gnome and shook his head again, this time marveling at George's bygone prowess.

"When I was just a youngster I used to go out with him and my dad. I'd collect scrap metal while they was trappin' rats, catchin' snappin' turtles, and shootin' ducks, pheasants, and rabbits. We ate the birds and rabbits and sold the turtles to restaurants for soup. There was a lot of wildlife out there." He began drying glasses, replacing them one at a time on the shelf next to the T-shirts. "Now it's different. I like it better in here these days." Hal looked around the bar where the line between then and now was blurred.

When I nodded and said, "I can see why. This is such a fascinating place," Hal beamed. Apparently nobody had ever told him that the bartender was supposed to do the listening while the customers talked. "See these," he said, stepping out from behind the bar and walking over to the former mantel. He picked up the framed flatware and brought it to where I sat at the bar. "This was scavenged from the pig farms when the New York restaurants used to dump their leftovers and leavin's out here. See, it's got markings on it." Opening the frame, Hal took out a fork and I read "Waldorf Astoria" engraved on the handle.

"My goodness," I said, at a loss for anything more original. "That's amazing. Tell me, what are those sticks over there?" As he crossed the room to replace the salvaged silverware, I glanced at my watch. Frank was nearly half an hour late. *Nothing's changed,* I thought, recalling the many times he'd been late for class.

"Those are the stakes they used to mark whose traps was whose. See this yellow one with the notches. This was my dad's. That one there was George's." Hal pointed to a maroon striped pole. "Before they had those, they could steal each other's lines of traps 'cause all them rusted old traps looked alike. They all let 'em rust so they'd be easier to hide in the water. But you couldn't tell one from the other. See?" Now Hal pointed to the row of identical rusted traps suspended over the bar.

Just then Frank O'Leary opened the door and stepped inside. He took off his sunglasses and blinked. I was surprised to see him out of uniform. In his jeans and white T-shirt, he looked a lot like the beanpole kid I remembered from years ago when he sat in my Intro to Lit class and dared me to engage his interest. "Hi, Professor B. Sorry I'm late. There was an accident in the tunnel and it tied things up all over. I was only ten minutes from here when we talked an hour ago." Frank sounded more himself now. "Coke please, Hal," he said, grinning at the bartender.

"Long time, no see, Frankie. How's it goin'? Here, on the house for old time's sake." The two men shook hands. Frank took the Coke and seated himself two tables away from where the gnome sat snoring softly and as far from the bar as he could get with his back to Hal. I sat opposite him.

Frank wasted no time in getting to the point. "Professor B, I heard in the precinct that you brought in some evidence on the Judd murder." I was about to nod when Frank rushed on, his voice soft, his eyes pleading. "Well, I also heard Falco's got orders not to follow up on it." If Frank noticed my eyes widening in disbelief, he gave no sign but just continued his whispered monologue. "And I know how you keep nosing around till you get to the bottom of things, so I figured you were still trying to nab the Judd girl's killer. Professor B, I don't want to see anything happen to you." His voice was

292

low, and urgency made it husky. My bewilderment registered because his next words were, "I can't explain. You'll have to trust me on this one. Just back off on the Judd killing. Let the squad handle it." Frank looked at his watch and took a long swig of his Coke. He put the glass down on the table, stood, and when he spoke again, it was in his normal voice. "Well, always good to see you, Professor B. I gotta get home now. We're going to Terri's mother's house tonight. You take care, now. See ya, Hal."

Frank was gone before I had a chance to say goodbye. As I sat there stirring the ice in the bottom of my glass with a straw and trying to make sense of Frank's furtive admonition, a crowd of uniformed security guards trooped in talking and laughing. I recognized none of them, but figured it wouldn't be long before Deatra and Hector and others who had been to Belinda's funeral showed up, and suddenly I didn't want to be seen there. Blowing air kisses across the room to Hal, I hurried outside. It wasn't until I stood next to my car squinting in the bright light and fumbling in my purse for my keys that I noticed my tires had been slashed.

Chapter 27

To: Bbarrett@circle.com
From: IgutierrezPI@juno.com
Re: Mejia family
Date: 06/07/01 10:46:24

Bel,

According to my sources, Maria Mejia was twenty-two years old when she was killed. She came here by herself from Bogotá four years ago. In Colombia she had worked as a cashier at an airport restaurant and studied English. She lived in an apartment near Journal Square with her cousin Marta Mejia, a woman in her early thirties who did piecework at an embroidery factory in Union City. According to neighbors, Marta returned to Bogotá after Maria's death because she felt safer there. I can't find any trace of her in Bogotá, but I haven't tried too hard. She may have changed her name. I'm still working on getting a copy of Maria's autopsy report. It seems to be "lost."

Raoul and I can meet at your house Sunday night as long as we tape the *Sopranos*.

Illuminada

"The idea of someone feeling safer in Bogotá than in New Jersey is interesting. Either my fears for Mark if he travels to Colombia are exaggerated or something is very fishy in Jersey City," I said after Illuminada repeated this information to Betty in the kitchen on Sunday evening. Before either of them could reply, we joined the men at the table where Sol was holding forth.

"So I get this call late in the afternoon, 'Sol, would you come and get me? I've got car trouble.'" Sol's imitation of me was dead-on and elicited grins of recognition from Vic and Raoul. "She gives me the address and I take off. I mean I look like Triple A, right?" His sarcasm was not lost on anybody around the dinner table. "I drive through rush-hour traffic you wouldn't believe for at least half an hour before I get to this godforsaken gin mill on the edge of the swamp and there's the car with the tires looking like they were put through a shredder. But the light of my life is nowhere to be seen." He pauses expectantly, relishing his moment in the limelight. "Just as I'm about to open the door to see if my beloved is waiting at the bar knocking back a tall one, she leaps out from around the far corner of the building and jumps into my car. Scared the hell out of me. 'Drive! Just drive,' she says. So I hightail it back to the car and peel out, leaving the Toyota there." Shaking his head and rolling his eyes, in the time-honored tradition of men confronted with seemingly incomprehensible female behavior, Sol reached for a fortune cookie.

"So you called Triple A and they towed Bel's car?" Of course, Betty, the group's resident pragmatist, needed to know at once how we had managed to retrieve my car. "I guess you had to get new tires."

"Yes on both counts. Triple A towed it to Greg's and he put new tires on overnight for me," I said, hoping to reassure her that the car had ended up in the competent hands of my longtime mechanic.

"*Chiquita,* why were you hiding?" asked Illuminada.

"Duh. I didn't want them to recognize me when we go back," I said, marveling once again at how the expression *duh* had come out of my mouth. It was another one of those contemporary additions to the lexicon that I found offensive and had vowed never to use.

Ignoring for the moment my assumption that we'd all go to the Rat Trap, Illuminada kept the questions coming. "And who do you think slashed your tires?" Of course, as our

296

resident professional crime fighter, she was focused on finding suspects.

"Possibly the animal rights people trying to drive Hal out of business by slashing his customers' tires." I said this just to get it over with, not because I believed for one minute that animal rights activists had slashed *my* tires. As if to underscore the absurdity of friends of the furry harboring antipathy toward me, Virginia Woolf sprang into my lap and arched her back, hoping to be scratched. I obliged.

"Well, no one at GuardNJ knows you're on this case, so I doubt if any of them did it," said Illuminada.

"But what about all those other suspects? The one-night stand and his jealous girlfriend? Or what about the childhood sweetheart the victim dumped? Or while we're at it, what about her pedophile stepfather? And let's not forget her vengeful cousin. To hear Betty tell it, there's a rogues' gallery of possible perps, Bel. I don't think you can just dismiss them totally on account of some gobbledygook the poor kid wrote," said Vic, transferring the last of the sesame noodles from the carton to his plate. "That's why I don't think you should hold your breath waiting for that hotshot detective you talked to to arrest Ramirez. And why did that rookie cop tell you to back off? I don't get that at all."

"I know you don't set a lot of stock in Belinda's journal, Vic. But they have to check it out." Illuminada spoke firmly. She believed in checking out every last possibility. If her own mother were a suspect, Illuminada would check her alibi. "As for Frank's warning, I agree. That is really bizarre. Why would somebody not want to pursue suspects working for GuardNJ?" She wrinkled her nose and pushed her empty plate away.

"Yes, Frank's warning was bizarre," I said. "And I hate to say it, but Vic may be right. Maybe Falco *didn't* think much of Belinda's journal. Maybe he was just being polite to a taxpayer trying to help." I sighed. Then in a different and very determined voice, I said, "So we have to get something else on Ramirez, and I have an idea. It still has some rough spots, but listen. How's this for a plan?" I could tell Sol was ready to dismiss whatever I said, but Betty got her Palm Pilot out and prepared to take notes, and that was the signal for everybody else to tune in.

I took a deep breath. "Okay, here goes. Sol calls up this retro guy I told you about, the one who owns the Rat Trap, and pretends to be a honcho director from our local cable TV station." I paused for a second, working out the details as I spoke. "He wants to include the Rat Trap in a documentary on culturally significant watering holes in N.J.: the Satin Doll, which is the real Ba Da Bing

Club, Rut's Hut in Clifton, and Maxwell's in Hoboken, and . . ." I hesitated, casting about for the name of another newsworthy bar.

"The Stone Pony in Asbury Park where Springsteen started," Betty filled in.

"Perfect," I continued. "So my friend Hal says yes, and we arrange to hang out there to interview and chat up the clientele. Sooner or later, somebody says something or does something that turns out to be a lead."

Vic sighed and said, "Maybe it'll work. Maybe somebody'll say something. That's the problem with being in the funeral business. My clients don't say much," he quipped.

"No, they don't," said Betty. "But there are advantages to living with the owner of a funeral home." Vic smirked as if to discredit in advance whatever intimate secrets of their life together his ladylove was about to reveal.

"Like what?" said Sol, clearing the nearly empty cartons of kung bo chicken, hidden dragon vegetable medley, cold sesame noodles, and steamed dumplings off the table.

"For starters, you always have access to an extra fridge if you need it, say on Thanksgiving or if there's a big sale." As Betty spoke, Vic looked relieved and began collecting and stacking empty plates.

"Are you saying that when we eat at your house, we're eating food refrigerated next to cadavers?" Sol's normally bass voice rose a pitch or two, indicating a combination of ex-aggerated disgust and incredulity.

"*Dios mio,* I hope you never get mixed up and, you know, bury the turkey and carve the corpse." Illuminada giggled at her own projection.

"You really do that?" Raoul's normally handsome features contorted in a grimace of revulsion. "You store food with the dead bodies? That sounds nasty." He shuddered.

"Sounds pretty kinky to me." I had to contribute my two cents. Actually, Betty was notorious for her efficiency, so using the cooler at Vallone and Sons Funeral Home to augment their fridge space was just the sort of thing she would do. "What's the other hidden advantage to putting up with this merchant of death?" I was hoping to steer the conversation back to the plan I had just formulated.

"Vic's got all these wigs and clothes and makeup. Every day can be Halloween." I barely caught Betty's last word as I carried the pile of plates to the sink.

"So you two wear costumes during sex?" Sol asked. "Antony and Cleopatra? Bill and Monica?" A wicked grin was evidence of how unlikely he thought it was that these two totally conventional midlife people would do anything of the sort.

"Right, Sol," said Betty. "Seriously, Vic can disguise Bel so the bartender and the old man and the GuardNJ people who saw her at

Belinda's funeral don't recognize her. And the rest of us can dress so we look like a cable TV crew." Betty tossed each of us a fortune cookie and began gathering unopened packets of mustard and soy sauce.

"*Caramba,* here we go again," said Illuminada, with a familiar spark in her eye. It was good to see her more like her precancer self. "You know, your scheme might work, Bel."

"It's totally off the wall. I'll do it because I know Bel and she's got that look, but trust me, we're wasting our time." Sol not only rolled his eyes, but shook his head as well.

I went over and gave him a kiss on the cheek because I appreciated his willingness to go along with a scheme he saw as crazy. In spite of his doubts, I was sure that if we hung out in a saloon with the people Belinda and Maria had hung out with, we'd learn something. Besides, the tiny slip of paper in my fortune cookie read, "You are about to accomplish something that will restore confidence in your judgment."

"So Bel, do you want to be a blond again?" asked Vic as we mapped out the details involved in implementing this scheme.

Sporting a blond wig and with four diamond studs glued onto one earlobe, a fake snake tattoo spiraling around my biceps, and so much makeup that even my mother would have had trouble recognizing me, I looked around the room. We all wore variations on the theme of black jeans and black T-shirts or turtlenecks. I clutched the clipboard and pretended to consult it. Since Vic had begun videotaping funerals and burials as a service to clients who wished to revisit these events, he provided the hardware and acted as cameraman. Illuminada also knew her way around the equipment, so she assisted him. Raoul and I were gofers, running back and forth from the van, fetching and carrying. Hoping to inspire confidence, Raoul spoke mostly Spanish and smiled a lot. When we weren't doing anything, which was most of the time, we sat around nursing thermoses of coffee. Betty paced the room with a cell phone to her ear and her Palm Pilot in her other hand.

Sol was a totally convincing interviewer, so Hal's face was wreathed in smiles as he answered question after question about the meadows men and their artifacts. Even the gnome awakened long enough to flash a toothless grin at the camera and explain how, as a kid, he'd trapped and skinned muskrats and hung their pelts on drying racks all over the house, trying his mother's patience.

It was early afternoon when the first group from GuardNJ finished their shift and drifted in. Raoul and I engaged them in small talk while Sol conducted interviews. He interviewed everybody who was willing and explained that whoever edited the film back at the studio would determine which ones to include in the version that would be broadcast. "Like *Survivor*," he said with a deadpan look, and everybody smiled. For the rest of the afternoon and into the evening, as the guards came and left, he asked forty-some people a few simple questions while Raoul and I worked the room, and Betty and Illuminada and Vic eavesdropped. "What's your name? Where are you from? How long have you worked with GuardNJ? Why do you come to this bar? What do you think of the history it embodies?" Vic made a great show of zooming in and out and getting angled shots and closeups. I could tell he appreciated having a live cast.

The woman I'd noticed weeping at Belinda's memorial service entered quietly with the last group. She agreed to participate only after another woman who walked in behind her said, "Aw, come on, Aurelia. Ya gotta stop mopin'" and dragged her over to the corner of the bar where Vic was seated during a break.

"Yeah. You walk around with that long face alla time, you look ugly. Lemme buy you a beer," said one of the guys, walking over to the bar and motioning for Hal to pour him a beer. "Here, now go talk to the nice man." He handed the glass of draft beer to Aurelia and gave her a shove that sent her halfway across the room to the corner where the interviews were being taped.

"*Gracias,*" she whispered and seated herself on the bar stool next to Sol's. Unlike the others who had preened, mugged, and gone to great lengths to praise the Rat Trap, Aurelia resisted Sol's efforts to put her at ease and replied to his queries in heavily accented monosyllables that she whispered with her eyes averted. When she finished and sat down at a table across the room, I made a show of collapsing into an empty seat across from her. "You don't like to be on TV?" I asked. "Do you feel all right?" It seemed a legitimate question in view of the fact that for so many Americans being on TV was a life goal.

"No, ees no' tha'," she said, making an effort to smile. As we talked, I noticed that there was no sign of Hector Ramirez. What if he had the day off? Would that unforeseen factor hamper or facilitate our efforts to loosen his colleagues' tongues? I waited for her to elaborate and when it became clear that she wasn't going to, I said, "Where's your boss? I was expecting to meet Hector Ramirez here. The man whose picture was in the paper, you know who I mean. The fiancé of the cashier whose body was found out here? Maria something?"

At the mention of Hector's name, Aurelia's

chin lowered and her hand began to tremble almost imperceptibly. "No. They transfer heem jesterday. They sen' heem to work at Cape May," she said softly, her face briefly transformed by the flicker of a smile which was at odds with the glance she shot over her shoulder at the man who had foisted the beer on her.

"You seem glad. I'm lucky. I've got a really nice boss, but I bet that Hector was hard to work for. He looked real mean in that picture," I said.

Then, just as it had at the memorial service, Aurelia's face fragmented itself into a composite of moving planes as she struggled to suppress a sob and to contain the tears seeping out from behind her closed eyes. I produced a Kleenex and handed it to her. While she dabbed at her eyes, I just kept on badmouthing the absent Hector. "Yeah, I thought he looked like a macho asshole. I don't know what a girl like that Maria saw in him. She was so pretty . . ."

Suddenly Aurelia reached into her purse and pulled out a much-folded scrap of newspaper. Smoothing it out on the table, so that once again I saw the lovely face of the dead cashier, Aurelia said, "She was my fren'. Like a seester." So Aurelia's tears at Belinda's funeral had been for her friend Maria.

"Yes, she was lovely. I'm so sorry you lost your friend." I spoke soothingly, hoping that even if she didn't understand all my words, she'd at least be comforted by my tone. "I know you would like to help find her killer," I added softly, extending my arm to pat hers. Then very softly, I said, "Here's my card. Call me." Raoul was standing over me doing a very good imitation of a man who's pissed off because his coworker has not been doing her fair share to unplug the equipment and load it back in the van. Under cover of his bulk, I pressed my card into her hand and repeated softly, "Call me. It's important. It's for Maria."

Aurelia had been the last person Sol interviewed, and her monosyllabic and heavily accented replies had reinforced his already dim view of the entire enterprise. "A total waste of time, if you ask me," he muttered as Raoul started the van.

Chapter 28

**Longtime Detective Promoted
Ralph Falco to Head
County Cop Squad**

In a brief ceremony at the county court-
house today, Detective Ralph Falco,
twenty-year veteran of Jersey City's Police
Department currently assigned to the
Hudson County Homicide Squad, was
promoted to captain of the all-county unit.
With a master's degree in criminal justice,
several medals for distinguished service,
and a long record of crime busting, Falco
brings both training and experience to the
top spot on the county's investigative team
specializing in homicides . . .

"Did you see the article about your friend
Falco in today's paper?" It was Betty on my
message machine. "He just got a big promotion." I'd heard the phone ring, but had
forced myself to remain prone on the floor
with my back arched and my hands behind
me gripping my ankles in what felt like a
pretty good rendition of the boa. Yoga had

proven to be a reliable and nonfattening way to relieve murder-induced stress. Besides, if I tried to extricate myself from this backbending posture too fast, who knew what damage I might do to my thinning bones? Once dubbed a human pretzel by a friend envious of my flexibility, I now had more in common with a potato chip.

After doing ten sun salutations, I enjoyed a final stretch and then played Betty's message again. I nuked a tea bag in a travel mug of water and, carrying the paper and the tea, strolled to the waterfront park a few blocks from the house. There in a post-yoga glow, I sat on a bench where I could see the Manhattan skyline across the river and marveled for the hundredth time at how the Twin Towers stretched to greet the morning sun. Then I read the article detailing Falco's promotion and sat quietly, sipping my tea, listening to the gulls, and trying to connect the dots.

Something was definitely fishy. The powers-that-be in this corrupt corner of the world would never promote someone with Falco's excellent qualifications. Their own under-qualified friends, family members, campaign donors, and "business associates" were always the candidates of choice for appointments and promotions. So what was the deal with Falco? Why *hadn't* he arrested Ramirez or at least reinterrogated him about his alibi? Sitting there in the sunshine, I forced myself to trace the line between the last two dots. Was this promotion a reward for protecting some behind-the-scenes big shot? That sorry scenario validated my sense that Belinda's killer and Maria Mejia's killer were one and the same and that a couple of GuardNJ employees knew who he was and, like Falco, wanted to protect him.

I was glad to have something to reinforce this interpretation of events because everybody had been pretty discouraged by the apparent failure of the previous day's effort. Illuminada, Vic, Raoul, and Betty had each taken off a day from work, and nobody had overheard anything even remotely connected to the killings. My brief chat with the tearful Aurelia was the closest thing we had to a lead, and even I had to admit that the chances of her calling were pretty slim. We'd pored over the video looking for an answer but found nothing useful.

After a while I returned home and turned on the VCR, prepared to watch the tape once more. When it was Aurelia's turn to be interviewed, her barely intelligible and perfunctory response to Sol's queries gave me pause, and I rewound a short portion and listened again. I had to admire the fact that, in spite of her limited proficiency in English, she understood his queries and resisted his efforts to engage her by responding politely but without elaboration or passion. She was smart and a little gutsy too. I wondered if she would call and if she knew anything useful. I certainly couldn't count on it.

I had some research to do. I called Sarah Wolf at the *Jersey City Herald* and got her machine. "Sarah, it's Bel. I need copies of all the articles the *Herald*'s ever run on Ralph Falco ASAP. Everything. Thanks."

Then I logged on to my computer. If I couldn't find what I wanted, I'd get Illuminada to look into it, but I suspected the information might be easily accessible, and I was right. There were lots of data on GuardNJ on-line, so with a little patience and a little surfing I learned what I wanted to know. GuardNJ was owned by somebody named Larry Janko, a name that sounded familiar. A photo of him also looked familiar. Sitting there I willed myself to remember where I had seen that face. After five minutes, I acknowledged a failure of will and printed out the photo to see if anybody else would recognize him. A little more searching revealed that Larry Janko not only trained and supplied guards for public spaces all over the Garden State, but also owned companies that installed electronic security systems in offices, malls, and homes statewide. The insecurity of New Jersey's residents and business owners had made this Janko very secure indeed. My cyber success brought a smile to my lips that turned into a scowl when the doorbell rang. Sol had gone to upstate New York for the day to baby-sit his grand-daughter again, and I wasn't expecting any-body.

I opened the door, but there was no one there. In the Saturday traffic streaming down the street, there were no clues as to who might have rung the bell. I checked for a rolled-up copy of *The Watch Tower* that would indicate the Jehovah's Witnesses had been in the neighborhood, but I found nothing. Nor was there a circular advertising specials at the local supermarket. Shrugging my shoulders, I went inside. I didn't have time to worry about underoccupied juvenile pranksters run-ning around loose all summer with nothing better to do than ring doorbells and run away. I wanted to shower and dress before Sarah got back to me.

Sarah always gave my messages top pri-ority, so I was surprised when I hadn't heard from her by midafternoon. Could she actu-ally have taken a day off? It was Saturday, after all. Even workaholics took off on the occasional Saturday. I tried her again, leaving another message. Then I left the house to pick up a few groceries. I didn't need to take the car, but I had a partial grocery list that I had made out, and I wanted to take that with me. I crossed the street and entered the vest pocket parking area we use. As always when I entered this personal parking space, I thanked God that it had come with our house so I never had to compete with the thirty-five thousand other residents of my Mile Square City for a place to park.

The sight of the windshield transformed my prayer of thanksgiving into a curse. "Damn!" I muttered and then quickly glanced around, realizing even as I did so that whatever teenaged terror had thrown the rock might be lurking behind the hedge. Seeing no one, I determined to ignore the way the hairs on my arms were standing on end and opened the car door and retrieved the Post-it note with my grocery list on it. As I glanced at the circles of glass that now decorated my windshield, I felt a blow on the back of my head and the circles became stars.

When I came to, I stood up and reached for the back of my head. Looking around quickly, I saw no one. With the hand that wasn't holding my aching head on, I locked the car and hurried back to the house, where I assessed the damages. The only one seemed to be the goose egg forming where I had been beaned. My purse was still over my shoulder and my wallet, cash, credit cards, and car keys were all in it. Pressing ice cubes wrapped in a towel to the bump, I called Betty and Illuminada and left messages asking them to meet with me the next evening. I didn't tell them what had happened, saving it for when we got together. Betty called back and agreed to host us, primarily to avoid trying to find a parking place in Hoboken. While I was talking to her, the doorbell rang. "Hang on for a second. Somebody's at the door." Holding the phone in a grip that had tightened with tension, I went to the door. I hoped my attacker had not decided to make a house call.

There stood a young woman with a *Jersey City Herald* ID card suspended from a black cord around her neck. Giving me the once-over, she said, "Bel Barrett?" I apparently matched the description she'd been given.

"Yes," I answered, enormously relieved to find that this time there really was someone at the door and that the visitor appeared harmless.

"Sarah Wolf said to give this to you. She said, 'Good luck.'" With that my caller handed me a manila envelope. I took it and muttered a thank-you. Before I could decide whether a tip was appropriate, my visitor was driving away in a car that had been double-parked in front of the house. "It's some info I asked Sarah for," I said to Betty, who was still on the line. "See you tomorrow night." I hugged the envelope to my chest, eager to read about the many virtues and daring exploits of Captain Ralph Falco. The afternoon flew by interrupted only by another phone call. It was the one I'd been waiting for. *"Profesora? Yo soy Aurelia Ortiz."*

I had told Illuminada only that I had car trouble, and she had offered to drive. We stopped to pick up some take-out on Washington Street. Carrying two large boxes of Benny Tudino's pizza, I pushed Betty's doorbell with my elbow. Illuminada was right behind me with a six-pack of beer. "This better be important, *chiquita*. Raoul and I were all set to watch *The Sopranos*. It's not bad enough you made us miss the show last week, now you have to make us miss it this week too." Illuminada was grinning. I was relieved when she didn't mention all the time she had wasted Friday. There was no doubt that, since her cancer diagnosis, my friend had lost some of her edge. I didn't have time just then to consider whether this was a good thing or not.

We lit into the pizza while it was still warm, washing it down with cold beer. It was perfect pizza, the crust thin and crisp and just faintly charred on the bottom, the cheese gooey, the oregano and garlic happily married, and enough tomato sauce to bind all those flavors. There was nary a trace of fresh basil, fresh tomatoes, fresh mozzarella or organic anything. The tomatoes were canned, the olive oil ordinary, and the herbs

314

dried. It was delicious.

"So what happened? You said you had a real breakthrough?" said Betty, wiping the last traces of oil off her hands and passing the roll of paper towels to Illuminada. I knew that any minute she'd be typing into her Palm. Her beer sat unopened in front of her. She was all business.

"I did. I had several breakthroughs. I got bopped on the head yesterday." I waited for their reaction and was not disappointed.

"Oh my God! Are you okay?" Betty reached over to grip my arm.

"*Caramba*, Bel, why didn't you call me?" Illuminada came over to where I sat and ran her fingers gently over the knob on the back of my head, causing me to wince. And then, before I had a chance to reply she asked, "Who would do that? Were you robbed? Was it some psycho student who didn't like his final grade?" RECC students, like students everywhere, did not always see eye to eye with faculty when it came to assessment. "Last semester a student filed a grievance against you claiming you failed her without due cause, remember?"

"I remember. That woman hadn't even been to class often enough to get a syllabus. I'm fine. I wasn't robbed and I'm sure it wasn't a student. The registrar hasn't even gotten their grades out to them yet," I said. The length of time it took for RECC students to get their final grades was legendary. "Besides, students file grievances, they don't vandalize property and commit assault."

"Did you see who did it? Where were you?" Illuminada was frowning as she spoke.

"No. I didn't see him. He snuck up behind me in our parking area while I was reaching into the car. But I'm pretty sure I know who did it." Both women looked at me expectantly. "It was the same person who slashed my tires, broke my antenna, threw a rock into my windshield, and rang my doorbell and disappeared." I recited the list of harassments I'd experienced recently, hoping to make my audience aware of how unlikely it was that these were random acts.

"Bel, if you don't tell us who you think it is, I'm going to hit you over the head myself," said Illuminada.

"I'm pretty sure it was Ralph Falco," I answered, delighting in the way their jaws fell open simultaneously. "Look, the way I see it is he's trying to scare me so I will stop trying to finger Hector Ramirez. He could have hit me much harder. He's not trying to kill me, but just frighten me off."

"He's not trying to kill you *yet* you mean," Betty said.

"What's his stake in all this?" asked Illuminada, on the trail of a motive.

"It's really sad. Look at these articles." I pulled out the manila envelope Sarah had sent me and spread its contents out on the table. "This guy's had a stellar career. He's put his life on the line at least three times to save somebody else. He's gone undercover to get evidence on drug dealers. He's got medals and commendations up the wazoo. Why would he suddenly let somebody bribe him? And with a promotion? He could have gotten promoted on his own."

"So, Sherlock, you tell us," said Illuminada, with only a trace of her usual impatience. She only called me Sherlock when she was really impressed by something I'd figured out. "I know you have an idea."

"See this?" I held up a picture of a young Ralph Falco in full uniform holding a chubby toddler. A pretty woman stood at his side. "This is from an award ceremony in 1982. I'll bet that toddler is about twenty now. And the woman must be my age. Who knows what expenses they might have? Maybe the promotion wasn't the only bribe. Maybe Captain Falco got a big chunk of change for deflecting suspicion from Hector and getting poor Jason indicted."

"So you're going to check his financial records?" Betty framed this as a question, but I could tell that she meant it as a directive. Surprise and concern had triggered her need for control.

"No. I'm going to talk with him. And you're both going to listen," I hastened to

317

add, because both Illuminada and Betty widened their eyes in identical expressions of incredulity and dismay. "Hold on," I said, raising my hands in front of my face as if to stave off their objections. "We can work this out after I tell you what else happened." I took a swig of beer. "I got a call from Aurelia Ortiz, the last woman Sol interviewed at the Rat Trap." It was hard not to say "I told you so," but I managed. "She'll testify."

"She's that mousy little thing with the heavy accent, right? The one who sounded like she ought to be listening to Prozac?" I never ceased to marvel at how Illuminada absorbed the details of a situation and how, unlike me, she remembered most of them. "Yes, that's her," I said.

"You mean the laconic Latina who acted like Sol was going to swallow her whole?" Aurelia had also imprinted herself in Betty's memory.

"The same," I said. "Aurelia Ortiz. Remember, I spent a few minutes chatting her up the other day? I recognized her from Belinda's memorial service. She stuck in my mind because she was weeping uncontrollably. I thought she might have been a new friend of Belinda's. Then at the Rat Trap she seemed quite depressed or maybe just scared. I figured Belinda's death must have been very upsetting to her. I also figured maybe she knew something, so we talked and I left

318

her my card." I spoke firmly, anticipating disapproval that I had broken our cover. When no one said anything, I added, "Well, she called me and I went to her house to talk to her last night."

"So what happened? What did she say?" Illuminada helped herself to a handful of popcorn from the bowl Betty had supplied and chased it with beer.

"Boy, I sure wish I'd thought to bring you with me. That woman does not speak much English and this woman does not speak any Spanish," I said. Seeing Illuminada's fingers poised over the table, now ready to drum with impatience, I resumed my story. "She lives in a small three-story apartment building in a neighborhood not far from RECC. I swear, everybody on her street was speaking a different language. Just walking from the cab to her apartment, I heard snatches of Spanish, Hindi, Arabic, and, I think, Russian. That area is a haven for new immigrants."

"Bel, we're not going to move there. Get on with it." Illuminada's fingers began to tap as she spoke.

"Okay. I'm sorry. Anyway, the door to Aurelia's building opened when I pushed it, and the vestibule was dark. I was peering at the wall trying to find a list of occupants, so I almost missed her. She passed behind me carrying a bag of groceries through the door to the stairwell. I started talking fast because you know how much city dwellers love to have people accosting them in dark vestibules. She looked at me and blinked and her eyes dilated. She pulled the bag of groceries in closer to her, and I could see her hand tighten on her purse. I realized that she didn't recognize me from the Rat Trap because I wasn't wearing that blond wig, but she did recognize me from Belinda's memorial service. I started explaining about the wig and that I really had been Belinda's *profesora* and she just stood there staring at me. I kept explaining. Finally she got it and she smiled this nervous little smile.

"All the way up the stairs, she kept saying, 'My house ees no nice' and I kept saying, 'No problem.' Suddenly I was so grateful for the existence of this ubiquitous catchphrase that everybody seems to comprehend," I said.

"Spare us the linguistics lecture, girl. Just tell us what she said." This time it was Betty. "It's getting late and some of us have to go to work tomorrow."

"*Dios mio*, at the rate Bel's going, we may still be here tomorrow." Illuminada yawned. "Just the recap, Bel, please. What did this woman see or hear?"

"Okay. First of all, she wasn't Belinda's friend. She was Maria Mejia's friend. And she didn't see anything, but she said Maria had told her she was going to leave Hector because he hit her fairly often and once he threw her down the stairs in his building. He was obsessively jealous. He told her if she tried to leave him he'd kill her." I was rewarded for my brevity by Illuminada and Betty's serious faces. Clearly the familiar saga of domestic abuse had upset them.

"But did she hear anything else?" Betty was aware that as sad as Aurelia's story was, so far it would not do anything to put Hector behind bars.

"Yes. She heard more or less the same thing Belinda did except she heard it in Spanish. She overheard Hector talking to two of the other guards . . ." I pulled a piece of paper out of my jeans pocket. "I made her write it in Spanish because her English is so limited. I wanted to be sure we got it right. You read it and translate." I handed the paper to Illuminada.

She glanced at it and said, "Roughly it decodes like this. 'You say anything about what I did to that bitch and you never work again. We're like cops. We don't rat on each other.'" She handed the piece of paper back to me. "Do you trust her? How did she get to overhear this?" Illuminada pointed at the paper now in front of me on the table. Her question was certainly fair.

"After Maria's memorial service, her cousin Marta invited the mourners to her apartment. Hector went even though Marta had not asked him. It was noisy, and Aurelia had gone through the bedroom and into the bathroom to call a cab when Hector and his buddies came into the bedroom to do a few lines of coke. They never knew Aurelia heard their whole conversation." I sighed, visualizing how Aurelia had shuddered as she recalled her friend's murderer soliciting help in covering up the brutal slaying. "But she told Marta and, afraid, Marta left the U.S."

"What about Belinda Judd? Did this little woman with the big ears hear anything about *her* death?" Illuminada was not going to let me forget the girl who had drawn me into this case in the first place.

"As a matter of fact, she did, sort of," I replied. "His latest girlfriend, Selena, who is also a guard, complained to Aurelia that Hector has nightmares and talks and yells in his sleep. Couple of nights after Belinda's body was found, he yelled out this. Here, read it yourself." I handed Illuminada another piece of paper.

"It says, 'Die you bigmouth whore. Why don't you just die? I'm tired of hitting you.'" As she translated, Illuminada's voice remained expressionless but her eyes flickered and her fist clenched.

"Last week he blackened Selena's eye. Aurelia thinks Selena will testify," I said, rushing to answer what I expected to be her next question.

"Well, is that all you wanted to tell us?" I

could tell from Illuminada's sarcasm that she was impressed because my half-baked idea about hanging out at the Rat Trap had led us to at least one actual witness and possibly two.

"That's all I have to tell, but I need to ask you two something. Look at this guy." I placed the printout featuring the photo of Larry Janko on the table. "His name is Larry Janko and he owns GuardNJ. Why does he look familiar to me? Do I know him?" Unfortunately, this question did not strike either of my two friends as odd because since turning fifty we had all lost enough brain cells to make identifying even the closest of friends problematic at times. Many times.

"Yes. I introduced him to you at Casa Dante. He was with Mo Dickman and the senator." Betty continued to provide context clues. "Remember when Maldonado kissed Illuminada's hand? Janko was lunching with those two." Only after a gleam of recognition finally illuminated my face did Betty stop, her own face lit by the satisfaction of having succeeded in her role as human memory enhancer.

"Of course. You're right. Now I remember. So he's pretty well connected. He wouldn't have to reach too far to find friends to help him reward a highly deserving local cop." I smiled the smile of the proverbial cat digesting the hapless songbird.

"Are you sure Aurelia will testify?" Betty asked, her backtracking reflecting her preference for solid evidence over theories about motive.

"She said she would. I believe her. She said Maria was like a sister to her, got her a job, an apartment, and gave her good advice. Aurelia called Hector an animal." I remembered how Aurelia had twisted a strand of her dark hair, looked me in the eye, and said, "I no escared no more. Thees is United Estates. They go' good cops here."

I hoped she was right, because I had a date with one of them tomorrow night.

Chapter 29

Press Release: 06/18/01
Attention: Sarah Wolf, Managing Editor,
Jersey City Herald

Top Cop Whacks RECC Prof
To Squash Bribery Charge

Much-decorated veteran police officer Ralph Falco, recently promoted to captain of the Hudson County Homicide Squad, killed RECC Professor Bel Barrett because she threatened to expose him for accepting a bribe. Barrett learned that Larry Janko, CEO of GuardNJ, gave Falco an undetermined amount of cash and "arranged" the aforementioned promotion in return for Falco's promise to impede the investigation of the murders of Maria Mejia and Belinda Judd. Janko feared that having a GuardNJ employee suspected of the crimes and charged with murder would end the firm's chances of being awarded the security contract for the mixed-use development planned for the Meadowlands.

Barrett learned that Falco suppressed evidence linking Hector Ramirez, an employee of GuardNJ, with the murder of Mejia, his fiancée. According to Barrett, Ramirez stabbed Mejia to death in his apartment after she threatened to break off their relationship because he was abusive. He drove her body to the parking lot of His 'n' Hers Shoes, where he put it in her car and made her death look like the work of a mugger. Coworkers at GuardNJ provided an alibi, thus eliminating him as a suspect.

Barrett also alleged that RECC student Belinda Judd, a new employee of GuardNJ, overheard a conversation among her colleagues implicating Ramirez, and by extension themselves, in this matter (see enclosure A, the evidence that Falco suppressed while pursuing the indictment of an innocent suspect, Jason Carillo). Ramirez realized that Judd was likely to reveal his guilt so he beat her to death in his car and dumped her body at Laurel Hill Park, where it was subsequently discovered. According to Barrett, Aurelia Ortiz, another employee of GuardNJ, overheard Ramirez acknowledge the first murder, and Selena Diaz of 244 Clark Street, Apartment 3A, can provide testimony linking him to both killings.

"Just bring the evidence and the witnesses

to the DA's office and let them go after Falco. There's absolutely no need for you to meet with him," said Betty. I sighed. It was hard to argue with her when she used that peremptory tone of voice. It was the voice of her inner control freak. She used it when telling her boss how to handle the RECC Board of Trustees or insisting that her son call her every time he landed safely at any airport anywhere.

"Betty, are you willing to help or not? I want to talk to him first." My wish to confront Falco personally made my own voice more resolute than usual.

"*Dios mios, senoras,* how long are you two going to argue? Bel could bring the evidence she has to the DA, but who knows how far the long arm of Janko reaches?" Illuminada had a point. It wasn't my point, but there was no need to go into what I hoped to accomplish at a meeting with Falco.

Betty relented with a grudging shrug. "Okay, okay. Let's do it Bel's way. I just hope that sad-assed excuse for a cop doesn't shoot you right in that hard head of yours, girl."

To prevent Betty's hope from becoming a prophecy, she and Illuminada made me swear I'd hand Falco the envelope containing the press release as soon as he got to Laurel Hill Park. "You tell him that if anything happens to you, a copy of this is on Sarah Wolf's desk and she will read it," directed Betty.

This had been a condition of their providing me backup because, as Illuminada said, "Listen, *chiquita*, Falco is like a God to the local police. *Dios mio*, I could call in favors all week, but no cop in the county is going to touch this one. That envelope is your life insurance policy." We planned that Falco and I would meet in the gazebo at Laurel Hill Park at seven the next night and Betty and Illuminada would be on hand. Sol was back at his daughter's filling in for a sick baby-sitter, and that was fine with me. It wasn't that I didn't want him at Laurel Hill Park, really. I just thought that I could communicate better with Falco without Sol or, for that matter, Raoul or Vic there.

Illuminada would be standing nearby between the gazebo and Snake Hill, where she could see us clearly. As a private investigator, Illuminada carried a handgun and practiced using it regularly at a local pistol range. She had assured me that her arm was no longer too sore for shooting. "Don't worry, I'll put a bullet in that *hombre*'s hand if he even looks like he's going to draw his gun. And if he so much as touches one of your graying frizzy hairs, I swear, I'll maim him." I thought her enthusiasm for this task was a little unseemly, but I was, as always, grateful for her support. Betty would also sit nearby on the wall at the kayak launch site, her cell phone at the ready. I didn't ask whom she planned to call. I just knew I wanted her there.

When I phoned Falco to set up the meeting, I noted two things. He was working late, and hearing my name, he immediately took my call. "Well, hello, Professor, good to hear from you. How can I help? Those RECC students giving you trouble?" His voice was silken and fluid. I forced myself to remember that only the other day this sweet-talking lawman had knocked me unconscious with a carefully calibrated blow. "You still playing detective?"

Ignoring his dig, I said, "I've got something else for you. It's really important. I need to talk to you. Privately." The way I weighted the adverb with a pause on either end of it made me feel like a siren in a Raymond Chandler novel.

"Sure, I could use a little private tutoring. Where and when?" His reply was light and bantering. He too sounded like a refugee from a noir novel who routinely made assignations with women he'd harassed and assaulted.

Remembering his appealing laugh lines, I had to struggle not to sound too coquettish when I replied, "The gazebo at Laurel Hill Park. Seven tomorrow evening."

"I'm looking forward to it, Professor. I won't be late for class." Before I could dream up an appropriate rejoinder, I heard a click and he was gone. I flashed a thumbs-up to

Illuminada and Betty. "Yes! Seven tomorrow night. Now let's figure out what I'm going to say."

"Whoa girl, from the way you talked to him, maybe we better think about what you're going to wear." I gave Betty a look that silenced her but did not stop her from exchanging glances with Illuminada.

Betty, Illuminada, and I drove to Laurel Hill Park in separate cars. I was the last to arrive. There were only two vehicles besides ours in the parking lot. The athletic fields and the playground were empty, but three canoers were beaching their boats. It seemed odd to be at the park without the UKC members. As I passed the spot where we launched the kayaks, I remembered Belinda huddling in my ruana, Belinda smiling up at Jason, Belinda paddling our kayak out of the reach of the deadly debris floating downriver. Thinking of her renewed my resolve. I seated myself in the gazebo to wait. The canoers pulled their boats out of the water and portaged them a few feet to the fenced-off area maintained for public use by the Hackensack Riverkeeper. In a few minutes they got into their cars and drove away. Now the area was deserted except for a woman sitting on a stone near the water facing Snake Hill and drawing on a large sketchpad. She glanced up at the craggy silhouette and, from time to time, made a few swooping motions with her arm as she transposed her vision of it onto paper. I wondered if Betty really could draw.

Between the gazebo and the river sat a bespectacled blond birder raising the binoculars around her neck to scan the sky and then lowering her head to consult a book. Since she knew most of the county police, Illuminada wore a blond wig and glasses so Falco wouldn't recognize her. She was doing a good imitation of an avian enthusiast even though I knew that she had little patience for this popular pastime. By seven-fifteen, there was still no sign of Falco. As the minutes dragged by, I became more and more anxious. What if he didn't show? What if he did?

Suddenly there was a roar and the dirt bikers rushed past on their way to Snake Hill in a cloud of dust and squawking gulls. When the air cleared, I saw a car pulling into the parking lot. Falco parked and got out. He was not in uniform. In jeans he looked like a slightly over-the-hill Marlboro Man. He leaned back into the car and reached for something on the front seat. It was a paper bag. I sensed Illuminada and Betty tense. Even though I knew that cops do not carry their weapons in brown paper bags, my own heart began to race, and I broke out in the first stress-induced hot flash I'd had in a long time.

Falco approached the gazebo. "So, Professor, you've got more evidence, have you? I figured that called for a celebration, so I stopped to pick up a little vino on my way here. That's why I'm late. Sorry I kept you waiting." He pulled a bottle of red wine and two plastic wineglasses out of the bag. I was not altogether surprised that Falco's agenda for the evening had not been all business. "Oxford Landing Merlot. Not a bad little bottle. Hold on a second and I'll open it." He reached for his pocket.

That's when I screamed. "Don't do that. Don't even move until you read this." All I could picture was Illuminada shooting off this guy's hand because he wanted to open a bottle of wine. My own hand trembling, I handed him the sweat-stained envelope I'd been clutching since I got to the gazebo.

He looked at me as if I was deranged. His earlier air of sociability became one of wariness. His tone was now the one he might have used to persuade homeless crazies to accept shelter on a freezing night. "Easy there, Professor. Why don't you have a seat? I'll read it. Is this more gibberish from the Judd kid?" Then, apparently rethinking his word choice, he said, "Don't get excited. Whatever it is, I'll read it." I sat down on the bench facing Illuminada and he sat next to me. The wine bottle remained unopened beside him along with the two plastic glasses. I stared at him as he pulled the single sheet of paper out of the unsealed envelope and skimmed the press release. I knew I was looking at a man whose life was about to change.

For the second time in minutes, his affect altered completely. Now his shoulders sagged, and he appeared to have stopped breathing. Looking sideways at me, he took a deep gulp of air and reread the press release. By the time he finished this second reading, the setting sun was shooting orange and pink streaks through a darkening sky. The dirt bikers had zoomed out of the park. Betty put away her pad, took a camera from her purse, and proceeded to photograph Snake Hill against a background of tropical stripes. Illuminada had disappeared from view, but I knew she couldn't be far.

"So what do you want me to do, Professor? You're calling the shots now," said Falco, all the ease and all the wariness gone from his voice. He sounded resigned. "You're probably wired, aren't you?"

Knowing that hidden recorders were the jewelry of choice for many in northeastern New Jersey, I ignored his question. Instead I posed my own, taking control of the conversation. "First I want to know why you did it. What made you, a decorated real-live hero, take money from Janko?"

"My kid brother Tony needs a brain operation. He's got Parkinson's disease. You know, like Michael J. Fox, only he hasn't got Fox's bucks. Tony's HMO will pay for only one side but he needs a bilateral. It costs around forty grand a side. He asked me for what he called a loan. Loan, hell. The poor guy's only forty, but he's not going back to work. He's got three kids." Falco sighed. "Do you suppose we could have that drink now, Professor? I could really use it." I shook my head.

When he continued speaking, his voice faded in and out. It was getting too dark to read the expression on his face. "Anyway, I just paid for my daughter's wedding and gave my son and daughter-in-law some help with a down payment on a house. I was tapped out. The day after Tony asked me for the money, Janko offered me fifty grand to kill the investigation. It sounds funny now, but I thought it was a sign from God. I figured I'd just slow things down a little and then, after Janko got the security contract and my brother had the surgery, I'd do it over right. But then you came in with the Judd kid's statement blowing Ramirez's alibi . . . Shit, I always figured Ramirez did Mejia, but I also figured his alibi was golden. And I never figured he'd kill somebody else. Then when the Judd kid got it, I told Janko that Ramirez was a loose cannon. I told Janko I'd take care of you if he'd just get Ramirez out of the area."

"So that's why you slashed my tires and knocked me out . . ." I spoke sharply, remembering the blow. "Why didn't you kill me? You could have. Nobody would have ever suspected you."

Suddenly he straightened up and said, "Look, I'm a crooked cop now. But a murderer? Sorry, Professor. You read too many of those crime stories. And I'm tired of playing one-way true confessions. I got a couple of questions for you. How did you know I was the one messing with your car? How did you figure me for the guy who knocked you out?"

" 'Cause it was the work of a pro. You hit me just hard enough to make me go down for the count, but not hard enough to do me any permanent damage. The same with all that stuff you did to my car. You could have blown it up with me in it, but you didn't. You figured I'd run scared and back off this case. Besides that," I added almost as an afterthought, "you never followed up on Belinda Judd's journal. I gave you solid evidence and you never picked up Ramirez." I leaned back against the bench. "Did your brother have the operation yet?" I posed the question as if it were natural to be sitting there at the river's edge chatting with a high-ranking law enforcement officer who has just admitted taking a bribe and suppressing evidence. When he nodded, I said, "Next question? It's still your turn."

"Yeah. What's in this for you? What the hell do *you* care who killed either of these women?" Falco spat out the questions, clearly upset that I was not only trespassing on his professional turf but also foiling his scheme to betray that very profession. "Why the hell didn't you stay in the classroom where you belong?"

"Look, Belinda Judd was a student of mine. I was very fond of her. I was upset when she was killed. Jason Carillo is also a RECC student who belongs to a club I advise. He isn't a favorite of mine, but he's not a murderer. I don't like seeing him in jail, his future blighted." I could tell that I was verging on the melodramatic. This was not the time for me to get on my soapbox and lecture this man on the multifaceted nature of community college teaching.

"Okay, Professor, I know a flaming liberal do-gooder zealot when I hear one. I used to be like you, wanting to save the world. I was like that until Carol died." His voice trembled and he lowered his head to his chest.

Decades of listening to students excuse their failure to complete papers, attend class, or study for tests by citing the illness or death of a loved one had toughened me. I'd heard enough hard-luck stories to know when I was being manipulated.

"I did my homework. I read how you lost your wife to cancer last year, and I'm sorry.

But lots of people lose loved ones without betraying their communities and endangering the lives of others. You said yourself that Hector Ramirez was a loose cannon. He might kill again the next time some woman doesn't like being thrown down a flight of stairs or smashed in the face. Your wife's death is no excuse." He glanced at me, shook his head, and ran his hands over his nubby crew cut.

"You must be a tough act in that classroom of yours. I bet your students think you're a hard-nosed bitch. But you know, I've always been a sucker for a tough broad. Carol was tough too. And when I first saw you that day in my office I thought you were really attractive. Not pretty, but attractive. You know how to talk to a man, and you had a kind of sexy sense of humor. And I know you felt the same way." I was grateful for the darkness so he couldn't see me blush. I *had* found him attractive. "You know, Professor, you are the first woman I've felt like that about since Carol. I even noticed you don't wear a wedding ring. The day we met, I was all set to ask you to have dinner with me when you started that rap about the Judd kid and what she heard. Until then I had thought that maybe, just maybe, you and I could —"

"We couldn't then and we can't now," I said.

"So what do you want from me? Why didn't you go right to the DA's office with whatever you've got?" He sounded piqued, as if I was taking up his time for nothing. Then before I had a chance to answer, Falco squared his shoulders and turned toward me. With a trace of his former flirtatiousness, he said, "I've got another proposition for you, Professor. What do you say I take the evidence you've got on Ramirez and his buddies to the DA, tell him I just put it together, get the Carillo kid out of jail, get Ramirez convicted, and we forget the whole thing? Everybody wins that way." He was leaning forward, his elbows on his thighs and his fingers interlocked in front of him.

"And Janko?" The scenario Falco offered was one I'd proposed to myself and rejected, but I was curious as to how he envisioned it working.

"Either he'll put me in cement shoes and give me swimming lessons" — Falco pointed to the river, a dark presence behind us — "or he'll keep quiet because he won't want me to talk about the deal we made. When I retire in a couple of years, maybe I can pay him back with my accumulated sick pay."

"No deal," I said.

"Why are we sitting here bullshitting? Take me in. That's what this is all leading up to, isn't it?" Falco rose to his feet, impatience making his voice gruff and rushing his words.

"I have a better idea," I said. "Sit down and listen." Turning toward him, I spoke slowly and deliberately. "I don't know why you threw away a career dedicated to saving lives, catching bad guys, and being a role model for other cops. It doesn't matter now. What matters is that I shouldn't take you in." I couldn't see his features, but I imagined his brow furrowed and his eyes perplexed.

"Stop playing games, Professor. What the hell do you want?" I could feel him turn toward me again.

"I want you to turn yourself in along with all the evidence, dummy," I said as if it were the simplest thing in the world. "That way you might get a more favorable hearing. You might even save part of your pension, or at least get a reduced sentence for solving the two murders and turning in Janko."

We sat there in a silence broken only by the cars rushing by on the turnpike just beyond Snake Hill. Finally Falco's voice rang out in the night with a false heartiness that made the hairs on my arms bristle.

"You've got a point and I've got no choice. Okay. You win. I'll turn myself in to the DA first thing in the morning. You have my word. Will that satisfy you?"

"No. I'm going to drive you over there now and wait in the car until you're inside. The DA's waiting. You can call your lawyer from

339

there." I spoke with more decisiveness than I felt.

"Why? I'd really like a last evening at home to straighten out a few things, call my kids, you know. I won't try to leave. You can even wait outside and take me in the morning." Falco had his head lowered and I could hardly make out his whispered plea.

"No way," I said.

"Why not, for Christ's sake?" he persisted.

"Because I'm afraid you might blow your brains out," I said matter-of-factly. "Let's go."

Chapter 30

To: Bbarrett@circle.com
From: Rbarrett@uwash.edu
Re: Thanks, Mom
Date: 07/02/01 06:10:16

Hi Mom,

Sorry I didn't have time to chat when I picked up Abbie J at the airport yesterday. The flight home was awesome, mostly because Grandma Sadie upgraded our tickets to business class, and we sat next to this totally cool guy in a turban. He's come here from Saudi Arabia to study aeronautics. He said Abbie J reminded him of his own little one, so he played pattycake with her and sang her songs.

The conference was totally awesome too. I learned a lot about the new research on stroke patients, and met really cool people. There were at least three of us PT moms partying, pumping, and dumping, which was pretty hilarious. We had a few hours free Sunday morning, so I went to the National Gallery by myself and walked around. It felt kind of strange not to be pushing a stroller or nursing Abbie J all weekend. I think I missed her much more than she missed me.

All your precious granddaughter wants to do since she's been home is drink from that orange sippy cup you gave her and tinkle in the potty "like Baba Bel." I found one of her diapers in the trash last night. She's never done that before. I wonder what it means. And she's talking in long sentences. She said, "Read to me a story with the moon like Baba Bel." Keith thinks it's so cute the way she chatters and sings now. She kept asking for "molee." Keith finally figured out that she meant guacamole, so he made some for her today, and she loved it. It's good to see her eating something besides bananas and crackers.

So thanks for making it all possible. I hope she didn't wear you out.

Love,
Rebecca

"*Dios mio*, this is embarrassing. I told you there's *no* need for you to waste your time sitting here every three weeks like I'm an invalid." Illuminada's voice crackled with annoyance as she glared at us from her seat next to the IV pole. The black silk turban she had begun to wear just last week accentuated the blaze in her eyes and the slash of scarlet on her mouth. But when she spoke next, her tone was deferential. "Of course, you know I don't mean you, Sadie. It's always a pleasure to see you."

Ma, who had insisted on coming this time "to give perspective," as she put it, sat in a chair to Illuminada's right. Betty and I sat on a small sofa across from her. On her left was Dr. Abdelaziz, Illuminada's oncologist, carefully calibrating the flow of lurid red orange liquid into the IV tube. In spite of her defiant words, Illuminada's face was pale and she looked tired. This was her second chemotherapy session, and the chemicals that would help to keep her cancer-free were already draining her energy, a side effect about which she had been forewarned but which frustrated her nonetheless. "Now instead of doing the work of three people, she does the work of just two," is how Raoul put it.

"I think it's lovely that your friends are here to keep you company," said Dr. Abdelaziz.

"The doctor is right, Illuminada. When I had my first mastectomy in 1946, I was too embarrassed to tell anybody. I was in the hospital for three weeks and the only person who came to see me was Sybil's father, may he rest in peace," Ma said. "Sybil couldn't come because they didn't let children visit hospital patients back then." Listening to her,

I knew again the terror and vague sense of shame I had always associated with Ma's long exile in the hospital. A few seconds elapsed before I returned to the present.

"And there was no chemotherapy then to fight the disease," Dr. Abdelaziz was saying, eager for Illuminada to appreciate her relative good fortune.

"If there had been, maybe it would have saved my other breast. I remember how shocked I was thirty years later when the doctor found a lump in my other breast . . ." Each time she said *other breast,* Ma's hand went to her chest in an involuntary motion that was both pathetic and brave. "What are the odds of that happening?" To every experience, Ma brought her gamblers' question. I knew that she was proud of somehow having beaten the odds, but I wasn't sure how her story of two-time survival was sitting with Illuminada.

I needn't have worried, for Illuminada said, "Yes, I *can* imagine. You are an inspiration to me, *senora.* And to my mother too, did you know that? Whenever she's going crazy with worry and making me crazy too, I remind her of you and she backs off." Illuminada grinned at Ma and made a kissing motion with her lips. Ma blew a kiss back.

"I hate to interrupt this love fest, but what are you looking so smug about, Betty? Did Vic drag you out of the shower and ravish you before breakfast again?" As I spoke, I saw Dr. Abdelaziz's eyes widen, but her hand remained steady on the IV. She struggled briefly to subvert a smile and gave up. Betty regretted telling us about a wet and wild moment she and Vic had shared, because we razzed her about it whenever she looked too pleased with herself.

"No, but Randy got a job!" Betty practically shouted this long-awaited piece of very good news.

"Thank God," said Illuminada, raising her eyes heavenward. "If he didn't get one soon, I thought you were going to give him yours. Seriously though, that's great. What's he doing?"

"He's going to be writing on-line training manuals for Trager and Heath. He'll be at their corporate headquarters." When Illuminada elevated her eyebrows in a question, Betty continued. "It's in the World Trade Center! He doesn't have to relocate. He can keep his apartment and take the PATH or the ferry. And they're paying him a little more than he got before plus they have a solid benefits package. He's really pleased. I'm so relieved."

"Mazel tov! That's wonderful news. It's always good to hear when one of the young people gets a break," said Ma. "And it's a blessing when a child lives close by," she added, just in case I wasn't aware of what it feels like to miss far-flung family members.

"Most of the time poor Bel and I only have pictures," she continued. "I just happen to have a few photos of Abbie J when she was here."

Dr. Abdelaziz carefully detached herself and the now-empty syringe of vermillion chemicals from Illuminada's IV tube and went to a counter where, behind a glass shield designed to keep the potent particles from floating free where we might inhale them, she injected a clear concoction into an IV bag. Apparently the red chemical, powerful enough to destroy cancer cells, posed a threat to our respiratory systems as well. In a moment, the doctor attached the transparent sack to the tube and suspended them both from the IV pole. "I don't need to keep such a close eye on this dose, so I'll leave you all to chat. Just let me know if you need anything." Looking around to be sure her injunction had registered, she turned and left the room.

"Abbie J liked the zoo, but she is still a little young to get it. What she really, really loved, though, was the toddler playground at Battery Park City," I said, staring at a picture of my utterly adorable granddaughter nearly naked and laughing in a fountain. "We spent over an hour there every day. She loved taking the ferry too."

"She is precious," said Illuminada. "Raoul thinks she looks like you."

346

"That little beauty looks just like her daddy. Look at those eyes and that chin," said Betty, returning the photos to Ma. She and Illuminada had previewed them on-line and we had already exchanged the conjectures and compliments appropriate to this ritual, but for Ma's sake, everybody went through it again. I could look at photos of Abbie J all day, so I was happy to accommodate too.

"Sybil, did you return Sofia's daughter's childproofing equipment?" asked Ma, never one to miss an opportunity to remind me of an obligation.

"No, but I'll drop it all off tonight on my way to Wendy's," I replied, not letting my minor irritation show.

"So how's Wendy doing now that she's brought her mom back here?" Betty asked. "That poor woman sure has had her hands full."

"Her mother is settling in nicely at the Arbors. It's a new assisted-living complex not too far from Wendy," I replied.

At the mention of the words *assisted living* Ma stood and made her way out of the room. "I'm going to look for the powder room. No need to come with me, Sybil. I can manage just fine by myself, thank you." Illuminada and I looked at each other, recognizing Ma's need to affirm her independence and stave off any thoughts I might have of installing *her* in an assisted-living facility anytime soon.

I nodded to acknowledge Ma's remark before I went on. "And Wendy is really pleased. The current grant for her precious Urban Kayaking Club is being renewed with additional funding for a couple of extra kayaks and a summer session next year."

"We know who she has to thank for that." Betty was never one to withhold praise when it was due, or criticism, for that matter. Her readiness to judge made her praise all the more valuable.

"I did the best I could," I said, trying to assume a modest expression. "Belinda's aunt is still grieving but a little more at peace, and her son Carl is satisfied too. He's stopped ranting about seeking revenge on Lyle Hendricks. I even heard from Jason. He left a message on my phone at school. He and Luisa plan to stop by my office in the fall to thank me in person and to show me the engagement ring he gave her. I guess everybody's happy except for Falco."

"And Janko. Janko didn't look too thrilled in that mug shot in the paper," said Betty. "Gina tells me that she heard he's keeping Mo Dickman up nights trying to get him off charges of obstructing justice and bribery. He may actually go to jail."

"Yes, I heard that too." Illuminada's grin was just a shade short of gleeful when she continued. "And I also read that the contract for security at the new development is out for bid and GuardNJ was not even listed among the bidders."

"Poor Falco," I said with a sigh, remembering those laugh lines. "He's sort of a tragic figure — bright, brave, good-hearted, and his good-heartedness became his fatal flaw and brought him down. If his wife hadn't died or his brother hadn't needed surgery —"

"*Caramba*, Bel, I don't want to hear the Shakespeare lecture now." Illuminada's eyes narrowed and her words were clipped. "If I die, I hope Raoul doesn't start taking bribes to cook his clients' books for the IRS. And if his brother hadn't needed surgery something else would have tempted him. Falco hung around too long in a place where taking a little piece of the action is just like breathing, and he finally joined the crowd —"

"Who's dying?" chorused Ma and Dr. Abdelaziz, practically colliding as they reentered the room.

"Let me detach your IV now," said Dr. Abdelaziz. "You're not going to die in the near future. You're doing very well and this treatment is precautionary, as I explained to you. How do you feel now?"

"I'm fine, thanks," said Illuminada, reaching for her purse as soon as her arm was free. She took out her green leather makeup kit and consulted her mirror. She straightened the turban, smoothed her arched brows, powdered away the circles under her eyes, and reddened her already red lips so they glistened.

"Come on," said Betty. "We're going to Second Spring, remember?" When both Illuminada and Ma looked quizzical, Betty explained. "It's a fancy wig boutique in Soho. Bel and I are treating Carmen Miranda here to the best wig moola can buy."

"Yeah, and then, if the antinausea drugs work as well as they did last time, they're treating me to lunch at Windows on the World," said Illuminada. "Why don't you join us, Sadie? On a day like today we'll be able to see for miles."

"You'll love it, Sadie. They put on a fabulous all-you-can-eat buffet up there." Betty tried appealing to Ma's well-known penchant for good food and lots of it.

"Thanks, girls, but Sybil already asked me and I had to say no. Today's the day Sofia and I read to the children in the hospital," said Ma. "I've got a date with a little boy with some awful kind of blood disease and I'm teaching him to play gin. He's pretty good too. But I'll take a raincheck." I sure hoped the folks at St. Mary's didn't mind that after a couple of sessions "reading" with Ma, a kid had a better than even chance of beating the odds.

Later in the gravity-defying elevator whisking us up one hundred ten stories to Windows on the World, Illuminada said, "I take it you didn't tell your mama about Mark's plans to backpack through Colombia. She'd be worried to death."

"Oh my God, in all the excitement of the Falco indictment, I forgot to tell you. Mark's bagged the Colombian excursion." I caught a glimpse of Betty's surprised smile. "Heidi, that marvelous new girl he's seeing, has an elderly client, a recent widower living on an island off the coast of Maine. His family's hired Heidi to help him break up his island home and settle into a retirement community in Mexico. And Heidi, bless her heart, has asked Mark to come along to help pack heirlooms and translate. He'll be on his way to Maine in a week or two."

"So the clutter consultant you were so undone over has turned out to be a guardian angel?" asked Illuminada.

"You better believe it. And she's not really a clutter consultant so much as a transition coordinator," I explained. "She helps rich people relocate or reorganize after . . ." The rest of my explanation was lost while we stood, stunned into speechlessness, gaping at the panoramic view that greeted us as the maitre d' ushered us into the restaurant.

About the Author

Jane Isenberg taught English to urban community college students for close to thirty years. She has been writing mysteries ever since she experienced her first hot flash. Her copies of *Modern Maturity* are delivered to her new home in Amherst, Massachusetts, which she shares with her husband Phil Tompkins.

Visit her website at www.JaneIsenberg.com.